She turned her he_____n the stool at the end _____. Not bad-looking, for a murdering piece of convict shit. Rosy brown, bald, long eyelashes, with a gap between his two front teeth. He looked almost sweet; that threw you off if you didn't know his history. Or if you weren't a cop.

Cooley was on death row for two counts of murder. He might have beat the first count eventually. He killed someone while driving drunk—arguably an accident. But there was the matter of the second count: He murdered a prison guard. Killed him with those gappy teeth. No way an incompetent public defender could claim *that* was a tragic error in judgment.

Now Cooley had a date with the needle in two years and change; and he and Grace shared Earl in a sort of spiritual ménage à trois—so Earl could teach them how to stay out of hell.

"You know how what feels?" Grace asked him coldly. "Facing an execution? Have you got disciples, Leon? Or have you already been put to death?"

Cooley was drinking a beer. Sweaty rings of condensation gleamed on the varnished wood—maybe like planets, God's vast universe. Earl wanted everything to be so cosmic, but when you were slogging around in the humanity, it really wasn't.

Also by Nancy Holder

SAVING GRACE

CRY ME
A RIVER

NANCY HOLDER

BALLANTINE BOOKS • NEW YORK

Saving Grace: Cry Me a River is a work of fiction. Names, characters, places, and incidents are the products of the author's imagination or are used fictitiously. Any resemblance to actual events, locales, or persons, living or dead, is entirely coincidental.

A Ballantine Books Mass Market Original

© 2009 Twentieth Century Fox Film Corporation

Published in the United States by Ballantine Books, an imprint of The Random House Publishing Group, a division of Random House, Inc., New York.

Ballantine and colophon are registered trademarks of Random House, Inc.

Fox logo and *Saving Grace* TM & © 2009 Twentieth Century Fox Film Corporation

ISBN 978-0-345-51594-0

Printed in the United States of America

www.ballantinebooks.com

9 8 7 6 5 4 3 2 1

To all those who embrace their Grace

Nothing is to be preferred before justice.
—Socrates

SAVING GRACE

CRY ME
A RIVER

CHAPTER
ONE

Feathers and braids in her blond hair, gray tank top clinging to her wiry frame, flared jeans slung low, Grace was throwing 'em back at Louie's and the jukebox was blaring "Born to Be Wild." It was past closing time and the windows were dark, except for the occasional flash of lightning. She couldn't hear the thunder, only the song, which, she supposed, made a great sound track for a girl like her. The pulsing beat egged her on. She bobbed her head and mouthed the words, letting the deep bass course through the soles of her cowboy boots as she pushed them against the rung of her bar stool.

The place smelled like stale beer, cigarettes, and a whiff of cooking oil. Louie kept it as nice as he could but a bar was a bar. Be it ever so humble, there was no place like Louie's when it came to getting shit-faced.

Thunder roared and the mirrors caught the lightning, reflecting light around the room. From somewhere in the ceiling, raindrops splashed on the bar—plink, plink, plink—like the echo of shell casings during a shoot-out. Grace dipped her forefinger in the water and pressed it against the varnished surface. *Grace was here.* The next raindrop washed her print away.

"Maybe it's time to build an ark," she said to Earl as she hoisted a shot of fine tequila to her lips. Saltshaker and lime wedge stood at the ready on a soggy paper napkin to her right.

Her burly cowpoke last-chance angel was hunkered on the stool beside her; he smiled a tad and said, "You'd need a little help with that."

"Naw." She threw back the tequila and it went down sweet. She shook salt straight onto her tongue and squeezed lime juice down her throat. She slammed the empty shot glass on the bar a little too hard. She loved getting wasted. She loved a lot of things Earl didn't approve of. "I don't need help with anything."

He cocked his head. Tousled salt-and-pepper hair framed his grave weathered face. His teeth weren't the best, which made him seem more real; nothing of God's was perfect, not even His angels. If you rolled that way. Thinking about God and so forth.

"That so?" he asked. "No help?"

"Not much," she said.

Instantly the jukebox song changed: *I get by with a little help . . .*

"Don't start with me," she said as she pulled a cigarette out of her pack.

"I started with you awhile ago," he drawled. "I just haven't gotten much of anywhere."

She grinned and pulled in smoke, let it linger, blew it out. A roll of thunder rattled the bar. She looked for Louie or someone like him to pour her another; then Earl was behind the bar, fulfilling her wish like a genie.

"Noah had help." He handed her the shot glass. "Building the ark."

"Yeah, and then God drowned their helpful asses." He knit his brows; he knew she was getting the story wrong on purpose. Noah's sons had helped with the ark and they were saved. Grace was not above redecorating the truth to make a point.

"And *everybody* ditched Jesus," she went on. "His disciples couldn't even stay awake on that stakeout the night before his execution."

"Man, I know how that feels," said a familiar voice.

She turned her head. Leon Cooley sat hunched on the stool at the end of the bar, nursing a longneck. Not bad-looking, for a murdering piece of convict shit. Rosy brown, bald, long eyelashes, with a gap between his two front teeth. He looked almost sweet; that threw you off if you didn't know his history. Or if you weren't a cop.

Cooley was on death row for two counts of murder. He might have beat the first count eventually. He killed someone while driving drunk—arguably an accident. But there was the matter of the second count: He murdered a prison guard. Killed him with those gappy teeth. No way an incompetent public defender could claim *that* was a tragic error in judgment.

Now Cooley had a date with the needle in two years and change; and he and Grace shared Earl in a sort of spiritual ménage à trois—so Earl could teach them how to stay out of hell.

"You know how what feels?" Grace asked him coldly. "Facing an execution? Have you got disciples, Leon? Or have you already been put to death?"

Cooley was drinking a beer. Sweaty rings of condensation gleamed on the varnished wood—maybe like planets, God's vast universe. Earl wanted everything to be so cosmic, but when you were slogging around in the humanity, it really wasn't.

"I started dying the day I was born," Cooley replied, grinning at her.

"Spare me," she snapped.

"That's what I'm trying to do, Grace," Earl said, back on the stool beside her. He put in a fresh piece of chaw between his lip and his gum. There was a plastic soda bottle in his lap for the spit. "Also, Jesus was not executed the morning they took him into custody at Gethsemane. He went to trial."

"Yeah, those Romans, they got 'er done," Grace said.

She winced; that was pretty blasphemous, even for her. She wrinkled her nose at Earl to show that she was just being . . . herself.

"You're upset because all those criminals you've been catching are going free," Earl said.

"Damn straight." She made a "gimme-gimme" motion at the sparkling bottles of hooch arrayed behind the bar, and her angel frowned.

"I think I'd better cut you off," Earl said. "Have you ever given any thought to the condition of your liver?"

"I don't need an ark. I know exactly when I'm dying," Cooley bragged.

"You're such a dumb shit," Grace said, taking another drag, feeling the smoke wind inside her like a slow-motion, benevolent tornado; holding it as it bestowed a millisecond of calm; blowing it slowly back out into the troubled world.

"Or your lungs?" Earl added.

"I'm a dumb shit because I know?" Cooley asked, shifting on the stool. "And you don't have a clue when and how you'll go?"

"I'll go out fighting," she assured him.

"That's what I'm afraid of," Earl said as a golden glow spread across her face and his feathery wings flared open. She stared at him, awestruck for just one instant—and then he, Cooley, and the bar vanished.

And Grace woke up in her bed in her house. Alone. She winced and touched her forehead. No, not alone. She had a hangover, unfortunately. She didn't think it was a result of the dream tequila; probably the actual Jacks and beers she'd sucked down last night. The squad's most recent case had gone south in court. That was six in a row. Another asshole was walking. There was no justice. . . .

The rain was pouring down and thunder rumbled above her. She wanted to stay in bed, but it was time to rise up, protect, and serve. With a yawn, she blew wispy blond bangs off her forehead and grabbed her bathrobe. Her mind kicked over as she considered where she'd dropped yesterday's clothes, and where her gun and badge were— nightstand drawer, good—and hustled barefoot into the kitchen/front room, where Bighead Gusman sprawled on his doggie bed.

"Hey, Gussy; hey, Piggy," she said as he lifted his head and panted at her. She opened the door and gestured for him to go on out. The raindrops beat a staccato rhythm on the cement, and Gus made a sound like a foghorn, plopping his massive head back on the soft padding.

"Don't blame you," she said. "It's raining like a son of a bitch. Let me know when you're ready."

She made kissy noises at him, grabbed a cigarette, a pack of matches from Toby Keith's bar in Bricktown, a bottle of extra-strength aspirins from the cabinet to the right of the stove, and took everything with her into the bathroom.

Her neighbor wasn't up yet so there was no one to flash. Popping the top off the container with her thumb, she tossed back a couple-four tablets as she turned on the shower and let it run hot. She climbed on in and let the water sluice down over her aching head, opening her mouth and gulping down some more relief. Her hangover would go away. It always did. She just had to work through it.

Grace put thoughts of her persistent headache on hold as she finished up her sausage sandwich from the drive-though and pushed through the glass door marked OCPD MAJOR CRIMES. She had on boots, jeans, a faded plum Henley shirt, and her sheepherder jacket, but she'd forgotten an umbrella. She was damp and she was chilly. And queasy. Maybe that greasy sausage sandwich wasn't such a good idea.

The familiar morning bouquet of acidic coffee and jelly donuts, breakfast burritos, and wet leather blasted her nose. Her stomach lurched again. Fluorescents cast the desks and swivel chairs in a pasty gloom. Phones rang; file cabinets slammed. The squad room at a quarter past her hangover wasn't a drowsy and slow joint to wake up in like some more civilized places of business; you got dropped back into the pinball machine the minute you showed up. And that was the way Grace liked it.

There was some anxiety in the air, though, and determination; Grace could smell it. Everyone was pissed off about how the D.A. kept losing their evidence-rich, loss-proof cases. Grace wanted to kick his ass. Since that was not an option, she wanted to kick someone else's ass— a bad guy's, maybe. Make that definitely. Next asshole who gave her attitude was going to be sorry.

Butch Ada was on deck, walking past the interview room where Grace had broken some felonious broncos in her day. Such as Six-Pack Johnson yesterday afternoon, when he gave up the bastard who was selling guns out of his pickup across the street from Webster Middle School. Johnson copped a plea for his part in that delightful business model; no big surprise, everybody would probably walk anyway. Shit.

Hand-rolled Stetson off, all-American haircut gleaming, Butch moved with an easy gait like he was herding some longhorns across the prairie. He held a cell phone to his ear, and gave her a wave as he said into the receiver, "Let me know when tox comes back."

Grace responded to his morning greeting with a salute. She dry-swallowed some more extra-strength aspirin and resolved to drink lots of water today. From the desk facing Butch's, Bobby Stillwater nodded in her direction, glossy black hair pulled back Native-American style, his reading glasses pushed down his nose. He looked grim and thoughtful as he studied a color photo on his desk. She could see it from where she stood: Backed by pine trees, a mangled arm extended from a pool of blood. A head lay beside a boulder.

Homicide, it's what's for breakfast, Grace figured. Maybe it was a new case.

She began optimistically reordering the day's priorities; like any other OCPD detective, she had too many open cases already. But a brand-new case—fresher than forty-eight hours—had a much better chance of closing than any of the lukewarm and cold cases piled sky-high on her desk. Everybody wanted a shot at the hot ones. Captain Perry was very fair about divvying them up, even if she loved Grace best.

And there she was, Kate Perry, walking out of her private office. Kate was Grace's relatively new boss, although they'd worked Vice together, making them job friends with some tight history, but they weren't going shopping together anytime soon.

Kate was wearing a dove-gray linen jacket and dressy jeans, silk T-shirt and some turquoise jewelry. As she sipped coffee from a white OU mug, her gaze rested on Butch for a second; she narrowed her eyes and looked back at Grace.

"So what've we got?" Grace asked the captain.

"A uniform caught a body in the Oklahoma River, near the Bricktown Canal," Kate replied, as Ham Dewey pushed through Major Crimes's front door. His honey-blond cowlicks were smoothed down; he had on a dark blue jacket, white shirt, and black trousers. Black shiny cowboy boots. Grace multitasked, giving most of her attention to Kate while checking out Ham's ass as he ambled up beside her. Her partner cleaned up great, and Grace's hormones appreciated the effort. Tasty as he looked, though, she liked him better naked.

Before Captain Perry could clear her throat in a pointed

and meaningful way, Grace swiveled her head back to her and blinked, pledging her complete and total attention.

"DB. River," Grace recapitulated.

"Lena Garvin's doing the autopsy," Kate continued. "Henry took his mother to that reunion in Wichita."

"*There's* a hot time," Grace drawled, privately reminiscing about the night she'd gotten wasted and seduced Henry on her floor. He'd just lost his old cat Molly, and Grace's family had revealed yet more dysfunction. That was reason enough to get drunk together; the screwing had seemed like a good idea at the time, but Henry had started sniffing around in hopes of a relationship. She'd let him down as easily as she could.

But she'd let him down.

"Lena Garvin," Ham grumbled. "Not the best." Henry was the best OCPD had, and he had the awards and dusty bottles of champagne to prove it. "Morning, Grace," he added, his voice a little warmer. His gaze rested on her face, and she looked away. There was a reason she didn't let men spend the night, not even Ham. Especially not Ham.

"Hey." Her head was pounding. Maybe if Ham had come over last night she wouldn't have drunk all that Jack and taught Gus how to twirl around in circles.

Maybe she would have drunk even more.

"Lena Garvin's who we have," Kate said neutrally. "The lab's checking out the deceased's personal effects. Right now he's a John Doe."

"How's it look?" Dewey asked the captain.

"Like a body in a river. That's all we know, Detective," Kate answered without a trace of sarcasm. In police work, there was a difference between connecting the dots and jumping to conclusions. Kate hadn't become the first female captain of Major Crimes by being sloppy. She handed Grace the case file and took another sip of coffee. "Not enough to go on yet. Young male, late teens, fully dressed. No note."

Grace flipped it open. Big colorful pictures of a bloated corpse pushing out of jeans and a flak jacket. Parts of the clothing were gone. So were parts of the body itself.

"Maybe a suicide, maybe a homicide, maybe he got drunk and fell in," Grace said. "Ham and me. We on the clock for this one?"

Kate raised a skeptical brow. "I seem to recall a solemn oath to get some of that paperwork off your desks. You've both got case folders piled so high, you'd be crushed to death if they fell over."

"We'll do it at lunch," Grace promised. Ham nodded. Who wanted to screw with forms in triplicate when there was work to be done?

"We got prints?" Ham asked, assuming it was a done deal.

"Not yet," Kate said, grinning faintly. Maybe she thought they were like little kids, demanding more candy and ice cream. Or maybe she saw herself before she got her own office, preferring the action to department meetings and budget bullshit.

"I'll get the prints," Grace said. "Ham, you check in with Rhetta. See what kind of forensic evidence she's got."

"On it." He turned to go.

"When's court?" Kate asked him pointedly.

"On it after court," Ham replied without a beat.

"We've got to win this one, if it belongs to us," Kate reminded Ham. "D.A.'s off his game."

"You got that right," Butch said as he disconnected his call. Ticking his glance from his crime-scene photos, Bobby blew air out of his cheeks, mirroring everybody's collective frustration.

Officially, their job ended when the D.A. took the case to trial. The police department gathered the evidence, caught the bad guy, handed him over to the court, and testified. It was the job of judge and jury to mete out justice. That was the party line. Inside the squad room, Major Crimes was extremely pissed off at the bad outcomes of their last six cases. Walk, walk, walk, probation, plea bargain down to practically no time, and another walk. Bullshit. Gang violence was way up in OKC, and the bad guys were laughing at the cops. Why not? At the end of the day, the D.A.'s office was going to let them back on the streets to do it all over again.

"We'll win this one, if it's a case," Grace swore. In her mind, she had already talked to Lena Garvin and was running the prints through IAFIS. Matching 'em in record time. With what? Butcher? Bomber? Bookmaker? Her headache vanished and her senses sang. A new case. A new day.

And tonight she was going to ride Ham until she dropped. *Cuz I'm a cowgirl, baby.*

"And I want your desks cleared—and I mean cleared— as in, there is nothing on said desks, at five o'clock today. *Not* like Longhorn Benny Arnold's trashy temple to his lost days of glory." Kate said it loudly enough for Butch to overhear, and Grace grinned over her shoulder to see if the barb hit home.

At his desk now, on another phone call, Butch half-smiled and tapped the oversized head of his Longhorn bobblehead. High noon in the bullpen. Grace knew it was incomprehensible to Kate that Butch had opted to quarterback for the University of Texas when he woulda, coulda, shoulda been a Sooner. Grace was on board with that; she didn't get it, either, and she'd slept with the guy. Repeatedly. In their long-term committed relationship of three months. Butch was good at pushing.

Like Earl said, life was full of mysteries.

*   *   *

Twenty minutes later, Grace entered the autopsy room. She was all duded up like a sci-fi movie extra in a gown, booties, gloves, cap, and mask, shivering in the cold. Cold kept bacterial growth down in the cutting room, same as in the big body fridge behind them. In other words, it let you rot slower.

Lena Garvin stood over the body, gowned, masked, gloved, her hands busy. Her gaze flickered up at Grace but she remained silent.

Grace had always been fascinated by the autopsy room. The tile walls held a large clock, shelves, books and paperwork, and human-anatomy charts—maybe in case the cutter got lost in all those organs and cavities, needed a road map. There was a scale to weigh the internal organs, which currently held John Doe's lungs. It had also held alcoholic livers, punctured hearts, shot-up spleens, and the fabulous detached penis of a porn star. Average human head weighed around eight pounds, same as a bowling ball. Porn star's penis . . . not quite eight pounds.

Bottles lined the shelves like patent medicines at an old-time travelin' show. In the drawers beneath, there was a hacksaw—no shit—and a whole passel of scalpels. Henry could take apart a body like a chef at Benihana's and look for clues the same way Rhetta could dissect a crime scene. But Lena was no Henry. She was a mediocre recent hire, and no one had warmed up to her much.

Grace joined Lena at the autopsy table and stared down at the bulging, battered corpse. The victim looked like a badly rotted balloon from Macy's Thanksgiving Day parade. The river current had dragged him along, and the fish had definitely been biting. There wasn't very much skin left on his face; his right eye was gone, and his left, intact, was glassy. Consistent with drowning as primary cause of death. In other words, he'd been alive when he'd gone into the river. But Grace wanted the deck stacked. She wanted conclusive evidence.

There was lots of head trauma that could go either way, pre- or postmortem. Lena hadn't opened up his skull yet, so his brain was not available for inspection. Drowning victims could bleed from head injuries even after death, because they died with their heads down and blood flow was subject to gravity.

Henry's stand-in had still said nothing by way of greeting. The room felt a couple of degrees chillier. Grace wondered what her deal was, but tried to stay loose and friendly.

"Hey, thanks for letting me come in," she said, even though it would have been unreasonable for Lena to refuse her request to observe.

"Sure." Hark, she doth speak.

"Did he hold his breath?" Grace asked. That would, of course, further indicate that the victim had been alive when he'd been thrown in the water.

"I've got froth," the other woman answered. "But you know that could happen from a drug overdose. Lungs were hyperinflated." She nodded at her scales. They looked like normal lungs to Grace. "I'm going to screen for diatoms. We'll see what the lab finds."

"You're screening for drugs, too?" Grace said carefully, not wanting to tread on her toes but unsure how far Lena would go to establish cause of death. Henry had once told her that screening for diatoms—algae— was an unreliable test for drowning. He usually ran it anyway, as well as a tox screen for drugs. Drug overdoses could look like drownings and vice versa.

Boil it all down, the only literal cause of death was oxygen deprivation. Starve tissue of oxygen, it died. But that was like saying the cause of death was dying. Grace liked all the answers that led to *the* answer. She liked as much evidence as she could collect. It was a form of ammo. She wanted to keep shooting until she hit the target.

"I'll do a full screen," Lena assured her. But there was full and there was full. "There's a lot going on with this corpse," she added, gesturing to the skull. Patches of fish belly–white skin puffed from the bone.

"You can see how glassy his eye is." Lena pointed to it; it gleamed like someone had put a shiny silver dollar on it for the ferryman. "More telling is the amount of water in the lungs. Classic wet drowning. You're right; he tried to hold his breath, which caused laryngospasm, but at some point he exhaled and drew another breath. Or tried to. Diatoms will tell us if he drowned in the same body of water he was discovered in."

Not according to Henry, Grace thought.

"Got it," Grace said. If he'd been alive when he went in, he wasn't a dumped body. It could still be a homicide, if somebody forced him in.

"Any sign of restraints?" She scanned his wrists, a combination of bone and shreds of flesh.

"None so far," Garvin said, shaking her head. "What with the bloat and the fish, it might be hard to tell."

"There might be metal particles or rope fibers embedded in the skin."

"Yes, Detective," the woman said in a clipped tone.

Whoops. Grace knew she'd better ease off. She moved ahead mentally to forensic evidence. Rhetta had his clothes and any other personal effects. Sometimes people who committed suicide put stones or other heavy objects in their pockets. A few tied their legs together, too. They knew that their instincts for self-preservation would likely overtake them, and if they could save themselves, they would. Grace understood that kind of anguish, but it was cowardly to kill yourself.

I'd never do it, she told herself. *No matter what happened to me.*

The average civilian thought drowning was a peaceful death. Yeah, about as peaceful as being waterboarded or suffocating with a pillow smashed over your face. If you asked a dozen people in a bar if they'd rather fall into an erupting volcano or drown, eleven of them were idiots unless you were asking the question in a cop bar like Louie's. Cops knew the score.

Cops *kept* score. She already wanted to win this one, if it was a real case. And she would. She'd do whatever she had to. Hell, yeah. That might bother Earl, but it sure as hell didn't bother her.

"How long was he in the river?" Grace asked.

"I'd say nearly a week," Lena replied. Grace heard the hesitation in her voice. "Degloving has commenced."

Lena gestured to the victim's extremities. The hands and feet were skeletal, with bits of flesh hanging off them. When a body was left in water for only a couple of days, the palms and soles looked wrinkled and/or covered with goose bumps. Longer than that, and the fat in the planes of tissue began to slough off the extremities like baggy socks and a pair of gloves. Hence: degloving.

"There's still some skin on the right forefinger," Grace observed.

Lena frowned at the body. "Yes," she said, flushing as if she realized she should have caught that. "We could slip that off, put it on someone's finger, and get a print that way."

No shit. That was what Grace had just said, wasn't it?

"Great. I'll wear it," Grace offered. "My hands are small. Like his."

A sharp nod. "I'll prep it and give you a call when I'm ready."

"Prep it?" Grace echoed uneasily.

"I think I need to dehydrate it in acetone overnight."

"Oh?" Grace blanched. She didn't want to lose that much time, and she wasn't sure this woman would get it right; maybe Lena herself wasn't sure either, so she didn't want any witnesses watching her screw up the whole thing.

Lena had her back up, that was for sure, stiff-necked and tight-shouldered: practically tapping her toes in impatience for Grace to get the hell out. Grace didn't move.

"Maybe we could try it first," Lena ventured, not looking at her. "Let me take another look at it." *Alone*, she meant.

"You got it," Grace said with a bright smile. She exited the autopsy room, took off her robe, gloves, and mask, and tossed them in the biohazard can. The squad needed a win. And with Lena Garvin on their team, someone should run interference.

She's gonna screw it up, Grace thought. As she passed by a window, the rain came tumbling down.

CHAPTER
TWO

After Grace left the autopsy room, she went to see Rhetta in the crime lab. Rhetta wasn't there, and by all appearances—the banker boxes on her exam table labeled with case numbers—she had evidence to process from six million other cases ahead of the floater. Ham was still in court, and if Grace went back into the squad room, her only alternative was her paperwork, which meant that it was time for a smoke in the stairwell.

Out she sailed, facing the concrete stairs where she'd had some of her best thoughts, stolen private displays of lust from Ham, and arguments with Earl. Her pointy-toed cowboy boots clanged on the cement as she climbed up; she stopped to pull a pack of Morleys out of her pocket and light up. Then, sitting down on a step, she drew in the sweet smoke, held it, let it out, and tipped back her head. Her temples were throbbing and she was dehydrated. Water, water, everywhere, so drink some, girlfriend. She thought about the day, and the dead thing on the table that once had been a kid. Thought about how badly it stank. That *thing* had once had hopes and dreams. Went to birthday parties, looked up at the stars and wondered.

Her mood darkened and she took another drag, trying to quiet her mind as it plotted and planned how to run the case. If there was a case.

She closed her eyes and picked a piece of tobacco off her tongue.

Then she felt a kind of sweet joy wash over her, and she smiled; there was Earl's wing tip, brushing her cheek.

"Hey, man," she said. She was grateful for the company.

He sat beside her with a spit bottle cradled on his knee. He was wearing jeans, leather walking shoes, a T-shirt that displayed what looked like an advertisement for a beach in a language she didn't speak, and a loose, unbuttoned work shirt over that. He inclined his head by way of greeting.

"Morning, Grace. Bet you ain't feeling so good," he drawled.

"I feel fine," she said, looking up at the ceiling as she took another drag.

"Half a bottle of Jack and a six-pack says otherwise," he countered. "Not enough sleep, fast food for breakfast . . ."

"Are you my mother's angel, too?" she asked him, sliding a mock-suspicious glance toward him.

He shrugged easily. "All I'm sayin', it's hard to do your job when you've got something else going on. Maybe you need to cut that gal some slack. You don't know what she might be dealing with herself."

Grace's dark eyes flashed. "First of all, I'm doing my job just fine. Second, Lena Garvin's this close to incompetent. Not because of some shit going on in her life, but because she doesn't know what she's doing."

"Oh, she don't?" he asked calmly, spitting into his soda bottle. "Seems to me she was following procedure."

"Oh, I see." She cocked her head, not exactly angry with him but maybe a little bit raw. Because he obviously had no idea what he was talking about. "I didn't realize there's a medical school in heaven and that you went to it. You want me to start calling you Dr. Earl?" She thought a moment. "Do angels have last names?"

"I don't," he replied. "I am aware, however, that

you've called me a whole string of names on occasion."
If he was offended, he didn't show it.

"I never have." She rose and tamped out her cigarette.
Then she squatted down to collect the remains.

"You don't know all the things you do when you're
drunk. And you were drunk last night, Grace. And you
have a hangover today. And if you have to run after some
crazy young kid who's got a gun and a grudge, you just
might have a little trouble doing it."

"Listen, Earl," she said, looking up with the shredded
cigarette in her hand. Then she paused. "Are you telling
me that's going to happen?"

But he was gone.

Of course.

The big Oklahoma sky dropped buckets of water on the
gussied-up brick buildings of Bricktown, the flower beds,
and the ducks bobbing in the deserted canal—no tours in
the driving rain, so no tour boats. The windshield wipers
of Bobby's four-by-four fwapped back and forth as Butch
popped a stick of spearmint gum into his mouth and offered one to his partner. Bobby shook his head.

"We found a leak in the living room last night," he told
Butch. "It's been raining down inside the wall for who
knows how long. We were moving the furniture out for
the carpet. Big patch of black mold."

Butch grunted sympathetically. Bobby and Marissa had
been saving up for new carpet for months. Bobby wasn't
big on buying things on credit. If something happened to
him, he didn't want Marissa stuck with a bunch of bills.

"I'm going to open up the wall myself, save some money
that way," Bobby said. "Maybe we'll get lucky. Could just
be some sheetrock, drywall, that kind of thing."

"Could be," Butch said. "Let me know if I can lend a
hand."

Bobby inclined his head. "Thanks."

Butch didn't say anything. He and Bobby were partners, and as far as he was concerned, that meant you helped out. He'd take a bullet for Bobby. When he'd partnered up with a married man, he'd wondered if Bobby would have done the same. Bobby had a wife and kids to think about. If Bobby stepped into the line of fire, he might leave behind a widow and two orphans. Might make a man hesitate when his partner needed an assist.

There was a fortune-cookie fortune in Butch's wallet, one from a first date about seven months ago: *He who travels light moves faster.* First date, last date. Stephanie had been a sweet girl, but there hadn't been any fireworks. She'd given him the fortune even though it had been in her cookie; made some comment about how she owned way too many shoes and never traveled with fewer than four suitcases; and smiled at him when he put the slip of paper in his wallet. She thought it was a memento. It was actually a friendly reminder.

Over the months, Butch had come to learn that he had nothing to worry about where Bobby was concerned. A man with family was a man hardwired to protect people. A man who didn't take unnecessary risks. Besides, when Bobby was on the job, he was no longer just a husband and a father. He was a cop, and a damn fine one.

"While we're in the area, I'll check in with October," Butch said. "See if he knows anything." October was one of Butch's informants. He called himself October because it was the month of his daughter's birth. His real name was Patrick Kelly, and he was their eyes and ears in a local gang led by a scumbag Butch had been after since before he became partners with Bobby. With all the squad's recently lost cases, Butch felt more motivated to go after loose ends. And October's big boy, Big Money Martinez, was loose as a goose.

They parked over by the ballpark and started canvassing the shops and restaurants for information on their waterlogged John Doe. Nope, nope, and nope, and couldn't they *please* do something about the homeless people who wandered into Bricktown at night?

"I think they come from that shelter," said a woman at the counter of an upscale fudge store. The store was decorated in egg-yolk yellow and cream, yellow wooden shelves holding stacks of white and yellow striped candy boxes. She wore her strawberry-blond hair in a geometric bob like Victoria Beckham's. "They deal drugs out of there, you know."

"Would you like to file a complaint?" Bobby asked her, looking attentive and polite.

She kept looking at Butch. Her cheeks got rosy. "Just . . . could you shut them down or something?"

"We'll look into it," Butch assured her.

"Thanks." Her voice was breathy and soft.

"So you didn't see anything, hear anything?" Butch prompted, keeping it professional.

"Like a *splash*? The thought that someone would have jumped into the water, just across the street . . ." She made a little "eek" face. "Scary."

"This area is heavily patrolled," Bobby reminded her. Bricktown was a prime tourist attraction, and OKC wanted visitors to feel safe to spend their money while they were there.

"Maybe so, but those homeless people still wander over here. And someone still managed to jump into the river," she argued.

"That's not confirmed yet," Butch said. "It could have been a boating accident."

She cocked her head. "Oh. I hadn't thought of that. Still, to think that there's been a dead body near my store . . ."

"Thanks again for your help," Butch told her. The

way he saw Oklahoma City, there were dead bodies near a lot of places. "Here's my card. Please give us a call if you think of anything."

She smiled, glancing from Butch to the card and back again. He knew that look on her face, what she was thinking. *Maybe I'll just call you anyway.* He stayed neutral. He wasn't seeing anyone at the moment, but he was enjoying the time off. If he could find a woman who understood what it was like to be a cop . . . a woman like Grace . . .

Cowboy down, he thought, with a soundless chuckle. *Travel light.*

"Would you both like a piece of fudge? On the house." She started to open the display case.

"That's very kind of you, but we're not allowed to accept gifts," Bobby said, finally stepping in to smooth things over for Butch.

She laughed as she shut the case and spread her palms on the counter, almost like someone about to be frisked. "Are you serious? What do they think, that I'll try to bribe you with a piece of rocky road?"

Something like that, Butch thought. *Give us some truffles, maybe a couple pieces to take home, next thing you're asking us to fix a parking ticket. The Big Rock Candy Mountain has some slippery slopes.*

"Maybe you boys can come in on your off hours sometime. Then you'd be regular customers, right?" Her hand strayed to her hair; she touched the ends. Butch wondered if she was aware that she was doing it. He kept his smile easy and let his partner—his *married* partner—do the talking.

"The next time I'm in Bricktown with my family, we'll be sure to stop in," Bobby assured her.

A little bell tinkled over the threshold as the two detectives exited the shop. Bobby gave Butch a look, and Butch didn't react.

"What do you *do* to these women?" Bobby asked.

"I didn't say anything, man," Butch protested.

"It must be pheromones. They smell that you're single."

Butch cricked his neck and moved his shoulders. "Maybe they just look down at my hand and see that there's no ring."

"You could wear a wedding ring. If you really wanted to fend them off."

"I don't like to wear jewelry. Specially not on the job," Butch said.

"What about that thing?" Bobby asked, gesturing to Butch's large UT belt buckle. A gust of wind flapped at Bobby's long blue-black hair, held away from his face with a silver clasp. Droplets smacked the pavement.

"Rain's going to mess up the crime scene," Butch said, ignoring Bobby's jibe, as he always did. "Wish we could find it first. If there is a crime scene."

Bobby nodded. "With you." He stepped over a puddle from the last batch of rain. "Let's see what October has for us. Day won't be a total waste."

"Day ain't over yet," Butch agreed.

One hour a day in the yard, five days a week. One hour of fresh air. Leon Cooley wanted to tip his head back and let the rain wash down over his forehead and cheeks. Rain made the world smell good.

But he didn't go. Word was the White Freedom gang had a hit out on him. It was about something he was supposed to have said a few days ago about some white prisoner's woman. He hadn't; he didn't give a shit about no white woman. Except maybe Grace Hanadarko and that fine friend of hers, Rhetta Rodriguez. People were skittish around him, assumed he had some kind of network of homeys outside to do his bidding. Like he might send one of his friends around to rape their girlfriends and burn down their houses. Shit.

Okay, so he knew one or two guys.

He'd messed up once—okay, twice, second time was an actual murder—and now it was the needle for him. Now he was counting the days, not because he was impatient—hell, no—but because he just wanted to know where he stood. Still, there was no sense rushing things, and he didn't want to go before he and Earl were finished with each other. Earl was trying to help him get right. Leon wasn't sure what exactly that meant, but he figured that as long as Earl was around, he hadn't gotten right yet. That scared him, bad. What happened if he got killed before Earl signed off on him?

"Hey, Leon," Earl said. He appeared, just like that, no wings of glory, wearing his jeans and shirt. He had on a T-shirt that read JUST SAY NO.

Leon realized only then that he had been pacing back and forth like a cheetah at the zoo. He stopped.

"Hey, Earl, did you bring me some smokes?" he asked.

"Smoking's bad for your health," Earl drawled, spitting tobacco juice into his soda bottle. "It'll kill ya."

"Okay, what is it today, some sermon, some lesson?" Leon asked, tensing up even worse. "You going to make me have another one of those dreams?"

"The one where Grace Hanadarko runs you over? Or the one where you two fly kites?"

"Shit, man." Leon huffed. "I thought you were supposed to teach me about God. So I can repent. And go to heaven."

"My job's to get you right with God," Earl concurred. "If you're in the mood to repent, you'd better take that up with him. I'm just FedEx—"

"—delivering the message. I know." Leon leaned against the wall. "So what are you here to tell me?"

Earl moved his head toward the frosted window. Bastards didn't even let Leon have a view. "You've stopped exercising."

"Some asshole's ordered a hit on me," Leon informed him, dull resentment boiling up in him. "Some Aryan-gang son of a bitch."

Earl shrugged. "Okay, then, so that's why you stopped exercising in the *yard*. But you can exercise in here. You used to. Doing all them push-ups."

Leon stared at Earl as if he had lost his mind. "I've got less than three years to live. Why should I bother?" He ran his hands over his bald head and dropped his hands to his sides. Even after all this time, caged up, it spooked him when Earl simply materialized inside his maximum-security cell.

"Well, you're alive *now*." Earl sat on Leon's cot. "What if you have a stroke? You want to spend the rest of your life drooling and peeing on yourself?"

"Earl," Leon protested. "C'mon, man. I'm not going to have a stroke." A chill ran down his spine. "Am I?"

Earl spit into his bottle. "I don't know, Leon. But I do know that God gave you a body to live in. You just have to do a few simple things to keep it in tune. Like a guitar."

"It's a lot of damn work," Leon protested.

"You want to be transferred to a prison ward where they leave you in shitty pajamas for a week at a stretch?"

"Who cares?" But when Earl put it that way, maybe he did.

"Life is sacred," Earl said. "It's the best thing God had to give you. Isn't it? Is there something better than life itself?"

Leon dropped his head, shook it. "I *knew* it. I knew you'd get around to that Jesus stuff one of these days." He blew out air. "God loved us so much He gave us His only Son."

"Today is not that day." Earl tapped his fingers on the

sides of the bottle. "Besides, you and I have been through all that. God doesn't care if you're a Muslim or a Jew or a Buddhist. He just wants you to have faith."

Leon huffed. "I *do* have faith, Earl. So why am I *here*?"

"Those two people you killed, well, you took away their gift. God sure didn't put you in here."

Leon began to pace again. "Then she should be here, too. Hanadarko. She hit me with her Porsche, killed me dead."

Earl spit in his soda bottle. "That was a dream. Didn't really happen."

"Yeah, it was a dream *you* set up so you could save her from going to hell. Bitch would have killed someone sooner or later. Then she'd be in here, same as me."

"That how you see it?" Earl asked, sounding genuinely curious.

Leon nodded.

"We don't know that, neither one of us. And as for not killin' someone, she has killed people. In the line of duty."

"Yeah, she does it, it's legal. But if you hadn't scared her—"

Earl crooked his eyebrow. "If I hadn't appeared to you, maybe you'd have killed another prison guard. Like I said, life is sacred to God, Leon. Everybody's life."

"You always got an answer for everything, don't you?" Leon began to pace again. He was edgy, pent up.

"I sure don't, and you know it. I'm just—"

"Don't say it!" Leon whirled on him. He balled his fists and clenched his teeth. He was so *angry,* so whitehot—

"Careful there, son," Earl said, his smile fading. "Your temper could get the best of you. It did before, didn't it? And I mean business about that stroke. You need to get your blood pressure checked."

"If God loves me so much, why doesn't he just take me

now?" Leon demanded. "How come I got to suffer like this?"

"Tombs come in all shapes and sizes," Earl said, making a big show of inspecting Leon's bare cell. Like it wasn't that bad. Like it wasn't four bare walls and a few pathetic pictures from magazines taped to the walls, instead of a living room with a plasma TV or a mall or even an alley full of garbage cans. "Stones roll away when you least expect them."

A flare of hope shot through Leon; just as quickly, he smothered it. Earl was a damn smart son of a bitch. He probably knew that part of Leon—a large part of him— had made a silent bargain with him. *I accept God, God lets me out of here through the front door. A free man with a long life. Hallelujah.*

"Whatever, man," Leon said dully. Then he narrowed his eyes and peered through his lashes. "Why did you come to see me today?"

"No special reason." Earl smiled. "Maybe I just missed you."

"Bullshit."

Earl shrugged. "Maybe God misses you."

"Hey, I haven't gone anywhere. I've been praying and all that shit."

"With your mouth," Earl said. "But not your heart."

"What, I'm getting grades in prayer now?" Leon scoffed. "I'm not praying right?"

Earl nodded. "God can't hear what you're saying. Not the way you've been praying lately."

The condemned felon turned his head. "I haven't felt like it."

"Leon, you got to have a connection with God. Prayer's like working out, only with your soul. You're getting flabby." Earl pursed his lips. "There's gonna be a white light and a tunnel. I'll be there to stretch out my hand.

But if you don't have the strength—the *faith*—to grab on . . ."

"Okay," Leon muttered. Earl was scaring him. "I'll pray." Earl said nothing. Leon looked up at Earl and blinked. "What, *now*?"

"No time like the present," Earl said. All traces of humor faded from his face. "It may be later than you think."

CHAPTER
THREE

Lena Garvin finally called Grace to tell her she was ready to get the print, and Grace called Ham. They didn't need him, but Grace wanted a witness regarding how well or how badly it went. He was out of court and in a surly mood when he met her in the autopsy room, thin little card strip for the single print and ink pad in hand. He told her that he had a bad feeling that court hadn't gone the right way. Again. The jury didn't seem to like what Ham was saying. It felt like they had already decided to let the defendant go.

"It's like we're cursed," he complained. "Like the juries all think we entrap these poor innocent citizens and work 'em over for false confessions."

"Assholes," Grace agreed. "Next case we catch, we'll boldface and underline it for them."

"Jesus," he grunted. "Civilians."

Pursing her lips, Lena slipped the cap of flesh from the corpse's forefinger over Grace's latex glove. Dead skin from a dead guy. *Tell me your name, kid*, Grace thought.

Then she let Ham roll her finger over the ink pad, then over the strip. Clear whorls. A good print. Go, Lena.

"Thanks, Detectives," Lena said briskly as Grace handed her back the dead guy's fingertip. They took off the clinical gear and left.

"So where'd it go wrong at court today?" Grace asked as they headed together back to Rhetta's.

"It wasn't just that." He glowered. "D.A. told me Joey Amador got probation at his sentencing hearing."

She stopped walking. "Shit, Ham. That asshole beat that old lady."

"But he's real sorry about it. And the judge bought it." He clenched his jaw and rubbed his right fist with his left hand.

"That was our win. You and me." She scowled. "We got a solid confession."

He gave his fist a punch. "Amador had better watch his sorry ass. The minute he violates probation, he's ours."

"Damn straight," she said. "We'll sic the beat cops on him, too. I'll bet he screws up by Christmas."

"Thanksgiving." He grinned at her, perking up. "Caught you staring at my ass while Captain Perry was filling us in."

She smiled to herself, saying nothing. Let him dangle. So to speak.

"You want to grab a beer after work?" he asked, his voice as warm as bourbon. "At your house?"

"Sure." She grinned at him. Good. *There* was a win.

Back-burnering her irritation with Lena and her disappointment over the Amador case, she spotted Rhetta through the glass of the crime lab and waved. Bustling Rhetta didn't see her. Grace's best friend since grade school had on white latex gloves and a white lab coat. Her chocolate-brown hair was up in a messy bun held back with a black headband, and she was wearing her big, thick glasses. Gold glinted in the light; Rhetta was a good Catholic, and she always wore a cross around her neck on a thin gold chain.

Ham's phone went off. He opened it. "Yes, Captain," he said. "On my way." He turned. "Captain Perry's got something for us. I'll check it out."

"Okay," Grace said. "I'll stay with Rhetta."

He handed her the print card and headed down the

hall. She admired his ass again, and then she went into the crime lab.

"Hey," she said by way of greeting, running her gaze over the shredded jeans jacket that Rhetta was scrupulously measuring. Rhetta was the best. Several objects were arranged in a straight line—a roach clip, four pennies, two quarters, and an unfolded piece of wet paper with seven numbers. That might be a phone number. Also, the initial *J,* but very elaborately drawn, in a sort of scrollwork. The ink hadn't smeared a bit, and the paper was in excellent condition.

"Was that on my vic?" she asked Rhetta. She took in the banker boxes, which had been moved to Rhetta's shelf, next to her picture of her kids in their Halloween costumes. A soldier with a fake plastic but no less impressive gut-shot wound, and a cowgirl. "You *did* give me cuts in line. Thanks, Rhetta."

Rhetta set down her ruler and beamed at Grace, the way she did when she was so excited she could barely stand it. She took the print card and laid it down next to the tattered denim.

"I did give you cuts and these are his clothes. Look at this, Grace." She tapped her boot heels on the floor, the Rhetta happy dance. "That piece of paper was in his pocket. He was in the river for what, a week?"

"Aren't you supposed to tell me?" Grace asked. "You're Forensics."

Rhetta jabbed her forefinger at it. "Grace, that's plain notebook paper. That should be a little ball of mush. And the ink should have run. It's cheap ink." She fluttered her lashes. "Don't you find that the least bit suspicious?"

"Suspicious, hell, yeah," Grace said. She gave Rhetta a wary look. "But I have a feeling our definitions of suspicious don't match up."

"Maybe Earl's involved," Rhetta said, leaning toward her Best Friend Forever. "Maybe it's another message."

Grace snickered and showed Rhetta the print card, which she set down next to Rhetta's microscope. Then she leaned sideways, examining the scrap of waterlogged paper without touching it. It was definitely in better condition than the cadaver it rode in on.

"Earl doesn't work that way. He told me police work isn't in his job description." Grace straightened up and smoothed her braids out of her eyes. "He couldn't even help me find Gus when he was lost."

"He *did* help you find Gus," Rhetta countered. "He helped you put up flyers, and how do you know he wasn't responsible for bringing him home?"

"Because my neighbor brought him home," Grace replied.

Rhetta let that go. "But you can't deny that he gave us all those clues to find Father Patrick Satan Murphy." Rhetta came down a notch when she mentioned the shithead's name. Father Murphy had started molesting Grace when she was nine years old; and he was dead now, which was a good thing.

But the man who had killed Father Murphy was dead, too—a suicide, no less. That weighed on Grace's conscience. She'd tried to give the guy a break, let him get out of town before the cops closed in to arrest him for the murder. Instead, he had a meltdown and shot himself. Wrong of her, and he had paid. No one knew, except Earl.

"No," Grace said emphatically, shaking her head. "Earl insisted he wouldn't be doing any crime busting." Still, who knew? Earl was an unpredictable devil of an angel, coming and going and flying her out to the Grand Canyon and the Parthenon. Serving her and Leon Cooley dream-booze and then lecturing her on drinking and smoking too much.

She punched the number on the paper into her cell phone. It didn't go through; the mechanical phone lady informed her it was not a working number. "I'll check this out," she said. "What else have you got?"

Rhetta pointed at the tatters of jeans jacket. "This is a men's small. There are fibers in the pockets, but not much in the way of personal effects. Except for that piece of paper."

"My brothers always had all kinds of shit in their pockets," Grace mused. "Maybe it's a jacket he didn't usually wear. Or someone else's jacket."

Maybe even the killer's. Maybe that was the killer's piece of paper, and his handwriting. And that number was John Doe's phone number, or the killer's number. Killer calls him to chat, tosses him in the river. . . . Grace started crunching the possibilities. Maybe there was no killer. No killer, no case.

"Get me whatever you can, Rhetta," she said. "See why that paper is in such good condition. If you stay on it . . . I'll make you spaghetti."

"Get thee behind me," Rhetta said, groaning with pleasure. "I still say it's divine intervention."

Grace pressed her lips together thoughtfully. "I think you're onto something." Rhetta's answering smile was smug. "I think God threw that kid into the river so you could get that phone number."

Rhetta's face fell. "You're mocking God."

"No, I'm not." Grace smiled sweetly. "I'm mocking *you*. Who knows? Maybe someone found the body and stuck the phone number in his pocket to help us out. Then threw him back in, like a fish. Catch and release." She'd have to reread the statement of the officer who had discovered the body to see if that was remotely plausible. She'd seen a lot of weird behavior in her life.

"Right. That's what I'm saying," Rhetta insisted. "Someone like Earl."

Grace sighed. "See, this is what Catholic school does

to people." She held up a hand. "Okay, I'll keep an open mind."

"Me too," Rhetta promised. And Grace was too much of a good friend to snort at her. Rhetta was a good Catholic. In Grace's opinion, "open mind" did not fit in that definition.

Bricktown.

Butch and Bobby sloshed past the fountain and the restored brick buildings, watching another straggle of tourists scurry into restaurants and shops to get out of the rain. The partners climbed back into Bobby's truck and drove east. Landscaped frontage roads and banks of flowers gave way to chain-link fences, tires, and a dark blue couch on the side of the road with a hand-lettered sign on it that read GRATIS.

They reached some old warehouse buildings sided with aluminum. No landscaping here, just weeds. Bobby rolled over gravel and parked on a rise in front of the one with the sign above the rusted metal door that read JEHOVA'S MINISTRY. The shelter featured boarded-up windows and a guy outside in an Army jacket everyone called the Count. All the scruffy man did all day was count the sections of the cracked sidewalk, and number them with a piece of chalk. Not in sequential order or any other pattern. He just wrote numbers on them. In spite of the rain, he was out there, shielding his piece of chalk and muttering to himself.

"I'll send October out if I see him," Bobby told Butch as the door of the shelter squealed open. They'd agreed that Bobby would canvass the homeless guys and the staff about the floater. Butch would stay out of it in case October wanted to meet. October was a sort of trustee at the shelter, had longer-term bunking privileges in return for keeping the place clean and doing odd jobs. He'd see

Bobby and get the message that Butch was waiting at their prearranged rendezvous point.

Bobby shut the door himself, and Butch sauntered past the Count toward the warehouses and Dumpsters on the east side of the street. The Dumpsters were collecting rain, creating sloshy garbage stew inside their rusting bodies. Staying in the shadows, Butch found an overhang and folded his umbrella. Checked his cell phone for the time of day and put it on vibrate. Then he waited. Rain puddled around his boots and he looked for higher ground. A rat scurried past. People thought detectives spent their days chasing down guys with guns. A lot of the game cops played consisted of avoiding garbage.

Storm clouds darkened, melting together to drive away the sunlight. It was a late afternoon like this one when he'd been driving, hydroplaned, and had the accident. He'd walked away and his buddy was paralyzed for life. Butch put that aside and stayed alert. October might want to be a good guy, but he was living a bad guy's life. Time would tell if he really could change.

Butch's patience was rewarded when he detected the telltale rhythm of October's walk. October had a limp—industrial accident, denied workman's comp; he let his temper get the best of him and trashed the foreman's office, and the foreman, too. Did a bit of time for it, and he could have come out of it just fine.

But once released, he moved onto the streets, and no amount of counseling or recidivism-program assistance could convince him to give straight life another try. Butch wondered what else had happened to October to drive him to such an extreme reaction, but Butch wasn't a social worker and October was a good informant. So.

Lightning flashed, and October appeared at the southern end of the alley. The short, leathery, twentysomething guy was a pulsar of compact muscle, tattoos, and acne scars. He was wearing a faded white T-shirt with a cross on it, an Army jacket over that, and a pair of jeans. He also had on a soaking wet red and black rag—his gang colors—that concealed his red hair.

"Yo," October said in his husky voice. He looked pretty good, for October. His gang, the Sons of Death, had set him up at the shelter to trawl for recruits. Butch had recruited him as well. Should Butch have told the guy who ran the shelter? Probably.

Butch nodded at the informant. He had a twenty in his left hand by then, and October ticked his gaze down at the money the way some men stared at heroin.

"Here's the deal," October said. "I'm moving up. I'm answering direct to Jorge. He reports to . . . you-know-who." Despite his nervousness, October thrust back his shoulders, proud of his accomplishment. Jorge was the number-two man. October had gotten a significant promotion.

Butch smiled grimly, not exactly able to congratulate him. The gang's number one was Big Money Martinez. One of Big Money's victims had been a thirteen-year-old girl named Priscilla Jackson. She refused to follow in her older sister's footsteps and hook for him. So he cut her into pieces. And fed them to his dog.

Butch knew Big Money had done it, but he didn't have hard proof. He had sworn that someday he'd bring that bastard down.

"Big Money," Butch said, and October swallowed hard. He licked his lips and glanced over his shoulder. Butch kept his right hand on his service weapon, holstered on his belt.

"Yeah, him." He looked down at the twenty. "That's for my little girl," he said. "Merrie. You'll give it to her momma, same as always." He adored his little girl.

"I will," Butch promised him. "If you help me out."

October frowned and crossed his arms. Uncrossed them. Shifted his weight. He was hopped up. "I am helping you out, man. I'm way in now, okay? I'm *connected*. So . . ." He pointed to the bill. "That should be a fifty."

Butch said nothing. He just waited.

"Merrie needs money," October said, gesturing to the twenty. "She's going to *have* things." His eyes blazed.

Who could explain the chaotic logic of the criminal mind? October loved his six-year-old daughter more than anything on the planet. But rather than get a real job, and find a way to reconnect with Merrie's mother, Janaya Causwell, October stayed on the streets. Then he endangered his own life to inform on his fellow gang members, including a man he feared so much he couldn't even say his name, because Butch threw some cash his way. For his daughter.

"Listen, here it is, okay? Jorge is moving me out of the shelter," October continued. "We aren't finding any good guys here."

"That's a shame," Butch deadpanned.

"I'm going to live with four other guys in an apartment. I'm going to give you intelligence on—on Big Money. You'll be able to take him down with the shit I give you."

"That remains to be seen," Butch said. If October could ever actually deliver. And didn't get himself killed first.

October took a long breath and licked his lips. Butch wondered what he was on. His eyes were jittering. "I'll get you what you need, Butch. So we'll need a new way to meet. And you're going to have to pay me a lot more money."

"You got something in mind?" Butch asked.

"Hundreds instead of twenties." October scratched at a scab on his cheek.

"About how we meet?"

"You don't come to my new place, ever," October said. "They see you, I'm dead."

"How're they going to connect you to us?"

"They see cops around any of us, they'll kill us all. Jorge already told us that."

"Does he suspect you?"

"No. That's what he tells everybody." October stuck out his chin in a way that reminded Butch of Grace's bulldog. "But he means it. I am risking my life, working with you."

Why the hell are you doing this? Butch wondered. But he just nodded.

"You can't come to me," October said. "And I can't call you at work anymore. So I'll need your home number." He pulled out his cell phone.

Like hell, Butch thought. He had a separate phone with its own number for people like October. He recited the digits, and October punched them very slowly into his phone.

"There's a message on there for a fake pizza delivery," Butch said. "If anyone tries it, they'll get the recording or else I'll answer as Tony's Pizza and Pasta."

"Let me try it." October dialed, listened, nodded. "Okay. Good." His eyes narrowed as he put his phone back in his pocket. "So if I need help . . ."

"I have caller ID. If you can leave a message, say the words 'stuffed crust.' I'll try to get you out," Butch said. "But no guarantees, October." Butch stayed straight with his informants whenever possible, trying not to promise more than he could deliver. Some cops led guys like October on, painting pretty pictures of a new start with WitSec—witness protection—and then dumped them like a bad date.

"Stuffed crust. Okay. And a backup signal, right?" October said, ignoring Butch's warning. Butch wondered what crime October had committed to advance in the ranks as he had. Made his bones, murdered someone? Someone else's son or daughter?

"Okay," Butch said. "Backup signal."

"If I can't call, or I can't talk, once I'm settled in I'll tell you where the nearest Dumpster is that you can see from the street," October told him. "I'll put a white towel on the handle."

There were 157 ways in which that could not work, but Butch didn't point that out. Instead he fished in his wallet for another ten. Then, as October started bouncing on his heels and cleared his throat, Butch brought out the real prize: Merrie's first-grade school picture. October had given it to Butch for safekeeping a month before. Wordlessly he handed it to October, who grabbed it from him.

"It's too dark out here," he whined. "I can't see it."

Two little piggy-tails, a missing front tooth, blue eyes, and mocha skin. Freckles. She was wearing a yellow T-shirt from Frontier City. Butch had given Merrie's momma some free tickets.

"C'mon, Butch," October said.

Sighing, Butch pulled a flashlight out of his jacket pocket and shined it overhead. So much for secrecy. He stood witness as October studied the picture, shifting his weight, and gave a sad little sigh that was totally at odds with the rest of his life. Tears glistened on his lined, pocked cheeks. Butch could see the love on his face, the yearning that softened him. That softness was Butch's secret weapon.

"Merrie." Even October's voice sounded different. "Only thing that keeps me going," he whispered. "She's it for me."

The do-rag gangsta man handed the picture back to the cop and stared at the wallet while Butch replaced the picture. October had explained that he didn't want anyone in his gang to know about his daughter. No shit, given what Big Money had done to Priscilla Jackson. For a gang informant, October was not traveling light, and that was how Butch really controlled him.

"Janaya knows the money comes from me?" October asked him. When Butch nodded, he added, "And . . . does she say anything?"

She sure did, but Butch was not about to repeat it. It was going to take more than a few dollars here or there for her to speak kindly about "that prick."

"She puts the money to good use," Butch reminded him.

"Yeah. Yeah, good," October said. "When you have kids, you'll see what it's like. Your heart lives outside your body. They become *everything*." He pinched the bridge of his nose. "She's the one thing I'm proud of. If anything happened to her . . ." He raised his face, unashamed of the tears that streamed down his cheeks.

"You'd help her, right, man?" he demanded. It was a question he always asked. "If anything happened to me, you'd step up?"

"Yes." It was the answer Butch always gave. And it was the truth.

"You're not lying to me?" October searched Butch's face. "I trust you, man."

"I'm not lying to you," Butch said. He checked on Merrie a couple times a month. She and her mother were doing pretty well. They were on welfare, but Janaya was hoping to get a job now that Merrie was in school. Janaya was erratic, but so far she had a handle on her weaknesses for men and drugs. At least both Merrie's parents cared about her. There were a lot of kids who didn't have that going for them, including kids who lived in the best parts of OKC.

Butch's cell phone went off. He checked the caller ID. Grace. He couldn't help grinning.

"Yeah," he said, turning away from October.

"Hey, Butch. Got a match on a phone number the floater had on him," she said. "Helping Hand Teen Crisis Hotline. I'm going to go check it out with Ham. What about you guys?"

"Nothing," he said. "So far."

" 'Kay," Grace said, and hung up.

"Time to shove off?" October asked him, trying to sound affable. Butch couldn't figure out how he could possibly have become one of Jorge's lieutenants. His mistrust of October increased exponentially. It had been a long time since Butch believed more than about 30 percent of what anyone on the streets told him. "Okay, let me go first. Give me a few minutes," October said.

And as usual, Butch wondered if this entire scripted meet-and-leave was some wackadoo maneuver laid down by October, if someday a herd of homeboys was going to jump Butch in the alley. Maybe even today.

"When are you moving out?" Butch asked him.

"I'm not sure," October replied. He could be lying; he could have forgotten. Or he could simply not know.

"Okay," Butch said. "Call me."

"I will." October looked hard at Butch, as if it might be the last time they saw each other. That was always a possibility.

Then the informant turned and melted back into the rain. After a couple of minutes, Butch ambled back toward Bobby's truck. Hand on the gun, eyes on the landscape. Watching, alert, owning the street, just in case.

The Count jumped out in front of him. His crazy eyes spun beneath bushy brows and above hollow cheeks; he waved his hands back and forth, demanding his attention.

"The world is coming to an end," the Count informed him with stinking breath. "God is going to flood the earth and wash away the unrighteous." He wiped his nose with the back of his hand. A wet smear of chalk smeared his upper lip like a plaster mustache.

"Seems like it," Butch said. "Thanks for the warning."

As Butch headed for the truck, Bobby appeared, shutting the shelter door. He shook his head as the two climbed into the vehicle.

"No one knows anything. A guy ODed in the shelter bathroom yesterday. The minister who runs the place swears no one's wandering over to Bricktown." Bobby started the truck. "It'd be a long walk."

"October's moving into an apartment with four other foot soldiers," Bobby said. "He got a promotion."

"He's going to get himself killed." Bobby turned on the defrost and increased the speed of the windshield-wiper blades.

"They all do, sooner or later," Butch agreed. "It's a suicide mission." He looked out the window. "It's not going to let up."

"No, it's not," Bobby replied.

CHAPTER
FOUR

"Okay, here's the weird thing," Grace said as she fished her hamburger out of the Johnnie's bag. She was talking to Ham on her cell while she was driving. The rain was heavy, so it was probably not a good idea to be doing so many things at once. "The phone number on the paper in the floater's pocket was written in a code. It took Tech about an hour to crack it."

"Why would someone do that?" Ham said. "I mean, it's a phone number on a piece of paper. In his pocket. Why bother with a code?"

"I guess he didn't want anyone to know he was calling a crisis line," Grace surmised. "Kids can be real paranoid." She took a big succulent bite of burger. Extra cheese, extra sauce, and onion rings as a side dish, too. It amazed her that she had had a hangover that morning, because it was all gone. Johnnie's was a bona fide holy grotto.

"Maybe he had a good reason," she added, downshifting as she reached a red light. The storm drains on either side of the street were overflowing, water churning against the curbs as pedestrians hugged the building side of the sidewalks. "To be paranoid, I mean. Maybe we're dealing with someone whose parents are high profile."

"So maybe they didn't file a Missing Persons," Ham said, following her train of thought. "We got no BOLO, nothing in the system to ID him. If their kid goes missing, they might send out someone private to pick him up and take him back to rehab and we never would know."

"Right, except the kid winds up in the river instead." She chomped a greasy onion ring in two and one half fell in her lap. Thank God she was wearing jeans. She slurped soda through her straw. Yeah, she was going to order a pizza for her beer session with Ham in a couple of hours, but she was hungry *now*.

"How'd it go with Captain Perry's lead?" Kate had ordered Ham back to the office because someone had called in a suspicious man wandering along the river.

"Turned out the guy was a jogger. Choctaw heritage. The caller thought he was a Middle Eastern terrorist."

Grace grunted. The way she looked at it, people in Oklahoma City deserved to be jittery. Timothy McVeigh and 9/11 loomed large in everyone's minds. But the hypervigilance did make for some interesting police work. She tried not to take the mistaken identity personally, as she herself was part Choctaw.

"By the way," Ham said, trying to sound casual, "I told her we'd both go in early tomorrow morning to get some more of those files off our desks." As usual, they had failed in their sworn oaths to get the paperwork under control. Captain Perry was not amused.

"Fine. You can go in *extra* early and do mine, too," she said.

"Yeah, bullshit."

"Hey, sucker, you're the one making bullshit promises." Grace took another swig of soda. "So I'm already at the address," she went on. They were in a race to see who got there first. Not very mature but oh, well.

"Liar. I am," Ham retorted.

"You are not." She grinned. "You're so full of shit. First one there gives the other one a blow job."

"You're on," he said.

The light turned green, and she was about to gun it when she caught sight of a kid about Clay's age walking a puppyish black Lab about Gus's size from beneath the shelter of an umbrella. She watched for a second, wondering about anyone voluntarily strolling around in this rain. Kid and pup looked reasonably happy. A horn beeped behind her.

She disconnected and paid better attention to the road.

Helping Hand was located in a strip mall off North Robertson. A nondescript two-story brick building with double rows of horizontal windows featured an ice-cream parlor; a deli; a combination cellular-phone and photocopy shop; and finally, Helping Hand, on the northeast corner. There was a tiny sign on the plain wooden door that you would miss unless you were really looking for it. Which was probably the point.

Ham pulled in nearly two minutes after Grace. As she leaped out of Connie the Porsche and dashed beneath the building overhang, she wagged her Johnnie's bag at him like a trophy and licked her lips suggestively. He laughed.

Then she tried Helping Hand's door, and found it locked. There was a buzzer set into the brick on her right; she pushed it. Ham grabbed her bag and ate the last onion ring, then wadded up the bag and expertly pitched it at a cement trash receptacle behind him. It went in.

"Yes?" someone said through the intercom.

"We're Detective Hanadarko and Detective Dewey," Grace said. She had called ahead.

They were buzzed in. Grace went first up a dingy, narrow flight of stairs. There was some graffiti on the wood paneling; someone had attempted to clean it off but hadn't succeeded. That was it, no pictures or plaques with uplifting slogans or anything.

"Cheerful place," Ham murmured.

"Yeah, no shit," Grace said. "If you didn't feel like killing yourself *before* you got here . . ."

There was another door at the top of the stairs; as they reached it, it opened. A thin, middle-aged man in a charcoal-gray sweater and a pair of gray trousers stood on the threshold. His graying beard was closely trimmed. A fluffy white-haired cat sidled up beside him and meowed at the visitors.

"Hello, Detectives," the man said pleasantly. "I'm Evan Johnson. And this is Ragdoll. I hope neither one of you is allergic."

They both shook their heads and entered a postage stamp–size foyer with a plain oak desk, a multiple-line phone system, and a desktop computer with a printer. An upholstered light blue chair was pushed back. White cat hairs dusted the desk. A cup of tea wafted peppermint in the chilly air. There was a framed needlepoint picture on the wall that said YOU ARE NOT ALONE. A framed business license: First Church of the Savior, Oklahoma City DBA Helping Hand Teen Crisis Hotline. Church-run, then.

Grace noted the lack of extra chairs, a couch, just the little office setup. It reminded her of her insurance agent's office. No frills.

"We're not a walk-in service," Johnson explained as he watched her take in the surroundings. He pointed at a door on his left. "Just phones. Our hotline volunteers work in two rooms through there. We have extra staff today. The rain makes it difficult for some kids." He smiled sadly.

"As I explained on the phone," Grace began, "we're trying to ID a drowning victim. He had your number on a piece of paper in his pocket, written in code. With the initial *J*." She handed him a printout of a picture Rhetta had taken of the miraculous item in question. "Is there anything you can tell us about this?"

Johnson took the paper and studied it. "Well, obviously, my last name starts with a *J*." He knit his brows. "As for the code . . ." He shrugged his shoulders.

"We think whoever did this, didn't want anyone to know he'd called you," Grace filled in. "That must happen fairly often."

"Yes. We get a lot of whispered calls. That's why we guarantee anonymity. On both ends of the line." He cocked his head. "I don't recognize this handwriting."

"So . . . when the kids call you, they don't know who they're talking to?" Grace prompted.

"We'll give them a first name, yes," Johnson said. "We try to connect with the caller."

So maybe the needlepoint line was a talking point for the volunteers, and not just some sentimental bullshit on their wall.

"Do you ever answer the phones yourself?" Grace asked.

He shook his head. "Not really. I do administrative work, fund-raising. We're nominally supported by a church, but they don't really have the funds."

"So it's unlikely a caller would refer to you as 'J.' Since your first name begins with an *E*."

"Unlikely," he agreed. "We have a roster of volunteers. Our phones are open twenty-four hours a day, seven days a week." As if on cue, a phone trilled through the door.

"It must be tough to find that many volunteers," Grace said.

"We go through thick and thin," Johnson replied. "Somehow it all works out."

For you guys, yeah, Grace thought, seeing the image of the floater.

Johnson went over to his computer and moved the mouse on its pad. "Here," he said, hitting a button. "I'll make a list of volunteers whose names begin with *J*. James Tallbear . . . Joe Varisse . . . Juanita Provo . . . I won't be able to give you their private information, but I can ask them to get in touch with you."

Ham looked at her. She translated his expression: *We can try to get a warrant if we need to.* She gave him a brief nod.

"We may wind up interviewing everybody," Grace said. "Or this may be resolved another way."

"Of course," he said. A piece of paper printed out and he handed it to Grace. Five names.

"And they won't mind talking to us?" Grace pushed gently.

"Not at all." He smiled at her. "We cover that eventuality in training. Our volunteers are highly altruistic. They really want to help troubled youth." He pointed to the sheet. "Joe's here now," he said. "Juanita comes in at two a.m. James is taking a break from working for us. Jackie's tomorrow at midnight."

Noted, Grace thought. "Lots of late-night shifts," she said.

"As you might imagine, our busiest time is late night through early morning. After the bars close and everyone else is in bed."

Grace was no stranger to underage drinking. "Of course." She folded the paper and eased it into her jeans pocket. "Can we check in with Joe?"

"I'll see if he's on a call," Johnson told her. "Excuse me."

He left them there and walked through the door. Grace scooted over to the window on the computer screen he'd left open, grabbed her little notebook out of her jeans pocket, and jotted down Joe Varisse's home address. Ham moved closer to the door Johnson had closed, listening. Footsteps warned her to scoot back over to Ham.

The door opened. A tall dark-skinned man stood on the threshold. He looked at them both with faint apprehension, then entered the room.

"Evan's taking my calls," he told them. He had a deep, melodious voice, like warm honey over warm oatmeal. Or something else warm. "What would you like to know?"

Grace blinked at the sound of his voice. She knew that voice. Then she broke out in a wide smile as it came to her. "You're Freeway Joe. You do the early-morning traffic on the radio."

He grinned at her. "That's me."

"I can't tell you how many times you have saved me from being late to work." She held out her hand. Looking amused, he took it.

Then he looped his thumbs in the pockets of his jeans. Sensing her unasked question, he said, "I volunteer because my little sister committed suicide about five years ago. She was eighteen. I figured if I could stop someone from doing the same thing . . ."

"I'm sorry," she said. There was a moment of uncomfortable silence, then she moved on to business. "I'm Detective Grace Hanadarko. This is Detective Hamilton Dewey. We're trying to establish the identity of a drowning victim. We think he called the hotline and talked to someone whose name begins with *J*. We're running a print and we're getting a sketch. So far, what we have is mid- to late teens, about five-seven, slight build."

Varisse tsked and lowered his head, as if taking a moment for the deceased. Grace liked that. "We only talk to them on the phone," he said. "We never meet face-to-face. The anonymity helps them open up."

He was talkative. Grace liked that, too. While she engaged him, Ham glanced through the doorway that Varisse had left open.

"We figured our victim died about a week ago," Grace said. "Anyone talk to you about drowning himself around then?"

"Most of our potential suicides plan to OD. Or they've got a gun," Varisse told her. "Mostly they want to go out listening to rock music. Something a little closer to home than drowning. So they can talk to us."

"They could take you with them on a cell phone," she pointed out. "Do you get many jumpers?"

"Funny thing about a hotline," he said. "A lot of experts argue that people who really plan to kill themselves won't call us. They'll just do it. We just keep them talking. As long as they're talking, we've got a chance."

"Speaking of talking," she said. "Maybe there's a room we can go to?"

"Maybe the deli downstairs," Varisse suggested. "It's a little crazy back there. . . ."

"That'd be great," Grace said.

"I'll check with Evan," Varisse replied. "See if he's cool."

Evan was cool. Grace filed away that maybe Evan did take the occasional call. In the deli, Varisse asked for hot tea with lemon, to pamper his voice. There were some neon-green flyers for Helping Hand beside the cash register. And some grape-colored ones for gastric-bypass surgery. Grace got some tea as well, and ordered everything bagels with cream cheese all around. Ham opted for coffee, and the three sat by the window. It was still raining; neon signs bled pink, blue, and red through the glass. Tires whooshed; the door opened and closed many times as people came in out of the rain.

"So what do you tell them when they call you?" Grace asked Varisse. "The ones who are threatening to commit suicide?"

He took a nibble of his bagel and chased it with tea. "That they'll probably fail. The majority of people who try to commit suicide survive the attempt. They wake up with pumped stomachs or a mental-health hold. Or severe internal injuries, brain damage, facial disfigurements from the gunshot. With lots of medical bills for their parents, legal problems, and freaked-out friends and relatives."

"And whatever's been bothering them is still there," Ham said.

"Yes." Varisse nodded. "Only they're even less equipped to deal with it because they've compounded the problem. We try to refer them to some real help."

"Still, it's pretty harsh to tell them that they're going to fail," Grace led.

"I take them past the point of suicide. Make them see that oblivion is highly unlikely. Tell them that if they've swallowed a bunch of pills, they're probably going to vomit before they lose consciousness. That they might go into a coma and get put on life support, and that their relatives might have to decide if they're going to pull the plug."

Grace nodded, encouraging him to continue.

"I ask them about their families. How they'll react to their death, or even a failed attempt. If they think they'll go to hell for committing suicide."

"Do very many believe that? That they'll go to hell?" Grace asked. She remembered the DBA on the wall. Christian organization.

"Some. Sometimes all they've got is me, on the phone." He sipped some more tea. The cup looked like a toy in his grip. He had muscles; he worked out. "They've passed their breaking point. They don't see any reason to go on. I try to make them see that it's just temporary."

"Do you tell them they might go to hell?" Grace asked.

"No. I'm not a religious person," Varisse replied. "We're funded by a church, but Evan has made it clear that we don't have to be believers. They're a pretty cool group."

"Do you go to their services, things like that?" Ham ventured.

"I don't even know where the church is," Varisse replied.

"If someone's ODing on the line, do you dispatch the paramedics if you can get a trace?" Grace asked.

He nodded. "And most of the time, the caller's pissed off at me when he finds out they've shown up. Callers like that are usually loaded—drunk or high. They're embarrassed. But once they sober up, a few have called back to thank us. Or their parents do. Make a donation."

"Do you record the conversations?" Grace added another packet of sugar to her second cup of tea.

He shook his head. "We don't have the resources for that. But each volunteer keeps a log of calls."

We could also subpoena that, Ham's look told her.

"Do they ever stop by? To thank you or leave a donation?" Grace shook in a third sugar packet. Ham watched her stir in creamer. More creamer. She smirked at him and added another packet of sugar.

"Evan discourages that kind of thing." Varisse looked down at his teacup. "Ongoing relationships. We try to help with an immediate crisis. We're not therapists."

Which wasn't exactly a *no.* And why did he break eye contact just then?

Ham had noticed, too. Grace knew it without even looking at him. After all, they were partners.

"So, say I'm thirteen and I call during your shift and you intervene," Grace said. "I decide not to kill myself. But what if I change my mind and call back? What if I get scared again? Will I get to talk to you?"

He looked back up at her. "Maybe, if I'm still on my shift. But I might be on another call."

"So if I ask for you?" she pressed.

"Sometimes there's two of us. Even three. We try to rotate the calls. But when it's just me, then you'll get just me."

"What if you find out I'm thirty-seven?" she asked. She was a tad older than that.

"That's about what I figured," he said, grinning at her. She sat up straighter. "We don't turn anybody away, of course. Youngest caller I've ever had was ten. Her stepfather was abusing her."

"Yeah, it can start early," Grace said in a low voice. She took a sip of her tea. It scalded her tongue. She took another sip.

"Do you guys ever listen in on each other?" Ham asked. "Say, you've got a tough call or you don't know what to say?"

"Not usually. When we're training, yeah."

"Are most of your calls people who want to commit suicide?"

"No. Less than half. Some people just need a connection. They don't know how to reach out to anyone real. We're at a safe distance. On the phone."

"E-mail?" Ham asked.

"No. There are some agencies that do that. IMs, chat rooms, texting. We're old-fashioned."

Time to double back. "So *do* you think they go to hell?"

Varisse shook his head. "I think we make our own hell. Right here." He pulled out his cell phone and looked at it. "I don't want to keep Evan."

"Of course not." Grace took one more sip of tea. Ham just left his coffee. They got up and hustled through the rain with Joe back to the door of the crisis center. Grace noticed that he had a key; he didn't need to be buzzed back in.

They went upstairs, finding Johnson back in the foyer. He told them another volunteer had arrived—Shirley Maxwell. She was already fielding a call in the back room. Joe Varisse had another hour, and Johnson was going to go home for the day.

"I'll put out an e-mail to all the volunteers and ask them to contact you," Johnson told Grace and Ham.

"Thanks. Anything they've got, any leads, would be appreciated," Grace said as she and Ham put down a quarter-inch stack of their business cards.

Johnson walked out with them, opened an umbrella, then headed toward a Dodge Caliber and got in. Through force of habit, Grace checked his plates. Oklahoma. He had a Sooner bumper sticker. No religious stuff.

"Damn," Grace said as she wiped some sugar off her fingers and fished out her keys from her jeans pocket. "There's not much accountability. Working alone, door keys floating all over the place. I mean, what if I was some sociopath who decided to tell every third guy who called me that he was better off dead? Ted Bundy worked on a hotline. How many women did he murder back in the day?"

"What if Joe's dealing drugs out of there? Or he hooks up with some vulnerable woman?" Ham looked up at the dripping overhang. "Something was going on with him," he added. "People like that, do-gooders, sometimes they have questionable boundaries."

Grace smirked. "Yeah, no shit, Detective."

He frowned. "Be nice, Grace."

She touched the buzzer without pressing it. "I'm just pushing your buttons, Dewey."

CHAPTER
FIVE

"Push harder," Grace whispered as Ham did his thing. They'd wrapped up at the office—no hits on the print, nothing from Butch and Bobby—and called it a day.

Now it was dark and rainy and sweet, in a raunchy kind of way.

There were wine bottles and booze bottles and cigarettes and pizza remnants all over the floor of her bedroom. They were writhing on their old stomping grounds, aka her bed. Grace's clothes were strewn from the refrigerator to the bedroom and back again. Ham's were in a pile in the bathroom. Nice long soak, a few bottles of wine . . . now he was on top of her and she was half out of her mind, it was so good. It was always so good. She died two, three times a night when she was screwing Ham.

And went straight to heaven.

"Oh, Grace, oh, God," Ham groaned. She knew that catch in his throat, felt him tense, and let her head roll back in the cradle of his palms. He spasmed hard. He was done.

And she was, too. Done and done in. The night had been glorious, candles and pearls, fluffy handcuffs and just a tiny bit of rough. Just fun rough.

Ham let out all the air, sighing hard, and she smiled. He gathered up her hair and kissed the side of her face, nibbling on her ear, and sighed again. Kissed her temple.

"Grace," he murmured, as if he couldn't say her name enough. He was getting awfully sentimental, so she slid out from his embrace and sat up. He reached a limp hand for her, easily dodged, and flopped his arm in the warm spot she had just vacated. Buck naked, she wandered into the living room.

"Where are you going?" he called.

"Gus has to go out," she replied. "Don't you, Gusman?" she whispered.

Gus was fast asleep. She nudged him with her toe and he didn't move a muscle. Didn't even blink. And damned if it wasn't still raining.

A blast of cool air kissed her as she opened the fridge and surveyed her beer supply. With a grin, she reached for a longneck just as Ham's hands slid around her waist. She felt his sex, still half tumescent, pressing against her back.

"That was nice," he said.

"That was hot," she corrected. She didn't do nice. They didn't do nice. Sex was sex, not a sashay through the tulips. Not even for Ham.

She left the beer in the fridge and shut the door. Since Ham had moved out on Darlene, it was harder to get him to leave at night. He'd promised things weren't different between the two of them, but they were. Moving out meant moving on or moving in, and she was nervous.

"Hey," she said, glancing at the clock on the microwave, "it's almost two."

"Yeah," he replied, sounding tense, as if bracing himself for the boot.

"Time for *Juanita's* shift on the hotline." She turned around in his arms, draped her wrists over his shoulders, and bumped against him suggestively. "We could call her."

"Dry run?" he asked, arching his pelvis against her. "Pretend to be strung out, scared . . ."

"We probably shouldn't mess with her. Don't want

any sort of entrapment dirtying our case. We gotta win this one." Grace rocked to their rhythm.

"If it is one."

They nodded in unison and stopped the sex dance. She left the warmth of his beautifully cut body and rooted around for her cell phone. It was tangled up in her bikini underwear. How come would remain one of life's mysteries. She found the hotline number and punched it in while they walked together to the couch. They sat down naked.

"Helping Hand," said a woman's voice, thick Hispanic accent. "This is Juanita. I'm here."

"Hello, Juanita, my name is Grace. Hanadarko," Grace said, giving Ham a nod. He sat back on the couch, putting a pillow behind his back. He had no idea that, on many other occasions, an angel had sat in that exact spot, chewing tobacco and munching on pizza with extra jalapeños and no mushrooms. "I'm a detective with OCPD. I'm sorry to disturb you like this, but I'm working on a case. My partner, Detective Dewey, and I left our business cards there at the crisis center."

"Yes," Juanita said, her voice rising a little. A bit nervous, talking to a cop. That was normal for most civilians. "I saw it. Evan left me a note and asked me to call you." She laughed shyly. "I'm sorry. I didn't realize he meant tonight."

"No. I'm just . . . up anyway, and he mentioned that you worked this shift." Ham snaked his foot under her thigh. She raised her leg so he'd have better access. "I have an unidentified drowning victim, and he had the center's phone number on a piece of paper. So I'm interviewing the volunteers to see if anyone can tell me who he is."

There was a pause. Grace didn't know if that was significant, or if Juanita was just thinking. It was so much easier to read body language than to speak to someone over the phone. Maybe they should have waited.

"We get a lot of calls," Juanita said. "Lately, I've been talking to more girls than boys. Unwanted pregnancies, boyfriend problems. A lot of their parents are losing their homes. That seems to be harder on the girls."

"It all seems so insurmountable when you're tired and scared," Grace said. "I'm not preventing any calls from coming in, am I?"

"No, we have call-waiting," Juanita assured her. "I don't think I've talked to anyone who threatened to drown himself."

"This kid was maybe sixteen, but he was small for his age. We're doing a composite based on forensic evidence." That was a polite way of saying based on his skull and pieces of skin and hair. "Once it's completed, we'd appreciate it if you'd take a look at it."

"Of course." There was another pause, and then she said, "Evan mentioned there was a *J* on the piece of paper."

"Yes." Grace cocked a brow. Ham looked at her. She held up her finger, and he got up and got two beers out of her fridge. She let the silence grow. Juanita was probably used to pauses on the phone. But maybe she filled them herself when they grew too long.

"I have another call," Juanita said.

"Okay, well, thanks. We'll be in touch." Grace hadn't heard any telltale beep, but that didn't mean anything—she might have missed it. She reached her hand straight up, and Ham put a cold beer into it. She clicked off her cell phone and set it on the coffee table. Lightning flashed. Rain fell.

Ham plopped down and took a swallow, looking over at her. She shrugged and started on the beer, while Ham started in on her, lazing his free hand over her breast.

"I'm not sure, but I think J-for-Juanita's a little nervous," she said. "We should stay on her."

"First, I'll stay on you." Ham's hand traveled to her

other breast, rough, warm fingertips on chilly, puckering skin.

"I need to get some sleep," she said, taking another drink.

"So . . . we can sleep."

"You need to go home," she insisted. "Those rats in the walls of your apartment will miss you."

"It's not that bad of a place." She heard the edge in his voice. He didn't want to leave.

Gus raised his head from his bed and told her in his Scooby-Doo way that he had to go weewee. Finally. Grateful for the opportunity to move away from Ham without seeming like she was moving away from Ham, Grace walked over to the side door and opened it. She made a little bow.

Gus flopped his head back down.

Thanks for nothing, Bighead.

Grace frowned. "Are you sick, man? Have you peed at all today?"

"He's fine." Ham started to reach for her. Then he sighed and set down his beer, scarcely touched. Wordlessly, he got up and walked past her; she smelled the yeasty scent of sex and hops as he went into the bathroom. After he peed, he didn't come out. He was getting dressed.

It is what it is, Grace thought as she watched the rain come down.

About three hours after Ham left, Grace's cell phone rang. She was asleep, fumbled, got it.

"Detective Hanadarko," Grace said.

"It's . . . Juanita. I hope I didn't wake you up."

I knew it. I knew something was up with her. Despite the low-grade hum in Grace's gut, she stayed neutral. "No, not at all. I keep crazy hours when I'm working on a case." She was trying to make Juanita think she was just like her. They were the same kind of people—people who would normally talk to each other, share confidences. Police work was a lot like working a crisis line: If you got people talking, you were getting somewhere.

"I . . . I thought of something." Juanita sounded shaky.

Stay easy, Grace. "That's great. Anything you can do to help me—"

"And I need to talk to you."

Bingo. Mucho bingo. *You are talking to me. But that's not what you mean, is it? You've got something. You know something.*

"Sure. You want me to come over there?" She waited a beat.

"I'm . . . no." Juanita's voice was low, breathy, as if she didn't want anyone to hear her.

"Or . . . you could come down to the office," Grace said, as if she was struck with sudden inspiration. She made her voice grow warmer, tinged it with a bit of excitement. "We might have a sketch today. I could show you the deceased's personal effects." *And interview you, with Ham or one of the guys behind our observation mirror, make sure I got our asses covered.*

"I sleep during the day." Juanita was losing her nerve.

"That's no problem," Grace said. She heaved a frustrated sigh. "I have a mound of paperwork to do. I'm so busted. I'm going into the office in a little bit to get it done before anyone comes in."

"Oh," Juanita murmured.

C'mon, c'mon, Grace silently urged her.

"Joe and I went down to that deli you've got there," she chattered on. "That's probably where I screwed up. I drank so much coffee I got wired. That was really dumb of me. I have enough trouble sleeping as it is."

"I know what you mean," Juanita said. "That's one of the reasons I don't mind the late shift." She took a breath. "Maybe I could bring you some coffee." Then she backtracked. "What am I saying? There's coffee at a police . . . at your work."

"Are you kidding? Our coffee is like battery acid. No one ever drinks it. We all bring in our own."

"Then . . . I could bring some, and maybe a couple of bagels. Or if you'd rather have a donut . . ."

Grace made herself not do her version of the Rhetta happy dance. But she did smile at Gus, who had opened one eye and was gazing steadily at her.

"Y'know, I've got the worst sweet tooth," Grace confessed. "I try to stick to the healthy stuff, like bagels, but you get what you want. Oh, hell, if they've got maple bars—"

"They do," Juanita said. "And chocolate ones, too." She waited.

"Damn. How about a couple of each? We can share. I just went to the ATM and—"

"Oh, please," Juanita said. She sounded almost cheerful. "Don't worry about *that.*"

"Well, thanks, Juanita. So, see you in . . . maybe half an hour?" Grace pressed. She carried the cell phone with her into her bedroom and gazed at the tornado of clothing. Shook her head and opened a drawer. Clean bikinis, cool. Clean bra. Two for two.

"Yes," Juanita replied. Given a task and a chance to be helpful, and committed to showing up with food.

Grace hung up and dialed Ham.

"Yeah." His voice was early-morning husky; it got her where she lived.

"It's almost seven. Juanita's coming in," she informed him. "And you have to do my paperwork."

He groaned, then laughed silently. So, no hard feelings for kicking him out. At least, none he was sharing.

CHAPTER
SIX

Tired but alert, Grace showered, dressed, and microwaved yesterday's leftover coffee. As she braided her hair, she looked around for Earl, to show him she damn well *could* wake up without a hangover, but he was probably off eating tabouli in Iraq.

The streets were slick, but Connie knew how to hug the corners. Grace got to 701 Colcord Drive in plenty of time and winced when she saw, really saw, all the folders on her desk. Poor Ham. Whistling under her breath, she scooped up the first five hundred pounds or so and hefted them onto his desk.

"Hey," said Bobby as he walked in. He was carrying a large brown paper shopping bag. She raised a brow. He said nothing, just walked over to Butch's desk and set the bag on his partner's chair. He opened the top drawer to the desk and pulled a colorful box out of his sack and stuffed it in the drawer. Pulled out another box.

Intrigued, Grace wandered over. The entire bag was full of various boxes of candy. Fudge, specifically.

She opened another one of Butch's drawers and placed the box inside. Bobby nodded his thanks.

"What're we doing this for?" she asked, grinning her lopsided grin.

"Butch broke a heart while we were out canvassing," he said. "She either owns or works in an upscale fudge shop."

"Fudgepacker?" she quipped as she examined one of the boxes. It seemed a little light to be a one-pound box of truffles. "This is an expensive joke, man."

"Sweet tooth," he said. "It would be if I'd bought candy at the store we went to," Bobby replied. He flashed her a smile. "And if there was fudge in any of those boxes."

She began to open the box in her hands, then stopped. She'd save the surprise for its intended target.

"I got someone coming in," she said. "Scared, I think. From the hotline."

Bobby folded up the bag and stashed it in his own desk. "Coming in willingly?"

"I think she wanted to meet me somewhere else. But after our string of bad luck around here, I don't want to screw it up, you know?" She jerked her head in the direction of the interview room. "You think you could observe?"

"Sure."

"Thanks, man."

Grace took the next pile of case files and transferred them to Ham's desk. Then she thought a moment and took back a stack, opened one, put on her glasses, and sat down. She had to reassure Juanita that she really did have to come in. Lessee, lessee. ADW. Assault with a deadly weapon. Black on black. She remembered the perp. Stared into his mean, dull mug-shot eyes and saw nothing there but a serious need for a time-out. In solitary.

"What time is she coming in?" Bobby asked her.

"Not sure. Soon," Grace replied. She checked the time on the face of her cell phone. It was coming on seven forty-five. "Maybe about now."

"I'll go get some coffee," said Bobby, leaving her alone in case her anxious citizen arrived.

"Thanks, man," she said. Added, "But don't drink it, y'know? That shit'll kill you."

They shared a smile and Grace called Ham on his cell.
"I'm almost there," he said.

"I'm here now. I think you owe me something." She
liked his dirty chuckle. "She's not here yet, but let me do
some girl talk with her."

"Got it." He sounded tired. "Grace, maybe *we* should
talk."

"Shit, Ham, we talk all day." She hung up.

"Not now, Earl," she said, just in case he felt like giving her a little morning pep-talk-slash-lecture about her
situation with Ham before Juanita showed up. But her
admonition was greeted with silence. She huffed, wish-
ing for a distraction so she could close the file folder.

And God answered her prayers, as Juanita Provo
hovered on the other side of the glass entrance to Major
Crimes. She was Hispanic, early forties, with a few curves;
bronze lipstick and eye makeup; wearing a navy blue raincoat over jeans, heeled boots, and a white blouse. She
cradled a cardboard take-out box in her arms loaded with
coffee and frosted donuts. Not a bagel in sight.

Grace caught the door and speed-dialed Ham. Juanita
smelled like roses. She smiled at Grace with big white
teeth.

"Hi," Juanita said. Yep, same voice.

"Hey. Wow, thanks," Grace said warmly. "Is this one
mine?" She eased the nearest coffee out of the container.
It was a strategic move: Juanita still had something to do
with her hands, and Grace had taken command of the
situation. She stood aside to let Juanita in. Watched her
assess her surroundings. Judging from Juanita's level of
curiosity, it appeared that she was new to the inside of
a police station.

"Hmm, that's good," Grace said, taking a sip. *Gack,*
where was the sugar? "We can go in here," she said,
indicating the interview room. "It's not all that comfortable," she added, "but it's private."

"Okay," Juanita said, still happy to be helpful. Her gaze strayed to Grace's and Ham's desks, which faced each other. "Wow, is that the paperwork you mentioned?"

Grace smiled. "Don't worry. I've got all day to deal with it. I'm grateful to you for the excuse to put it off for a little bit. So if you feel like, y'know, *chatting* for a while . . ." She raised her brows: *please, please, please*?

Juanita's face clouded, as if she was being brought out of a warm bubble of girl-to-girl camaraderie into the colder reality of why she had called Grace. If people thought Grace would play nice because she was a girl, Grace was happy to let them think that. She officially did not notice Juanita's change in demeanor and walked her into the interrogation room. Pushed the button to make the light go red, signaling that the room was occupied, and shut the door behind the two of them.

She set her coffee cup on the table. Juanita blinked at the handcuff ring in the center while she put down the carton. At the two-way mirror.

"It's not much," Grace agreed. "Would you be more comfortable at my desk?"

"Oh, no, this is okay," Juanita assured her. She brightened. Falsely. "Do you want chocolate or maple, to start?"

Grace's cell phone vibrated inside her jeans. She guessed that Ham had arrived.

Grace took a chocolate frosted bar and sampled it. Fat, sugar, and cocoa. You couldn't go wrong with that. She gave a little moan and pulled back her chair. Juanita sat down, but she didn't take a donut. Grace pretended not to notice as she flashed Juanita a guilty little grin and took a maple bar, too.

Juanita smiled a little, and picked up the other maple bar. She broke off a little bit and put it in her mouth. A tentative sort. Grace would be gentle.

"You must be tired, after your shift." She drank some coffee.

"I . . . there was a boy," Juanita began.

Here we go. Grace took another sip of coffee. Then she looked at Juanita.

"His name was Zack. He called . . . a lot." She looked at her maple bar as if it might tell her what to say next.

"And did he mostly talk to you?" Grace asked her.

She nodded. "Evan doesn't want us to form attachments. We're not therapists and we're not always there. So if someone calls expecting to talk to the same phone volunteer, but can't, it adds to their sense of powerlessness."

"Makes sense." Grace tore off more maple. No, wait, it was time for some chocolate, no, for both. God, she was hungry.

"But . . . he was so . . . ," Juanita trailed off.

So you broke the rules. Told him your schedule. "Trouble at home? Drugs?" Grace asked.

"The thing is, if it's not him," Juanita said, "I don't want to violate his privacy."

Or get in trouble. "That's perfectly understandable," Grace said calmly. "People take a big chance when they open up to you. I respect that."

She waited. Juanita sat quietly.

"So . . . was it drugs?" Grace asked, trying to set up a scenario. That's what cops did, built up a picture, a scenario, for the interviewee to participate in. So the subject could add detail or correct the officer. And then, eventually, some of the interviewees realized they had tipped their hand or outright confessed. Juanita dipped her head.

No, Grace translated.

"Bad home life?"

"He stopped calling about a week ago," she said, gazing up at Grace with a stricken look.

Grace's cell phone vibrated again. She debated. Juanita was maybe about to have a breakthrough. Maybe the call was urgent. Maybe the best thing was to let Juanita take a moment.

"Excuse me," she said, pulling out the phone. It was a text message from Ham: SKETCH.

Wow, that was fast, she thought approvingly. *Maybe Earl is helping us.*

"Juanita," she said, "I know that at Helping Hand you talk to people on the phone. But maybe you saw someone hanging around in the parking lot, or sitting in the deli. We have a sketch. I'd like to show it to you."

Her eyes got huge. "Of the . . . does he look? . . ."

"No, no, it's what our John Doe looked like before," Grace said. She leaned forward slightly. "You'd be helping us out if you could tell us if you ever saw him around."

"Okay." Juanita cleared her throat. "Yes."

"Excuse me," Grace said, pushing back her chair. "I'll get the sketch and I'll come right back."

The woman crossed her arms and nodded. "Okay."

Grace left the room and saw no one in the bullpen. On a hunch, she entered the observation room. Ham was sitting in the chair nearest the door with an open folder in his lap, revealing the sketch. Kate, Bobby, and Butch were there, too. Grace took the sketch from Ham. Wide, light eyes, big forehead. Sharp nose, weak chin. Long hair, no particular style.

"Hi, Zack," Grace tried experimentally.

"Look at her," Butch said.

Grace looked through the mirror at the drab, unfriendly room. Juanita's head was bowed and her fists were clenched.

"She's praying," Grace said. "For this Zack? Or for herself?"

"Go find out," Kate told her, looking serious and determined.

"On it."

Grace strode back toward the interrogation room, then forced herself to slow down. She took a deep breath and put on her game face: sympathy, hope, sorrow. She gave the door a little knock and went on in.

Juanita raised her head and slid her hands into her lap. Straightened her shoulders. Licked her lips.

"Now, this is just our best guess," Grace began. "But we've got a young man in our morgue with no name, and we'd like to know who he is."

Gently, she placed the sketch down in front of Juanita Provo. The woman sucked in her breath and sat back in her chair. Her eyes widened, welled.

"Oh," Juanita whispered.

Hello, Zack, Grace said to the sketch.

"Does he look familiar?" Grace ticked her gaze to the observation mirror.

"I . . . yes," Juanita ground out, farther back in her seat. "He . . . are you sure . . . he's dead?" she rasped. Then she touched the center of her forehead with a trembling hand. "I mean . . . I don't know what I mean. . . ."

She covered her mouth with her hand; Grace was afraid Juanita might throw up, and she glanced around for the metal trash can, which they mostly kept in the room to slam down on the table and scare the living bejesus out of the hard cases.

"Zachary. He went by Zack." She made a choking sound deep in her throat. "Oh, God, we . . . I . . ."

Had phone sex? Robbed a liquor store? "You met," Grace began. "It was against the rules, but you saw him. You know that this is Zack." She flickered with triumph as Juanita shifted in her chair. Score for Hanadarko.

"He had no one," she said. She began to cry. "He was so lost."

"That's okay," Grace said. "You take your time." Grace grabbed one of the paper napkins from the deli and handed it to her. Juanita took it and wiped her eyes.

"Terribly lost," Juanita said, sobbing hard, once. Then she caught herself. "I told him to pray."

"That's good," Grace said.

"Pray for it to go away."

Say what? Grace waited. And waited.

"Pray for it to go away," Grace echoed. "It" what? Their love for each other? His heroin addiction? "Juanita, what was wrong?"

"He thought he might be a homosexual." Now the words ran together, as if she had to get them out quickly or she might never say them. "So I told him if he lifted his heart up to Jesus Christ, he could be healed. He could be *normal*."

Grace's blood pressure rose. *So this kid comes to you, confides in you, looks to you for help. And you give him a line of fundamentalist bullshit?*

She clenched her jaw. "How'd that work out for him?" she bit off, then shut her eyes—because of course that was the wrong thing to say. She tried again. "Is that the policy of the crisis center? To pray with the callers?"

Juanita wept. Grace was afraid she was going to lose her. She opened her mouth to assure Juanita that she, Grace, prayed six times a day and most especially at noon for troubled youth, when Juanita spoke again.

"No. We're funded by a church, but it's nondenominational." Then she amended. "I mean the hotline's supposed to be secular. If they ask to pray on the phone, we do it, sure, anything to give them some time to cool down. But I . . . I knew this was against their policies."

Their policies. She was already putting distance between herself and the center. Probably assumed Evan would boot her ass.

"So when Zack called because he was confused about his sexual orientation, you indicated to him that being gay is not okay?" Grace gritted. Wrong thing again. She hadn't had any sleep. "I'm sorry," Grace began, but Juanita spoke over her, moving her anguished gaze from somewhere in time to right here, right now, and Grace's face. She flared a bit.

"It's *not* okay. It's a sin. And I wanted to save him. Jesus could have lifted that burden from him, if his faith was strong enough."

Then she dropped her head again, as if she knew she shouldn't even bother trying to justify her actions. The crown of her head gleamed under the fluorescents. Grace wanted to smack her, balled her fists beneath the table. *I have to be like her. She'll open up.*

"You were trying hard to help him. You must have met with him, prayed together," she said, her training winning out over the big red blur of anger fuzzing her mind.

Juanita nodded. "Yes. We met."

Grace picked up her maple bar, trying to remind Juanita that they'd had some good times here in the interview dungeon confessional. "At church?"

The woman shook her head. She was biting the lipstick off her mouth. Balancing-act time; Grace had to get the most bang for her questions until Juanita melted down or stopped talking.

"He didn't want to go to a Catholic church," Juanita said.

"And you're Catholic?"

"*Sí.*"

Grace caught the code switching—moving from English to Spanish—and knew Juanita was starting to lose it. The more stress she was under, the more likely she was to really put it out there. Or fold up her tent. But there was more. Grace was certain of it.

"That must have bothered you," Grace said, getting out of her chair. She walked around the table. "I'm Catholic.

I've got a brother who's a priest." *Who is a sanctimonious asshole.*

Juanita looked dubious. Grace very much regretted her outburst about praying away the gay. For that she assigned herself four folders of paperwork. No, two. She cleared her throat and perched on the corner of the table. "And I have a sister who's a lesbian," she said. She was lying of course, she needed to stack the deck so that Juanita would show her hand. "I've got some tough family dynamics."

"Oh." Juanita nodded. She wrapped her napkin around the forefinger of her left hand. Grace noted the absence of a wedding ring.

"He . . . people at school made fun of him," she said. "He was small, and girlish. He talked about being more macho. He really wanted to change."

"But . . . he couldn't," Grace said sadly, going for the cheese-out manipulation. "Not in time, anyway." A beat. "Did you suspect he was going to do it?"

Juanita jerked. "Suspect? . . ."

"That he was going to commit suicide." Grace crossed herself. "The one unforgivable sin."

"Oh, Dios *mío*," Juanita whispered brokenly. "Zack, *mijo.*"

"You shouldn't blame yourself," Grace said. *Even though I sure as hell do.*

"I—I didn't get through to him." Juanita sniffled. "He died in a state of sin."

Grace shook her head slowly. "Sometimes people are so broken that we just can't fix them. But at least you tried."

"People don't fix other people," Juanita said. Her quavery voice suddenly became very firm. "Only God can fix them. But they have to offer themselves to Him to fix."

"You're right. I didn't say that well," Grace allowed.

She put a hand on Juanita's shoulder. "This must be so hard on you. When you say he had no one else, are you saying he had no family? Do you know his last name?"

"No," she replied. Too quickly.

"Please think hard," Grace urged softly. "We need to find his next of kin. Arrange for his burial."

"Oh." She chewed off more lipstick. Tightened the napkin around her finger like a noose. Grace figured Juanita was trying to dodge the aftermath, put some space between her and the boy she had failed to save from going to hell. And the crisis center, which would probably give her hell.

"We've sent his prints out," Grace said. "They'll come back sooner or later." That was probably a lie. There were about 150,000 cases listed in the ViCAP system. Victims, perps, suspects. There were over 300 million people in the United States.

"I—I think his last name might be Lacey," Juanita blurted. "He said it once to me."

Yes. Grace nodded thoughtfully. "You've got a good memory. Do you remember if he talked about parents? A brother? Sister? Someone with a name? Do you remember the name of his school?" It wouldn't be too hard to track him down now.

"His father is a truck driver," she said. "He's gone a lot."

"What's his mother's name?" Grace asked her.

"I don't know." She started to cry. "*Por favor,* please. This is all I know. I've been up all night." The tears came harder. "Please, let me go home."

Grace had no choice. She couldn't charge Juanita with anything. Accessory to suicide, yeah, maybe.

"Thank you so, so much for coming to me with this," Grace said, keeping the door open for Juanita to come back. "I know it was hard. But what you did today is going to help us."

Juanita sobbed. "He is gone from God. He's gone from God."

"We don't know that," Grace soothed, squatting beside her chair and rubbing Juanita's arm.

"He didn't die in a state of grace. I—I thought I could do some good. I thought . . ."

Grace's anger built again. Juanita was more concerned with her own complicity than the fate of Zack's immortal soul. *Typical Catholic bullshit,* she thought.

"Talk to your priest," Grace said, taking Juanita's hand. *Confession is good for the soul. He'll probably make you feel even guiltier, and you can wallow in it. That'll take your mind off being fired from the hotline.*

Juanita nodded. "Thank you," she said.

"Oh, and here. For the donuts," Grace said, handing her a ten. "Please."

"No, no," Juanita said, but she took it and stuffed it in her purse. She left, still crying.

As Grace shut the squad-room door, Kate, Ham, and Butch filed out of the interview room, grim-faced and angry, like her. Grace kicked a trash can.

"Zachary Lacey, whose father drives a truck," Captain Perry said.

"I'll contact the schools. The Oklahoma Department of Public Safety can get a match against the commercial driver's license records," Bobby said, heading for the phone. Grace checked the wall clock. Nine straight up. Offices were open.

"God, she might as well have pushed him in," Grace said.

"You call a help line, thinking you're safe from judgment," Kate concurred. "If they had a religious agenda, they should have advertised it." Her look took in Grace and Ham. "Did you get a sense that this Joe Varisse was on the up-and-up about that place refraining from spiritual counseling?"

"Maybe," Ham said. He turned to Grace.

"They're like that, those religious groups," Grace bit off. "Pull you in, then once they've got you . . ."

Then she turned away. Turned back, and looked at Ham.

"Once we find out which school he went to, let's talk to the kids who were mean to him. Shitheads."

Ham nodded. "Got it."

And Butch opened his top desk drawer. Saw the candy box and opened it. A sound chip activated and the room was filled with a woman's voice shrieking, "Butch, oh, Butch, oh, my God!"

Everyone started cracking up as Bobby darted over and opened the other drawers and the other candy boxes. More women joined the ecstatic chorus. Then a sheep baahed and a cow mooed, long and low and contented.

As laughter joined the cacophony, Butch just shook his head. Then Bobby reached into a box under his desk and said, "Who wants fudge?"

CHAPTER
SEVEN

Pizza, popcorn, a pound of sour gummy candy, and two liters of root beer.

Let the games begin.

Grace popped in the DVD of the horror movie Doug would probably not want Clay to watch while Clay settled in. They were both wearing their pj's. Clay's were a faded T-shirt from the Cowboy Hall of Fame and a pair of gray sweats. Grace had on baggy white men's flannels with blue stripes.

Gusman nosed at the pizza box on Clay's lap. With a giggle, Clay pulled off part of the crust on his double-super-triple-extra-meat-worshipers' pizza slice and let Gus hoover it in. Clay's giggle became a full-throated laugh, and Grace smiled fondly at the two of them. She sat down next to boy and dog, and Clay handed her a piece of pizza. They were using paper towels for plates.

Grace picked up the remote. "So, previews or no previews?" she asked.

"Previews. There will probably be a lot of cool gross ones," Clay said. His dark eyes, so like his dead mother's, sparkled with anticipation. He still had his baby dimples. He was so cute.

She grinned. "Previews it is."

They watched in silence as a zombie chewed the top off a woman's skull. With a roar, he began to eat the screaming chick's brains.

Zachary Lacey's autopsy's done, Grace thought. *Cause of death, drowning. Shit.*

"Does it ever bother you when you see dead bodies in real life?" Clay asked her. "Like, all mangled?"

Like your mother was when I found her?

"Yeah," she said. She glanced over at him. He was rapt. "But it's worth it, Clay. It helps me catch the bad guys."

He processed that. She narrowed her eyes.

"Are you going to have nightmares over this movie?"

"No way," he said, blanching. "I've been waiting for months for this to come out on DVD."

She reached out to tousle his hair, but he was getting to an age where that was a patronizing gesture, maybe. Instead she jostled him with her hand and chomped down on sausage and spiced taco meat.

"Your dad say anything about this movie?"

Clay looked even more worried. "He doesn't even know it exists."

"Good." She picked up the remote and turned up the sound. "Let's keep it that way."

He laughed. "You're cool, Aunt Grace."

Ripping open the bag of sour candy, she moved her shoulders and cricked her neck. "Yeah, well, that depends on your definition, Clay."

"You're fun. And you listen to me."

The image of Father Patrick Satan Murphy, her priest and her molester, bloomed in her mind's eye. He had taken her for ice cream and to the movies, and a dozen other "fun" places. And he'd listened to her in the confessional. Murphy was the man her entire family trusted with not only her physical safety, but the care and nurturing of her immortal soul. Her direct line to God the Father and the Blessed Virgin, mother of all. Father Murphy took Grace's virginity when she was nine years old.

Nine.

So this kid Zack calls for help, and some bitch tells him he's got to pray for God to change him so God can love him. Sweet.

"Clay," Grace said, "you've got a lot of people who care about you, man. And if there was something that was bothering you, *anything,* you could go to one of those people and tell them about it, right?"

He crammed some popcorn and gummy candy into his mouth. "Sure, Aunt Grace."

Right. And your uncle, the priest, would tell you it was bad to be gay, and your grandmother would change the subject, but at least I can teach you to tell someone. If I'd told someone, I would have stopped Father Murphy.

Or maybe . . . no one would have listened to me. Maybe they would have blamed me. Look at all those other kids the Church betrayed. All those damn bishops. They didn't just turn the other butt cheek. They looked the other way.

Her stomach lurched as she glanced at Clay, safe in her house, eating a bunch of crap, watching a movie. So many people loved him. Wanted the best for him. But . . . would they be able to give it to him?

She caught her lower lip as her chest tightened and she was filled with something that made her tremble. How on earth would she help him make his way to adulthood? Become a man?

"He's got a father for that," Earl said. She jerked her head up. Clay was curled up beside her, and Gus was snoring against her thigh. Earl lounged in her easy chair with a bag of microwaved popcorn in his lap. An old re-run of *Law & Order: SVU* was on.

"What happened to the movie?" she asked.

"You both conked out and it was giving me the willies, so I popped it out and turned this on. But it's pretty gruesome, too." Earl made a face.

"I recorded the game," she told him. "You could watch that."

He raised a brow. "Which game?"

She laughed silently. "You are clearly not from Oklahoma." She gathered up her hair and let it fall. Dropped her head back against the sofa.

"A father," she said. "You mean Doug, his dad." She looked over at him. "Right?"

He changed the channel. Yet more crime-scene investigators were hunkering down around a dead body. Sighing, he surfed on. "You don't know what I mean, Grace."

"Maybe I do. Maybe that's the same father who lets airplanes crash into buildings and sixteen-year-old boys drown in rivers because they're gay."

"God's real sorry about Zachary Lacey," Earl said, looking hard at her. "I am, too."

"Sorry because he was gay so he went to hell?" she tested. If Earl could confirm Zack's sexual orientation, she was one step closer to the finish line.

"Grace, please." Earl was aggrieved.

"Well, people *can* do things that send them to hell. You said I was going to hell."

"Zachary Lacey was a sweet kid," Earl said. "Or so I've been told."

And I'm not. "Then why did you guys let this happen to him?"

Earl sighed. "You just don't get it, do you, child?"

"No. I don't, Earl. I sure as *hell* don't." She snaked her way off the couch and stood. Gus and Clay remained as they were. "I'm tired."

"No, you're thirsty." Earl turned off the TV. "You're thinking of going to the fridge and grabbing a beer."

"So? My ranch, my rules, man." She bowed her back, stretching out the muscles and staring up at the ceiling.

"And a bottle of tequila," Earl added. "That's on your mind, too."

Grace huffed and straightened, prepared to give him a stink eye. "Again I say . . ."

But he was gone.

"Good," she said aloud, sounding petulant and immature even to herself.

She went into her bedroom and came back with a soft cream-colored blanket that she arranged over Clay and Gus. Gus's legs pumped and he wheezed; he was doggie dream-jogging. Then she closed up the box of leftover pizza, walked into the kitchen, and opened the fridge. There were the lovely beers. Screw him. She crammed the pizza box on top of a brick of cheddar cheese and reached her hand in for a nice longneck.

Then she looked at the clock on the microwave, its red eye beaming behind the receipt for the pizza and some packets of Parmesan cheese. Damn. It was four a.m.

She shut the fridge not because Earl had shamed her but because she didn't feel like drinking a beer this close to starting a brand-new day. With her luck, she'd catch another FBI's Ten Most Wanted and get busted down for drinking on the job.

Taking another peek at Clay, she stomped into her bedroom and climbed into bed. She rolled over on a pack of matches and got them out of her way. Wondered who was talking to whom at Helping Hand and if they were doing more harm than good. She'd tried to talk a kid out of jumping off the bleachers at his school. Failed.

They were mean to him at school.

Grace ruminated on that awhile. She had to get some sleep. She fluffed up the covers and closed her eyes, but they popped back open. She tensed all the muscles in her body, hard, and relaxed them one at a time.

She sat up and lit a cigarette. She wondered who else couldn't sleep at four—make that four thirty—a.m. Maybe Rhetta was up, milking Holy Cow, worried about how to pay for the farm. Making lunches for her

kids. You couldn't call moms with kids at four thirty
a.m. It scared 'em. And it woke up the kids.

Grace tamped out the cigarette and lay back down
again. Counted sheep.

"Maybe you'll do better if you count your blessings,"
Earl said.

They were back in Louie's, and the water was rising
around her ankles. It was icy and it made her bones
ache.

"Shouldn't we start bailing?" she asked him. "This
place is filling up fast." She squinted against the lightning
that flashed in the window. "And it's still raining."

"It's always raining someplace on Lifeboat Earth,"
Earl said.

The alarm woke her up and she realized she'd had another dream. No Leon Cooley in this one, thank God.
No hangover, either. She never had too much to drink in
front of Clay. *Bleah*. Too much popcorn and sour candy,
though.

She got up and made her signature rubbery pancakes.
They stuck to the pan but, hey, she'd cooked breakfast.
Clay got up and took a shower, put on his Catholic-school
uniform, and took a few bites of pancake.

"Can I have cold pizza instead?" he asked her.

"Sure. I'm having that, too," she replied.

She picked up a cup from the pile of dirty dishes, rinsed
it out, and poured coffee in it. She took a slug and then
got the pizza out of the fridge. Flipped open the box and
gestured for him to help himself.

"Can I have a cup of coffee?" he asked.

"No." She glanced at the clock on her microwave.
"Uncle John should be here in about ten minutes. Be sure
to brush your teeth." She poured him a glass of milk.
Then she took a slice of pizza. "And you might not want
to mention our choice of movie to him, either. Even
though we fell asleep before the really good parts."

"How do you know?" he asked.

"How many horror movies do you think we've watched together?" she demanded. "You don't know the best gory stuff comes later?" She showed him her teeth and chomp-chomp-chomped.

"Chmp, chmp, chmp!" Clay tried to be a zombie while at the same time not chewing with his mouth open.

They smiled, coconspirators.

The best gory stuff.

It was difficult to say which was harder on the friends and family of missing persons. Sometimes when you told them their loved one was dead, they thanked you. They had to face the fact that Cousin Mo was gone, but at least they knew. It was the not knowing that made it so hard. It was hell not knowing. That was why so many people had risked their lives to retrieve all the bodies out of the Murrah Building as fast as possible.

Time to meet the Laceys.

Grace entered the interview room and looked at the seated couple. She felt the tension rise as she came in and sat down. Ron Lacey was a burly man with a full beard, and he kept his Owens Field ball cap on. His eyes were too close together, and Grace reminded herself that just because that made him look kind of stupid, it didn't mean he was. His jaw was tight and he had that flat, resentful expression some people got around cops. It didn't matter if she could help him. He detested her just because. Maybe to underscore that point, Monsieur had chosen to wear a faded Harley-Davidson T-shirt. Harley bikes went for around fifteen grand, for starters. She sincerely doubted he owned one.

Cherie Lacey, his wife, sat huddled beside him with the long scarlet fingernails of her right hand wrapped around his bicep. Younger, with blond hair straightened into a stylish cut. She had on way too much makeup, and was wearing large hoop earrings with hunks of glass or maybe cubic zirconium dangling from them. She wore a leopardskin-print tank top and spiky black boots decorated with loose boot bracelets studded with brass roses and more sparkles. Her eyes welled with tears, and she was holding an unlit cigarette between the slender fingers of her left hand, which was shaking.

"Hello, Mr. and Mrs. Lacey," Grace said in a soft voice. The couple was facing the two-way mirror. "I'm sorry to have to call you down here like this."

Cherie Lacey glanced at her husband. He stared stonily at Grace. Cherie licked her lips and toyed with her cigarette. "Where's Zachary?" she asked. Her voice twanged pure Texas. Grace should have made Butch do this one.

Ron Lacey stayed quiet. Waves of hostility rolled off him like body odor. Despite no match on the print, Grace was fairly certain that his son's body was lying in the morgue; Grace wondered how Daddy would react when he found that out.

For the time being, the mom was the one who was more engaged, so Grace concentrated on her. "When was the last time you saw your son, Mrs. Lacey?"

"He's my stepson," she replied. "It's been about a week."

A week. Potential match, Grace thought. She kept her face neutral. "Did you file a Missing Persons report?"

Cherie blanched. "Well, I—"

"No, she didn't," Lacey interrupted, "because he runs away a lot. Little shit."

Beneath her coat of makeup, Cherie's forehead was wrinkled, as in maybe she was a little older than she first appeared. "He usually comes back after a couple of days. I didn't want to get him in trouble at school, so I . . . I called him in sick." She blanched. "Was that, um, illegal?" She swallowed hard and grasped her husband's arm tightly. The frown lines on his face softened as he laid his hand over hers. She didn't look back at him.

"Maybe not if you call him in for a couple of days," Grace replied. "But he's been gone a full week, ma'am."

She swallowed, contrite. "I know. But Ronnie was on the road, and I wasn't sure what to do."

"You're a trucker," Grace said. "Long haul. You were in Nebraska." It would be easy enough to verify if she needed to.

His too-close, stupid eyes practically crossed. He must be fun in a bar fight. "So?"

"Just sayin'," Grace said evenly. "Making sure I understand the big picture."

He glowered at Grace. "There is no picture here, cop. This is family business. We'll raise him our way. They only care if he's in school so they can get money from the government."

"Sir," Grace said, then forced herself to take a breath, "we have reason to believe that your son is dead, sir. We have a body in the morgue, and there's been a positive ID of a composite sketch by someone who knew him."

"No," Cherie whispered. "Oh, no, dear God, no."

Grace opened her file folder and laid the sketch faceup on the table. There were also color pictures of the bloated horror they'd fished out of the river, but she kept those facedown and out of sight.

If she was looking for some grief from the man, or shock, she didn't get it. Although Cherie Lacey caught her breath and covered her mouth, Lacey's expression never wavered.

"Zack," Cherie whispered. "Oh, my God, that *is* Zack. Ronnie, oh, no, *no*." She burst into tears and he patted her, almost reflexively, as he waved his free hand dismissively at the sketch.

"That's just a drawing," he said. He gestured to the folder. "What else you got?"

"I have very disturbing pictures," Grace replied. "It's possible we have the wrong person. As you say, this is just a composite sketch, done by a police artist with a computer. But whoever it was, he drowned, and he was in the river for a week."

"Oh, no, no," Cherie moaned. *"Ronnie—"*

"We don't know it's him," Lacey said, sounding impatient. "I want to see the other pictures. The *real* ones."

Grace considered. She could not let her instant dislike of this man color the way she treated him now. It was highly likely his son was dead, and the photographs would stay with him for the rest of his life, unless his heart was coated with Teflon.

"I need a positive ID, but I need to warn you that you may not be able to do that from any pictures that we took of the body." Grace looked down at her folder. "The body is not in good shape," she underscored. "We could try other ways, a DNA match." Unless the kid wasn't his. Where was Zack's natural mother in all of this?

"I can take it." Lacey started to reach across the table. Like he was in charge. Grace placed her hand on the folder.

Cherie hiccupped. Her face was dead white.

"Mrs. Lacey," she said, "you're not obligated to look at these pictures. Since Zachary was your stepson, I suggest I show them just to your husband. So if you'll kindly look away."

"Can . . . can I go out of the room?" she asked.

"Yes," Grace said. "If you want some coffee, just ask someone. They'll be glad to help you."

Cherie hurried past Grace in a cloud of drugstore vanilla cologne, probably the next aisle over from where she got her blond hair.

"Mr. Lacey, may I ask you where Zachary's biological mother is?"

"No idea. She split on us when Zack was nine. We got a few postcards at first, birthday cards, that kind of bullshit. Then they stopped coming." He glared at her. "And I *did* file a Missing Persons on her, and you people came up dry. You can check all that."

Maybe that was why Ron Lacey hated cops. Although Grace doubted it.

"Just show it to me, goddamn it," he bit off at her.

Grace took her hand off the back of the first picture— the close-up—and flipped it over like the bottom card in a game of blackjack. She felt she was being brutal and she didn't want to be; she didn't want to make this man pay because he was a redneck asshole who didn't seem concerned about his son at all. He was looking at her, not at the picture, and she realized he was staring at her breasts.

"There," Grace said, sliding the photo toward him with her forefinger.

He had the decency then to stop leering at her and glanced down at the picture. He went white. Stared. Kept staring.

"Is that your son, sir?"

He was silent for a long time. Grace wondered if he'd gone into shock. Then he bobbed his head once.

"I think so. Yeah."

She wanted his voice to sound raw with emotion. She wanted to be able to say someday that in that moment, he aged ten years. But he didn't. She reminded herself that grief did funny things to people. Juries had convicted innocent people because they didn't behave "right" during their trials. And she was not here to convict him. Just to figure out how and why Zack Lacey had died. Maybe in the process she could figure out how and why his mother had disappeared.

Circumstantial, she reminded herself. *I'd run away from this asshole, too.*

"Where'd you find him?" he asked finally.

At last. Some interest, Grace thought. "I'm so sorry for your loss," she said. She meant it. "A police officer on patrol found him in the river." She didn't disclose anything more than that.

He frowned at her. "A week ago? And it took this long to let us know?"

"He was found two nights ago, sir." Grace picked up the photograph. "There was no ID on . . . with him. Just a phone number for a teen-crisis hotline. He's called it a number of times. Do you know why, sir?"

"He called a *what*?" The man stared at her.

"A crisis center." Grace made herself sound soft and confused. "Do you have any idea what he was upset about?"

"No." He was back to stiff-jawed. And by the pink in his doughy cheeks, she was pretty sure he was lying. "What now? You send his body . . ."

He trailed off, and she got the feeling he was more embarrassed that he didn't know the term for "funeral home" than he was freaked out that his kid was dead.

There was something going on here. Something she did not like. At all.

"We have a few more tests to run," she said. Henry was back tomorrow, yes. "We want to make absolutely certain that no crime was committed against your son."

"A crime," he echoed. He frowned again, and then his lips parted. "Someone killed him?" He sucked in his breath. She couldn't tell if he was bullshitting. Or if he knew someone killed him.

"We don't know that, sir," Grace said. "We're trying to determine that. So we would like to keep his . . . remains . . . here for just a little longer."

He looked past her shoulder. Grace guessed that

Cherie was looking at him through the window. "Are there . . . storage fees? If you keep him for more tests?"

No way, she thought, incredulous that that would be his first thought. *No effing way. I thought I'd seen and heard it all.*

"No, sir."

"Then . . . I guess . . ." Now he did look down. He sighed and wiped his face with his hands. His shoulders rounded. Grace made no sound. Even though no clock was ticking, she heard one; maybe it was her heartbeat. Maybe Lena Garvin would give the body up. She'd say she'd done all the looking necessary and they needed the room in the morgue. And she'd be right. But Henry would be there tomorrow.

"I guess he's not going anywhere," the man said.

"Thank you, sir."

She got up and put the photograph in the folder. "I'm sorry," she said again, turned, and left the interview room.

Cherie was perched on the edge of Butch's desk, wiping her eyes with a tissue. Butch was leaning back in his chair with his hands wedged under his armpits. Classic body language.

Then Cherie turned and saw Grace; her lips parted and her eyes widened. Grace pursed her lips, and the woman burst into tears.

"It's Zack, isn't it?" she wailed.

"We believe so, ma'am," Grace replied. She was aware that Butch, like Grace herself, was watching Cherie closely as she sobbed.

"I need to ask you to step back into the interview room, just for a few questions," Grace said, gently and sadly.

The woman nodded and slid off Butch's desk like a snake. Grace walked her back in, and Cherie hurried over to her husband and threw her arms around him.

Lacey kind of sagged as he held her. Grace gave them some time and then she broke it up.

"I'm so sorry, but I have to ask you a few things," Grace said. "We want to know why this terrible thing happened to your child."

"I'm going to sue that damn shrink," Lacey blurted.

Grace blinked. "Your son was seeing a psychiatrist?" *And you thought it was odd that he called a help line?*

"So he could get his meds," Lacey said. "Antidepressants." He threw the word like a punch.

"So he had a problem with depression," Grace said.

"I read up on those things. They can make kids go crazy, commit suicide." Lacey's right eye twitched. "That's what you think happened, isn't it? That he killed himself? God*damn* it. Damn it, damn it to hell!" He made a fist and slammed it hard on the metal table. Again and again, as Cherie cried harder. Grace was glad to see some big emotion out of the man. It was better than pussy-footing around.

"Do you know why he was depressed?" Grace asked. "Did it have anything to do with being gay?"

"What?" Lacey froze. "Shut up," he snapped at Cherie, who was still crying. To Grace, "What the hell are you saying? My son is not a faggot."

"That's why he called the crisis line," Grace told him, her voice low, her expression sympathetic. "He was afraid he might be a homosexual."

"No way. No way," Lacey yelled. He jumped out of his seat. Grace half-expected him to launch himself over the table at her. Jeez, no wonder Zack had kept it to himself.

"Ronnie, please. Oh, God, Zack," Cherie wept.

He turned on Cherie. "Shut the hell up!"

Grace observed, waiting to see if he went physical on his wife. Or if she flinched in fear that he might. No action. Grace kept watching. The veins on Lacey's neck were bulging. The stepmom's emotional behavior hadn't altered since Grace had dropped the bomb. Cherie was devastated over his death. Pure and simple.

"How did you hear this?" he demanded.

Grace had a feeling that if she told him, he'd storm over to Helping Hand with a bazooka. So she said, "We have some privileged information at this time."

"I am suing them," he said. "Turn my boy into a faggot—"

"We have no indication that your son was gay, sir," Grace cut in. "Only that he was very distressed."

"What else did he tell them? They're liberals, right? Goddamn—"

"We are doing everything we can to figure out what happened to him," Grace said. "Please, Mr. Lacey, let us do our jobs."

"I want to see him," Lacey said, swinging his attention back to Grace. "Let me see him. He's my only son."

And my only son is not a faggot, Grace supplied.

CHAPTER
EIGHT

"So is that the deal, Earl?" Grace asked her angel as they shared a cigarette and a chaw in the stairwell. The Laceys were gone. And Lena Garvin wanted to get rid of Zack's body, just as Grace had predicted. "God doesn't want us to, y'know, be bad because of His ego? *His* kids can't be screwups? Talk about conditional love."

"God wants you to be happy, Grace," Earl said.

"Christians aren't perfect, just forgiven," she intoned.

"Something like that." He spit into his soda bottle.

"Well, that must be such a relief. For the Christians." She stomped out her cigarette and put it with the rest of its buddies on top of the ledge. Then she flung open the door.

Two more hours on the day shift. She sailed into the autopsy room and hovered on the perimeter, to find a new body lying on the aluminum table, female, cuts across her face; and Lena Garvin speaking into a transcription microphone. Busy girl.

"I'm releasing Zachary Lacey," Lena said, making a point of switching off the mic. "Does the next of kin have a funeral home picked out?"

"Tox screens come back?" Grace asked.

Lena shrugged. "Not yet, but what does that matter? We don't need the remains any longer. Is that all?"

"Actually, no," Grace said. "He was on antidepressants. Can you check for that, too?"

"Sure. But there's no need to keep the body. We've got plenty of samples to work with."

Samples.

"But there might be *other* things," Grace pressed. "Things we haven't thought of yet."

"I have completed the autopsy," Lena insisted, shooting Grace a dirty look.

Grace took a deep breath. "Can't you keep Lacey in the fridge one more night?" she asked, bracing herself for a blast. "I got a feeling. I really do."

I got a feeling that you missed something, and Henry will be back tomorrow. And you know that is what I'm saying, and please, Lena, God, you have to know this is not personal but I want to, I don't know, make sure this kid, this dead kid, gets justice. So, yeah, I am asking you to give me permission to let Henry take a look.

Lena looked from Grace to the cadaver on the table and back to Grace. Then past her. For a second, Grace had the sense that Earl was in the room. Maybe he was Zack's last-chance angel, too. Maybe he'd help her out with the investigation for once.

Maybe every time a pig snorts an angel gets his wings.

Then Lena narrowed her eyes and said, "Okay."

"Thanks," Grace said, startled. "Thanks so much." Without realizing she was going to say it, she added, "Come to Louie's tonight. We go there after work."

Lena sighed. "Fine."

Grace smiled at her. Really smiled. "You can follow me over."

Zachary Lacey had been a student at Franklin High. The final bell had just rung and the kids were all filing out. It wasn't raining, but battleship-gray clouds hung as low as they could go. The streets were wet. Water dripped off bushes and trees.

The kids who were racing toward the parking lots—texting, putting in their earbuds—were just a handful of years older than Clay. Grace realized with a start that when she imagined Clay in her mind's eye she still saw him much younger. Would he sustain any more major trauma in his young life? If anyone ever hurt him, she hoped she got the same judge who gave Joey Amador probation when she got put on trial for assault and/or murder one.

She and Ham couldn't do any searching without a warrant, which they didn't have, but they could ask questions. All the kids carrying enormous backpacks that made them look like hunchbacks. Which ones had been mean to Zack? Who wasn't mean in high school? *Rhetta.*

Grace and Ham visited with Ms. Miller, the well-groomed principal, but it was obvious pretty soon that she didn't really know who Zack Lacey was. The sketch didn't ring any bells. After she checked his schedule, she lined up some of his teachers for interviews. Zack was: quiet, an underachiever, absent a lot, sweet. Everyone was shocked. No one saw it coming. Of course not, because they were mandated reporters: If they saw signs of abuse or distress, they were legally obligated to let someone know. And no one had.

Somehow, the word got around that there were cops on campus and that Zack Lacey was dead. Word always got around. Kids walked slowly past the window that looked into the principal's office, where Grace and Ham were conducting their interviews. Lookiloos, into the drama.

Except for maybe one kid, who appeared and then reappeared in the window. Five-five, maybe a hundred twenty sopping wet, purple-black with long eyelashes and West Indian features. He had a cap on rally style and jeans probably as loose as was allowed. Gold necklace, baby gangsta wannabe. Grace saw that Ham saw him, too; and her partner took over when she excused herself from their interview with Mr. Tranh, the vice-principal.

She trotted down the hall with its diversity mural and a pretty good painting of a mustang, Franklin's mascot. Then she zoomed outside and raced up to the kid while he was still watching the window. When he saw her, he started to bolt. But he had on a big-ass backpack, which probably slowed him down.

"Hey, man," she said, pulling back her jacket so he could see the badge at her waist. "I'm Detective Grace Hanadarko. Did you know Zachary Lacey?"

He stopped. His back was to her. She saw kids looking and figured he wanted the ground to swallow him up. Just as she was about to repeat the question, he turned around, nodded. His lips were trembling. Zack's death mattered to him. A lot.

"Listen, I'm really sorry," she said. "You two were close, right?"

He looked left, right, superanxious.

"Can we go someplace, sit down?" she asked. "I need some help. People want to close the lid on this, say he was just some redneck kid with problems who jumped in the river—"

His mouth dropped open. He blinked at her. There were flecks of gold in his eyes. She caught the merest whiff of marijuana. Noticed it but let it go. For now.

"Is that . . . is that how? . . ."

All she had to do was reach out one finger and push him; he'd fall right over on his ass. A stiff wind blew, nearly doing the job for her. She put her hands in the pockets of her sheepherder's jacket.

"Yeah, that's how," she said. "I'm sorry, man."

She watched him tense, working against tears. "A coffee shop," she suggested. "A place where we can just talk, you and me."

"I got nothing to say to you." He took an unsteady step backward. He wasn't just upset. He was *scared*.

"I won't use anything you tell me against you," she promised. She saw his stony refusal and pulled out her business card. "At least tell me your name." He remained silent. "All I have to do is describe you to your principal." She crossed her fingers that he would care.

He reached out a hand for the card. "My name is Antwone."

Yeah, baby. Go, baby. "Antwone . . ."

"Yeah." He turned his back and strode away. Her card was in his right fist. She kept watching, her concentration on that fist. He was close to the gutter; if he threw it . . .

He still had it in his hand when he loped across the street.

"Could be nothing, could be something," Grace told Ham as she drove toward the station. "Kids are skittish. Like colts. But he was definitely afraid."

"You smelled weed on him. Maybe he was afraid you could tell he was stoned."

She shrugged. "Maybe he was afraid I'd assume he was Zack's boyfriend." Her cell went off. It was Butch's ringtone, so she said to Ham, "Grab it."

"Yeah, Butch," Ham said. "Huh. Okay. Yeah, we'll take it. Give me the address." He whipped out a three-by-five notebook with a pen stuck through the spirals from his jacket pocket. He pulled out the pen with his teeth and pressed the phone against his ear so he could write. "Yeah, yeah, got it."

He hung up and looked over at Grace. "Butch and Bobby went to see Zack's shrink. Doc knew about as much about him as the school principal."

Grace let Connie cling and squeal as she took a corner. "In other words, nothing."

Ham tapped his pen against the notebook. "The way they saw it, the psychiatrist—Dr. Metzner—would just rubber-stamp his prescription renewal for Prozac. But Metzner did mention that Zack's family is Catholic. Their parish priest is named Pepera. Butch set up an appointment with Pepera in his parish office in twenty minutes, but he just got a call from an informant. I said we could take it."

"Sure," Grace said, revving Connie's engine. "Where's he located?"

"Back across the river. Take the Forty."

Grace took the big bridge, passing over near where the North Canadian River became the Oklahoma River, which fed into the Bricktown Canal via a lock. They were near Del City.

"There's the turn," Ham said.

She roared into the parking lot and sat a minute while Ham got out. She wasn't a big fan of Catholic churches. Earl said that was okay. Johnny, her priest brother, said it wasn't. She was a baptized Catholic. Accountable, then, for lack of team Holy Spirit.

She got out and locked Connie. Raindrops pelted the top of her head, and she thought about dashing back to the car for her umbrella. Her beloved Porsche 911 sure was clean from all the rain.

Father Pepera had an office in the parish hall. A modestly dressed middle-aged woman wearing a crucifix—might have been a nun or just a secretary—checked in with him by phone from her desk and told Ham and Grace she would escort them.

Ham and Grace walked on terra-cotta tile through a Navajo-white hallway. They passed a statue of the Virgin Mary and a painting of Jesus walking on the water while the apostles sat in their fishing boat, looking frightened. Ham jerked his head at it.

"This rain keeps up, we'll be getting to work in rowboats," he said.

"I had a dream I was building an ark," she told him. He chuckled. "I didn't let the D.A. on the thing," she added. "He drowned."

"No lawyers on the ark," he agreed.

Or priests, she thought as the woman rapped sharply on a door with a nameplate that read FATHER PEPERA. *Except maybe Johnny, if he asks nice.*

The door swung open. The man was sitting behind his desk. He was pale, and there was a blotch on one of his sagging, lined cheeks, looked like a melanoma. He was almost bald, and had very bushy white eyebrows. Grace spared a second glance at his jowls and his droopy earlobes. Here was a man beloved by gravity.

"Yes, Detectives," he said in a flat voice.

She flashed her badge. "Hello, I'm Detective Grace Hanadarko and this is—"

"I know. We spoke," he said.

He'd spoken to Butch, not to either of them. She figured there was no need to correct him. A detective was a detective. But she did have to make sure they did things by the book, so she introduced Ham.

By their lack of interest shall ye know them: A detective was still a detective. There were over ten thousand recognized saints in the Catholic Church. Pepera probably knew all their dossiers. But cops? Interchangeable.

"We have a drowning victim named Zachary Lacey," she continued.

"The suicide." She could have chiseled words into a stone tablet with his voice.

She stopped, glanced at Ham. He remained pokerfaced. That was the right way to go, for sure, so she did, too. But she was beginning to have a funny feeling at the base of her spine. Like her vertebrae might pop out, she was holding things in so tightly.

"We're investigating the situation, Father," she said. "We don't know yet if he took his own life."

Father Pepera did not defrost. "I thought that was what Dr. Metzner was told. If he did kill himself, I won't say Mass for him."

Grace's lips moved but she couldn't make a sound. She was stunned down to her toes. "But . . . the Church—"

"The Church has left it up to the conscience of the parish priest," he replied, folding his hands and laying them on his desk. "And I will not say Mass for anyone who commits such an atrocity."

He gazed up at her. There was a defiant gleam in his eye, like he was enjoying being an asshole. Like he was daring her to say he couldn't run his own show. *My parish, my rules.*

Ham took over while Grace fought for composure. "Father Pepera, this is a juvenile. He was only fifteen, and he was under psychiatric care."

"He was sixteen," the priest countered.

Are you shitting me? Grace wanted to yell at him. But she didn't. She licked her lips. "We've spoken to his parents. He was taking antidepressants, and sometimes they have side effects. Suicidal thoughts—"

He shook his head. "They are only nominally members of this parish. I haven't seen any of them in church for months. We take care of our own, Miss . . ."

"Hanadarko," she said, fighting to keep the sharpness out of her tone. "Father . . . sir, as I said, we haven't determined if he took his own life."

"Well, if he didn't, then I'll bury him," he replied. As cold as that.

Grace stayed on target. She had lost it with Juanita. She wouldn't lose it here. "If you could remember anything that might help us. Was he in Faith Formation, was he—"

His phone rang. He looked at Ham and Grace. "I can't help you. His grandmother might be able to offer you some insight. She was a parishioner here until a few years ago. Still sends me a Christmas card every year."

"Do you have an address or a phone number for—" Grace began, but he picked up the phone, giving her a look that indicated her dismissal.

Grace turned her back and marched stiff-legged out of his office. Ham followed, shutting his door.

"Stay cool, stay cool," he urged her as she strode down the hallway. Her boot heels rang on the terra-cotta tile as she marched into the office of their escort. The woman was typing. She had the radio on low, classical music.

"Hi," Grace said, sugar sweet. She smiled at the woman. "Father Pepera suggested we get in contact with Zachary Lacey's grandmother."

"Lovely woman," the secretary said, beaming. "She used to run a prayer-quilt group. She made the most beautiful quilts."

"How long ago did she move?" Grace asked.

"Oh, it's been at least ten years," the woman said.

When Zack was six. "Would you by chance have her phone number? Address?"

The woman hesitated. Grace smiled harder. "It's all right. We're investigating the death of her grandson, Zachary."

The woman knit her brows and peered up at Grace through her lashes. "Did that boy . . . do himself in?"

"We don't know. We need to ask Mrs. Lacey a few questions to help us understand what happened." Grace waited. Cops did a lot of waiting.

"Well . . ." The woman brightened. "I'll get in touch with her and ask her to call you. How's that?"

Less direct, but better than nothing, Grace thought. "That would be great," Grace said. "Let me give you my card. Ham?"

He pulled a card out of his wallet. Grace took it and handed it with hers to the secretary. She was amazed at herself, masking her fury, playing nice. Nice would get them so much further. But as soon as it was safe to, she was going to rip Father Pepera a new one.

"Thank you," Grace added, as the woman pulled out the center drawer beneath her keyboard, pulled out a paper clip, and clipped their cards together. Then she placed them beside a coffee cup with an image of a stained-glass window on it and words written in flowery lettering: *When God closes a door, He opens a window.*

Grace flushed, said nothing. *What if God locks all the doors and sets the building on fire?*

"We're in a little bit of a rush on this," Grace said. "The family wants a Mass and, well . . ."

The woman looked grim. "It's all this divorce and easy living," she said in a low voice. "People don't have a sense of responsibility anymore. Sin is very real."

"Yes, you're right," Grace said evenly, bouncing her head like Butch's Longhorn bobblehead. "But we want to straighten this out for Zachary and his family."

"Of course." Now Church Lady was the one who sounded insincere.

When they got out of earshot, Grace let loose. After she ran out of names to call Father Pepera, she invented new ones. She called Johnny and demanded that he come to Louie's, then changed her mind and asked him to meet him at her home instead. Ham looked a little crestfallen—her priest-brother at Grace's house equaled no booty call—but he said nothing as they climbed into Connie.

They returned to the station and Grace slammed out of the car. She was seething with a burning, white-hot

mighty fury that was made no better by the sight of a
dozen little pamphlets hanging from the ceiling above
her desk. They had been attached on lavender gift-wrap
ribbon, and they had titles that read *GAY? NO WAY!*
I WAS SAVED BY JESUS: I WAS GAY; HEALED BY
JESUS; HOMOSEXUALITY: LOVE THE SINNER,
HATE THE SIN; ARE YOU SAVED? And the best one,
to which were attached aluminum foil "wings" on either
vertical edge: *LUSTFUL THOUGHTS: PRAY!*

Made no better at first, until she corked the fury with
an appreciative snort. Their elaborate prank did what
cop practical jokes did best, took the edge off, and she
grinned at Bobby, who was seated at his desk, talking
on his cell phone as she and Ham cracked up. She half-
expected there to be a strap-on in her drawer, but in these
days of sexual-harassment worries, probably not.

"You won't believe what happened," she began, but
Bobby held up a hand as he stood. He wasn't smiling.

"I just got a call from Butch. He's got an informant
named October who has a little girl."

"Merrie. Yeah, I know about that, man," she said,
waving her arms so her mobile of religious tracts would
flutter around. Ham picked up a purple feather boa
from the seat of his chair. And a tube of hemorrhoid
cream.

"Hey, my brother's gay," Ham protested mildly.

"And we love that about him," Grace assured her
partner. Although at the moment, Nick kinda detested
her for sleeping with his married brother.

"Merrie's missing," Bobby went on, patting himself
down, digging into his jeans pocket for his car keys.

Grace turned. "Missing as in . . ."

Bobby shook his head. "Mom went to pick her up
from school and she wasn't there."

"What?" Grace and Ham traded looks. Looks that
said, *Oh, shit.*

"I got a call about another case, had to come in; Butch is out there now, looking for her," Bobby said. "I'm going, too."

Grace glanced at her cell phone. "Hell, we're off the clock in ten minutes," she said. "All I had left was to check in with Evan Johnson about Juanita's extracurricular, off-the-books spiritual-counseling service." She raised her brows at Ham.

"I'm in," he told her.

"You call Butch for the plan. I have to make a quick stop," Grace said.

She left the squad room and went to the autopsy room. Lena was there, bent over another corpse. With a start, Lena jerked away from the body and moved her gore-covered, latex glove toward her face, then dropped her arm to her side and averted her head. But Grace saw what she was trying to hide: Lena was crying.

"Hey, man," Grace said. "What's going on?" For a split second Grace put Merrie on the table, but that didn't make any sense. She looked down at the body. It was a black man, maybe thirty. Didn't look so good. Looked dead. She wondered who would get the case. She looked back up at Lena.

"Nothing," Lena said, not meeting her gaze. "I can't go to Louie's."

"Good," Grace replied. She gave her head a shake. "I mean, that's why I'm here. I can't go, either. I came to let you know."

"Okay." Lena stepped closer to the autopsy table. Possessively. "I'm doing this one on overtime. Captain Perry asked me to."

And so . . . is that why you're crying? Is your boyfriend pissed because you blew him off?

But Grace didn't ask those questions. She just nodded and left the room. And felt even less confident of Lena's corpse-side manner.

CHAPTER
NINE

Ham checked in with Butch—no change in Merrie's status—and he and Grace got into separate vehicles. Bobby was already gone. Grace found a pack of cigarettes under a circular for the local big-box pet store and lit up as she screamed down the darkening streets of OKC. She called Butch herself because she needed friendly voices at a time like this, plus she was hoping for miraculous good news. He was at the shelter where October lived.

"October's not here," Butch told her. "He moved out this morning. I'm questioning the other residents, to see if anyone knows where he went."

"He's missing, his kid's missing. You think he took her and split?" Grace asked. "Who's with Merrie's mom?"

"I went over there first but I didn't stay long. Maybe you could go talk to her, see if you can get anything." He paused. "Something's up over there. Her place is a mess."

"On it," she promised him. "Where's Ham?"

"He's going to Merrie's school, to check out if anyone saw her leave," Butch said. "Teachers are supposed to wait for the parents, make sure the kids are accounted for. I was closer to the shelter."

Triage.

"Bobby's going over to Big Money's territory, see if he can turn up anything." Butch's voice sounded tight.

"Got it. We'll find her, Butch." She knew what he was worrying about: that Big Money had discovered October was a traitor. Bowel Movement had cut up a thirteen-year-old, and he'd never gotten called on it. Stupid D.A. No one was afraid to do anything to her town. Goddamn it—

Calm down, she told herself, as she barreled on over to Merrie's blasted-out hovel of a building; trash, condoms, and urine in the hallways, graffiti everywhere. Jesus God, what a place to raise a kid. Her thoughts flew immediately, as they often did, to Clay.

"Hey," she said, when Merrie's mother, Janaya, opened her door. Janaya took one look at Grace and broke down.

"Oh, my God, my baby, my baby," she wailed.

In a movie, Janaya's place would be spotless and she would be wearing humble if modest attire. She would work as a waitress and go to church every Sunday. But Janaya's boobs were hanging out of a V-neck sweater, and her jeans were so tight Grace could see the outline of her sexual parts. Her F-Me heels were so high, Grace half-expected her to fall forward on her massive chest and bounce back upright.

Grace shuffled through half-dressed Barbies and big brightly colored plastic toys and trash and dirty paper plates that smelled like rot and cat urine; and high heels and some makeup; and her boot heel came down on something that broke like glass. Maybe a crack pipe. Maybe a plastic syringe.

"He took her, I know he took her," Janaya said, sobbing.

The remains of some Mexican fast food littered a threadbare couch. Grace cleared two spots and flashed her badge, gestured for Janaya to sit down. Janaya stayed on her feet, nominally. Grace remained standing as well.

"I'm Detective Grace Hanadarko," she said. "I was sent over here—"

"Butch," Janaya said. "He's looking for her." She nodded, vigorously.

"You didn't pick her up from school," Grace began, pulling out her notebook. "You got there a little late and she was gone."

"Oh, my God, all right, I was a few minutes late!" Janaya shrieked, taking a step away from Grace. She teetered on her shoes. "But no one's supposed to take her. Don't you know anything, bitch?"

Grace lifted a sticky towel off the couch and set it on the floor. Didn't drop it. Tried to show respect. This was a frantic citizen. "I know you're upset—"

"*Upset?* Patrick takes my baby and you think I'm *upset?* I'll kill that son of a bitch. I will do it."

Grace held back what she was thinking: that the best-case scenario was that Merrie was in October's possession. No. Best-case scenario was some playdate Janaya had forgotten about and Merrie was at a friend's house, eating cookies and watching a Disney movie.

"Butch was getting him out of that life," Janaya said. She swayed; Grace reached out a hand and grabbed her forearm. "He was going to help him find a job."

Is that what Butch told you? Grace wondered. She set that aside. It wasn't important right now.

And then her cell phone rang. Civilian ringtone. Still supporting Janaya with her right hand, Grace grabbed the phone out of her jeans pocket with her left. "Detective Hanadarko."

"It's Antwone," a hushed voice confessed.

Shit. "Antwone," she said. "Hey, man. I'm glad you called." She waited. Janaya went completely still and stared hopefully at her, and Grace fought her instinct to shake her head, tell her no, this had nothing to do with her baby.

Kept waiting for Antwone to speak.

"Antwone?" Grace pressed. "You still there, man?"

"Yeah." His voice was muffled. "I'll meet you. I—I have a job at a bowling alley. I get off at eleven."

"Cool. Gimme the address." She waited some more.

"Maybe we can meet a few blocks away," he said. "There's a taco stand."

"I won't act like a cop," she promised him. "At your bowling alley."

"They saw you at school."

"Okay." She had no idea if she could keep the appointment, but she wrote down the name of the taco stand. Janaya kept watching her. "Listen, Antwone, I'm on a case and I may not make it. Can I call you at this number?" It was blocked, but that would not be a problem.

Janaya wilted and turned away. Grace stayed with Antwone on the phone.

"Um," he said, "I guess."

He was scared and he wanted to talk. Her crime-dar was blaring. But Zack was dead, and so far, a six-year-old named Merrie was not.

She hung up and said, "Janaya, have you gotten calls on your cell phone? Who's called you today?"

Janaya was going glassy and dazed. Her light brown cheeks turned bright red and she broke eye contact. "I lost it. I don't know where it is."

So what was the truth? She pawned it? Stole the one she had had but the battery wore out?

"Do you have a phone line here?" Grace looked around the room.

"It's, um . . ." She licked her lips, sandpaper on an emery board, stared at Grace as if Grace herself knew the answer and might be willing to share. As Grace blinked *No clue,* Janaya started crying again. "It got cut off. This is not the way it's supposed to be!"

No shit, Grace thought.

* * *

Butch had canvassed the shelter, down among the gray men. The director of the shelter informed him that October had left with a duffel bag in his arms, apparently walked down the street, and got picked up elsewhere. Then the director took Butch to task for concealing October's "criminal affiliation," and Butch humbled himself as expediently as possible. That done, he walked out the squeaky front door.

Wearing a trash bag as a rain poncho, although it was not currently raining, the Count was scribbling away on the sidewalk, and Butch could still smell him from ten feet away.

Butch had just pulled out his cell phone to check in with the rest of the squad when the Count looked up at him and said, "Oklahoma plate." He had rheumy alcoholic eyes and if he had six teeth he had half a dozen. He tapped the wet sidewalk with his chalk. Butch looked down at the smear of letters and numbers. He pulled out a notebook and jotted them down.

"Did you catch the make of the car?" Butch asked him.

The Count started writing on the pavement again. Butch watched.

123456789987654321.

"Was it a big car? Was it white? Red?" Butch prompted.

246810121416.

No matter. He could call it in. His cell phone rang. It was Bobby.

"Nothing yet," Bobby shorthanded.

"I have a license-plate number," Butch told him. "I'm going to run it. I'll call you back."

"The car's a '64 Chevy Impala. Lowrider classic," Butch told Grace. "Registered to Lawrence Shimoda, who reported it stolen almost exactly a year ago. Mr. Shimoda is not answering his phone and I went by his place. There's a For Rent sign on the front door."

"Okay," she said.

The five detectives in the Major Crimes squad were all cruising like sharks through the chum of Big Money's kingdom. It did not look as run-down and scummy as the part of town where Janaya lived, or the environs of the shelter, even. You had your basic graffiti on the mailboxes as well as a few signposts, trashy alleys, but the cars were not the worst and the yards were not the grossest. Why go into a life of crime if the best you could hope for was what you already had?

So . . . it was nondescript. Forgettable. Lacking the high drama of, say, shooting heroin under your tongue or your first murder. Tired old houses and middle-aged apartment buildings. No *CSI: Miami* here, baby. No sound track. Still a '64 Chevy Impala done right could be a classic, collectable automobile. High end, *muchacho*. She thought about Ron Lacey and his Harley T-shirt. Most gang members didn't even make minimum wage. But they might wind up with a stolen Electra Glide.

Grace called Captain Perry to bring her up to date. Then she called Butch again. "There's an APB out on Merrie," Grace told him. "No BOLO on October because what if his gang doesn't know about his kid?"

Butch grunted, thanked her, and hung up. She knew he knew that moving cautiously with the media made sense. So was Butch wrong, mixing it up with a guy with a little girl? Would she have done it?

"Yeah," she said aloud.

She called Johnny to tell him not to show at her house. She also told him what Father Pepera had said.

"That's not Church policy," he said. "I've said Mass for a suicide victim myself."

She hadn't known that.

"Well, he's insisting that it's up to his conscience."

"I'll talk to him."

"Put the fear of God in him," she advised him. "Plus, Johnny? He's an asshole."

He ignored that. "I'll get back to you," he said.

She and Ham checked in on some of Big Money's known hangouts—a strip club, a coffee shop, a chop shop. But again, they couldn't really lay it out there, either, because they were still stuck with not wanting BM to make the connection between October and his daughter. No one had anything, not even in exchange for money or get-out-of-jail-free passes.

Thanks to Captain Perry, Downtown put a lot more cops on the streets to search for the little girl. Nothing plus nothing still equaled nothing, and Grace and Ham kept the pressure on as best they could. But some nights the bad guys were like bits of mercury, dribbling away if you pushed on them at all.

After wasting money on food they didn't eat, the two left Noodletown, a Korean restaurant. Hepped up on green tea, Grace checked the time. It was ten thirty. She was supposed to meet Antwone at eleven.

"You know what I'm not liking?" she said to Ham as they headed for their cars in the little parking lot. "I'm not liking that Janaya lost her cell phone. And she didn't have a landline. So no one is able to contact her. I mean, I called all the people on the list she made for me." She stepped over a puddle. "And I called the number she gave me as the one for *her* cell phone. But I had to suggest that we do that."

"Yeah," he said. "That's bullshit. But she's high, scared." He ran the scenario. "She's sitting in her apartment, and her kid is missing, and she's not asking friends to make calls, check around." He looked at her. "It's wrong."

"I'm going back over there," Grace announced.

"No. I'll go. You go meet up with Antwone." He put his hand on her shoulder. "Grace, we're doing everything we can for Merrie."

She hated her feeling of defeat. Hated it. Raindrops smacked the top of her head, and she batted at them angrily, as if they were doing it on purpose.

"I'll call you if something breaks," he promised her. "I'll go over to Janaya's now."

She nodded. Although she had concerns over Lena's handling of Zack's autopsy, she had full confidence that Ham would do it right. She flooded with deep, sincere gratitude that he was her partner.

So she drove to the taco stand, driving by first to make sure there was no posse waiting to jump her or any other surprises. She saw Antwone sitting at a picnic table by himself; a couple sat at the next table, making out. He was studiously avoiding them.

Shadows slid over Connie as Grace got out and walked calmly toward the kid. He raised his head and saw her. She saw his back go up. Another raindrop plopped on top of her head, and she half-raised her hand to signal to him that she saw him and she was cool.

Yeah, right. Like he thinks I'm cool.

Deer, meet headlights. She revved up her cop brain because something was going on and she was not leaving until she found out what it was.

"Hey," she said. "Thanks for coming."

He didn't reply. Pot fumes rolled off him. Damn, not the sharpest tool in the shed. Maybe he'd had to build up his nerve to talk to her.

"Let's just make it easy on us both," she said gently. "I know you want to tell me something. So tell me. Please."

Antwone hung his head.

"Antwone," she prompted, and then she realized he was whispering. She leaned forward, and she had a flash of déjà vu, sitting in the confessional at church, telling Father Murphy she'd lost her temper at Paige during dinner, all the while knowing he was going to screw her when she finished.

"Zachary was my . . . my boyfriend." He whispered it in a rush. "We had to be so careful. We couldn't tell anyone." He glanced up at her. His eyes fluttered shut as if he were fainting; his brows knit together into one unibrow of torment. His chest rose and he took in a ragged breath, punctuated by a high, agonized gasp as his lower lip trembled. Grace had seen a lot of hurt in her day, an awful lot of pain, and this kid was in hell.

"They hated him. And *I* loved him. I was the only one, but I was . . . we . . ." He crumpled forward, resting his arms on the picnic table and pressing his forehead against the backs of his hands. "Oh, my God."

Grace waited, a witness to his agony. She would watch him cry all night if it would help her figure out what happened to Zachary Lacey. She would do whatever it took. But she wouldn't let herself feel what he was feeling. A cop had to carry a chip of ice in her heart, observing, assembling the clues. Now would be a perfect time for a full confession, or for Antwone to unknowingly dump a treasure trove of useful information on the table.

"How much did they hate him?" she asked. *Enough to kill him?*

Antwone cried awhile longer. Grace waited. *C'mon, c'mon,* she pushed. *Tell me the thing that will break this case.*

She stayed detached and watched, trying to decide if his grief was genuine or if he had killed Zack and was putting on the sobfest of his life. She doubted option number two. He was here, after all. He had come to her for help.

"Hey, man, you'd be surprised how many people I know who are secretly gay," she said, placing a comforting hand on his arm. He pulled away. "I mean, they told *me* they're gay, but they're keeping it a secret." *Stupid, Hanadarko.* "You got to give me something to work with, Antwone. What do you know about Zack that we don't know?"

"Man, if my daddy knew I was here sitting with you . . . ," he began.

If Daddy knew you were gay . . .

"He was going to this church, this crazy, big-ass church," he told her. "That place scared the shit out of me, all the rolling around and shaking. He said it was working, that he didn't think he was gay anymore . . . that he was . . ."

Going to stop loving you? So you killed him? Grace thought.

"Did you go with him?"

"Hell, no." He pushed his fists against his eye sockets. "But he wanted me to." He licked his lips and took a deep breath. She kept watching. There was more.

"Can you give me the name of the church?" she asked him. "Was there anyone there he hung out with?"

"Pastor Marc, the youth pastor. That dude's gay. I'm sure of it."

"How sure?"

The taco-stand lights went out. In the darkness, Antwone stared at his fingernails.

"I—I didn't know I was . . . that way . . . until I met Zack. We were partners and then . . ." He trailed off as if he realized he'd just said too much. "I gotta go." Pushing the flats of his hands on the table, he began to rise. This was it. She was going to lose him. She thought fast and furiously.

They were partners. They had something going on? Were they in a band together? Business? Debate team? Grace's heart sped up, like a big cat after a kill. Moving from the prowl to running it to ground.

The truth.

Now she had to be careful. He just might outrun her. She had to corner him.

"You were new at it," she said. "You didn't know how the streets work."

"I don't know what you're talking about." He took a step back and crossed his arms over his chest.

But he didn't walk away.

"Was it just to friends, at first? A little bit of weed?"

He shook his head hard. "We—I'm not into that."

"Give me the name of your connection," she said. "A first name will help. We watch most of them. We may already have you on camera buying from him." She was lying. "But if you tell me yourself, I'll help you, man. I swear it." She kept her face open and honest, in case he could see her in the oily murk of the taco stand. "If this guy hurt Zack . . ."

Clouds scuttled; the moon came out and kissed his dark downy cheek. Her heart broke a little for him but she kept herself in check.

"I gotta go," he said.

Shit.

"If this guy hurt Zack . . . ," she repeated.

He turned and began to walk away. She started seeing his future in front of her eyes: dropping out of school to avoid arrest; hitting the streets full-time. Hustling, stealing. It was like watching him die. Like losing him to hell.

"Antwone, Zack wouldn't have wanted—"

"How do you know?" he demanded, whirling around. He burst into tears. "He had *nothing*. His dad beat the shit out of him."

New data point.

"And something was weird about his stepmother. He was onto her. He told me he was going to prove that she was lying." He added all this in a rush.

Yeah, Antwone, keep going. Gimme clues. Gimme ammo.

"What about the gay youth pastor?" she asked. "Marc. He in on any of that?"

Antwone's face hardened. "*He's* an asshole. Zack thought he was so great."

She tensed and tried not to show it. "Did Marc try to make a move on Zack?"

"I don't know. I just know Zack started acting different after he started going to that church. He kept telling me Jesus could fix everything." He narrowed his eyes. "I don't think Jesus can fix shit."

"No argument here," she agreed. She could almost hear the flapping of Earl's wings. "Did you know he was on antidepressants?"

"He threw that shit away after he accepted Jesus as his personal savior."

"But . . . was he still depressed?" Her cell phone vibrated. She let it go. "Depressed enough to kill himself? Or do you think he might have accidentally fallen into the river while he was stoned? Maybe . . . fishing?"

"Shit," he said. "Zachary and me never went fishing in our whole lives. I gotta go." Before she could protest, he fixed her with a look. "I have homework."

"Please. Stay." She raised her chin. "Listen to me. You're telling me stuff, good stuff. I'm going to use it. But I'm not going to use it against you." As his lips parted, she raised her left hand out, gang style. No weapons here. *Cuz you got nothing, too. I take what's left, you'll be dead in five years.*

He licked his lips and looked left, right, as if someone might be there with a lifeline to provide his final answer.

"Zack died," she said. "Maybe he did it himself, but maybe not. And if he didn't, I want to find out who did."

"You don't understand," he muttered. "You're a *cop*."

She held out her hands. "Man, who understands better than me? I live in the same world. I know the rules. I just don't play by them. Is your father in a gang?"

He stiffened. "My father went to prison for a crime he didn't commit."

Yeah, tell me another, Antwone Senior. "That happens," she said. "I took down one of the FBI's most wanted and then someone falsely reported I was drinking on duty. She was a chick who was pissed off at me." Maybe that was not so clever, proving that it was hard to trust authority figures.

His lips parted. "That sucks."

"Tell me about it. But it got put right. At least for me. I want to put it right for Zack."

Tick . . . tick . . . tick . . . She thought about checking her cell phone. But she sensed that, this time, she shouldn't break eye contact. She looked him straight in the eye.

Finally, Antwone's shoulders sagged. "Flaco," he said, and told her the story of how he and his "partner"— what a word for a gay teenage drug dealer—had bought drugs from a known OKC dealer. His face went blank and sullen the way Ron Lacey's had; he was defiance incarnate, daring her to leap across the picnic table and cuff him. But there were tears in his eyes, and she knew it was all bullshit. He was still sweet, still hopeful, still . . . good.

"I know him," she said. "He's an asshole."

Antwone smiled a little, very tentatively, and the sun came out. Maybe he could crawl out of the pit. Maybe she could give him a hand up.

"He was cool with us," he said finally.

Ya-huh. Probably gave you all the weed you could smoke in return for selling it to your classmates. But never any money.

"I may have more questions," she said. "Give me your address." Before he could refuse, she added, "The school will give it to me if you don't." She pulled out her notebook, glancing at her cell phone at the same time. Ham.

"I'm only doing this for Zack," he said.

"That's cool, man," she said. *Whatever works.*

Antwone gave her an address and left. Grace called Ham back.

"October doesn't have her," he said. "He called Butch with some information, and Butch could tell he doesn't know she's missing. And Butch didn't fill him in."

Shit. "You tell Janaya that October doesn't have her?"

"I think she knows," Ham said. "I think she's involved with the disappearance."

"Are you still with her?"

"We've got a uniform watching her place. I need to get some sleep." He hesitated.

My house is not a hotel. And bed warmers don't sleep over.

"Walk me through it," she said. "While it's fresh."

"It was the lack of interest in staying connected. She doesn't seem focused on finding out where Merrie is. She kept insisting October had her, and she wouldn't entertain any other possibility."

"Well, addicts can be like that," she said. "Glom onto something and work it to death. God, Ham, did you see her apartment? Where's Social Services in this? Did Butch ever contact them?"

"Merrie's school was watching Janaya, she was late a lot to pick Merrie up, but there were no signs of abuse. Butch said he never saw her place look so bad. You know how addicts are. They do okay for a while and then something sends 'em over."

"Like killing their kid because their new boyfriend's jealous, doesn't like sharing Mom's attention."

Ham took over. "Or she tried to make her stop crying a little too hard. Freaked out. So we search the Dumpster for empty bleach bottles and get a cadaver dog."

Grace's stomach lurched. That could not happen to little Merrie.

Oh, but it could.

"Butch is sure October doesn't know she's missing?" she asked.

"October called to tell him he was moved in, but he was afraid to give him the address."

"That's helpful." She actually meant it. Any new information was helpful. "Antwone was Zack's boyfriend. They were dealing."

"You think it got Zack killed?" Ham asked.

"It usually does, sooner or later," she replied. "Henry's coming home tomorrow. I'm going to ask him to take another look at the body."

He sucked in his breath. "Lena Garvin's not going to like that."

"We had a meeting of the minds," she said. "Something's up with her, though. She was crying in the autopsy room. Not over that. She was already crying when I came to tell her we couldn't meet up at Louie's tonight."

"Well, it could be a woman thing," he ventured. Grace made a sound like a snorting pig. "C'mon, *you* get moody."

"I never do," she said gleefully, raising the decibels on the snorts.

"God, I hope we find that little girl." She heard the tension in Ham's voice. "I'm thinking about all those mothers who kill their kids. There's gotta be a special place in hell for them."

"Do you think she's capable of it?" Grace asked him.

"No one surprises me anymore. Except you."

"I'll see you in the morning," she told him, and disconnected.

CHAPTER
TEN

"Okay, listen," October whispered into the phone.

Seated inside an all-night coffee shop in a booth all by himself, Butch listened. Hard.

"You-know-who is going to a buy on Saturday night. It's gonna be big. So he's going himself. Here's where it's going down." He rattled off an address and Butch blinked, hard. It was on the same street as the shelter, in the row of warehouses where Butch had waited for October so many times. Damn.

"Are you going to be there?" Butch asked him.

"I don't know yet."

"What's your new address?"

There was silence. October cleared his throat. "I'm not sure."

October's reluctance made a kind of sense. Big Money was not going to be on October's turf when and if he went down. But if the cops came into October's house, there was a good chance dots would be connected. Conclusions would be drawn. And October would get a bullet to the back of the head. If he was lucky.

"Did you give the money to Janaya?" he asked Butch. "The eighty bucks?"

"It was thirty." Butch closed his eyes. He still wasn't going to tell October that Merrie was MIA.

"Okay. But you know this is my big score, this information on the buy," October declared. "I am giving him to you. That should be worth at least . . ." He took a deep breath. "Five hundred dollars."

So cheap, Butch thought. Less than two weeks' salary, even at minimum wage. Was that why guys like October went south? They couldn't even imagine themselves making it in the everyday world? It had to be hell or heaven, but never life on Earth?

"Butch? Am I right? Five hundred?"

"Yes. I think you're right." Butch waved away the tired waitress as she trudged toward him with a coffeepot. He was the only customer in the entire restaurant.

"No shit?" October blurted. "And you'll give it to her?"

"I think, for that much, I'll put it in a savings account for Merrie," Butch said. From the looks of things, Janaya could cook five hundred dollars in five minutes.

"Hey, wait a minute," October protested.

"Or if you'd rather I give it to Janaya, I will."

"Yeah. So give it to her before Saturday, okay?" In case Butch got killed, he meant. "And bring lots of friends," October whispered. "*He* will."

"Got it." Butch thought, *This could be it. The time I finally nail Big Money to a tree.* It was supposed to be his quarterback moment. Goal line in sight, his team had the ball . . .

But it felt like that night when he'd walked away and his buddy hadn't.

He hung up, stood, and dropped five bucks on the table. Merrie's school picture came out with the five-dollar bill, and he gazed down at the snapshot before picking it back up. Then he got in his car and took a drive.

Grace had hung up with Ham, but she hadn't gone home to her bed. She'd stopped in a grocery store and

bought a cup of caffeine at the coffee bar and a chew
toy for Gussie in the pet aisle. Then she drove the streets
of Big Money's hood, looking for the lowrider Impala.
Shapes and shadows moved and blended in the alleys
and darkened windows: gangbangers, thieves, and other
criminals. Kids looking to belong to something, anything.
Anyone. Silhouettes of lives disintegrating before her
eyes. And when the dawn came and the sidewalks rolled
back out, the husks of their bodies would turn to dust in
the sun.

No Chevy, no Big Money. She thought about calling
Butch, but he had her number if he wanted to talk;
and maybe he was catching some z's, although she
doubted it. After a time, she returned to Janaya's building and chatted with the uniforms assigned to watch the
woman. The wind smacked her cheeks to help her stay
awake; she walked the block, feeling her heart spinning
in her chest.

The rain began to pour down, and Grace leaned back
her head as she patrolled, getting soaked clean down to
the bone. There had to be something she could do for
Merrie. There was always something to do.

And you wonder why I drink, she thought, picturing
Earl. Wet and shivering, she kept walking; hell with the
storm, the darkness matched her, black on black. Trees
shifted in the wind. Bushes shook, as if some gigantic invisible monster crept among them. Crime and evil and
death. Where was St. George the dragon slayer when they
needed him?

The uniforms were in their car, drinking coffee and
watching. She walked past them again, giving them a
wave; then across the street, squinting up at the apartment she figured for Janaya's and saw that the lights
were on. Was Momma pacing the floor, or was she getting high?

"This is bullshit," she said aloud, and she walked up

to the graffiti-covered front door of the building. Once upon a time it might have been orange; now it was air-brushed layers of colors outlined in black. Everyone on the planet had tagged it; so sad that this was their Iraq, Afghanistan.

The door was locked and she wasn't about to break and enter. She waited about thirty seconds before a black guy stumbled through the door. He blinked and smiled, revealing gold teeth, about to say something when Grace showed him her badge. He muttered a few choice expletives and gave her a wide berth as he staggered out into the rain. He looked so stoned, she wondered if he even knew it was raining.

Janaya lived on the third floor; Grace made a lot of noise on the concrete stairs so the dealers and hookers could take it elsewhere if they felt like it. One tender-loving couple didn't feel like it; on a mission, she moved past them wordlessly.

She banged on Janaya's door. Sure enough, there was loud hip-hop music, and it took a long time for said door to open. Janaya was higher than a kite.

And when she opened the door, there was a cell phone in her hand.

Grace lifted her badge off her belt and felt the jangle of her handcuffs without bringing them into play. Part of her mind was playing the scenario before a court of law—child abandonment, endangerment—but it was more important to find the kid than bust her mother. Not invited, she did not enter Janaya's home.

"We know everything," she said. "We tapped your cell phone. That you don't have."

The woman crumpled and began to cry. "It just happened, it happened and I . . . I didn't know . . . what to do."

Someone came up behind Grace; she turned to find Butch behind her. He was as wet as she was, and beneath his low-slung cowboy hat, his eyes flared as he took in the situation. She gave him a sharp nod.

"Janaya, may we come in?" he asked calmly. Warmly.

"LaKeisha has her," Janaya said to Butch. "I got there to the school and I . . ." Her knees went out from under her and, as before, Grace held her upright. "I was a little late and, well, I've been late before, so LaKeisha got her. I couldn't find the phone and now I got it and she called me all screaming 'Where the hell you been, girl?'"

Grace wanted to do the Rhetta happy dance. She wanted to break into a rebel yell. Butch's shoulders straightened.

"Are you going to take her away and give her to Patrick?" she asked fearfully. Her eyelids fluttered and her words were slurred. She was flying. "Because he's straightening out his life?" *And I'm not,* the unspoken ending went.

Grace slid a neutral look at Butch. He whipped out his cell phone, ready to make the calls that would get them to Merrie, and Social Services would take it from there.

"We need LaKeisha's phone number and location," Grace said to the weeping, addled woman.

"Am I going to jail?"

For possession at the very least, Grace thought, but she said, "We need to find your baby."

"Merrie," she ground out, as if she were dying. Which she was, inch by inch.

Good, Grace thought. *Die faster.*

"Butchy," Merrie said against his shoulder as he carried her out of LaKeisha's apartment. She smelled like cookies. She had fallen asleep watching *Lilo & Stitch*. LaKeisha's older daughter had given her a little stuffed dinosaur she had named Cherry. Janaya often told Merrie she was as sweet as cherry pie. She was half asleep, with Cherry in the blanket with her, waving tiredly at

LaKeisha and her four daughters, two of whom were crying.

The teacher at Merrie's school—a white teacher—had mistaken LaKeisha for Janaya when LaKeisha came by from picking up her own daughter at the same school. LaKeisha had realized that Janaya hadn't shown up. Her friend was already on thin ice with the school for showing up late a few times too many. So LaKeisha put her arms around Merrie, and the white teacher didn't say a word, just waved.

After she left the school, LaKeisha had called Janaya, who hadn't answered. Figuring Janaya was too high to talk, she took Merrie home and kept trying to reach her momma. For hours. She sure didn't call the cops because that was not what folks did.

When she and Janaya finally connected, Janaya didn't tell her about the police search; and when the authorities came by, to her place, LaKeisha was infuriated. She had asked Butch if Patrick was going to get custody of Merrie, and he'd told her he didn't know. Social Services was involved now.

"Well, he should get her," LaKeisha had informed him while one of her daughters took Merrie to go potty. "She a junkie bitch ho, and that's all I got to say about her."

When Butch had carried Merrie out of the house, he'd put her into the car of a social worker who'd promised the little girl that she could see her momma real soon. The social worker assigned to the case looked a lot like Michelle, the girl he'd taken out one time, who had pretended to hang herself at work out of unrequited love for him. Everyone had been in on that one, too.

Butch hadn't wanted to hand Merrie over. He didn't want her with strangers. He knew Grace was appalled at what she'd seen at Janaya's, and he had been, too. Last time he'd been there, the place was pretty good. Not perfect, but not the disaster it was now. Janaya would be evaluated, and maybe there were some programs for her that would enable her to retain custody and maybe there weren't.

Saturday was three days away, and he needed to tell his captain that Big Money was within his sights. But if October got wind of what was going down with his baby and his former woman . . .

Butch had Janaya's cell phone. Janaya had agreed to give it to him. He'd checked the calls and was taking the SIM card to Tech in the morning to see who she'd been talking to. What a tangled web . . .

He stripped down and got in the shower, let the stress and the frustration and, yes, the guilt, sluice off with the soap and the hot water. The guilt stuck.

Ham got a call from Grace that Merrie had been found. He'd been lying in the bed in his apartment, running scenarios for new searches for the six-year-old when his cell rang. They shared the joy and then she hung up; and he thought very briefly about phoning Darlene. But it was late and he was tired. So he lay down and ran scenarios for how to solve the Zachary Lacey case. If they had a case.

Grace spent the first part of the morning driving around South Rob looking for Flaco. She didn't find him at any of his old haunts, which raised alarm bells—maybe he'd left town because he'd committed a murder. But maybe he was in bed, asleep. It had stopped raining and the early-morning birds started trilling; dawn was close at hand, and you couldn't squeeze blood from a turnip no matter how hard you tried. In other words, even Supergrace needed to rest.

She went home and gave Gus his new chew toy. He was properly appreciative, even taking it outside when he went weewee. She took a hot bath, complete with candles and bubbles, and thought about calling Helping Hand to see who was doing what.

Merrie was found; her parents were nonfunctional; but the research indicated that kids did better in their families of origin pretty much no matter what. She smiled her wry, crooked smile at the thought of her own family of origin and gave props to Johnny for his reaction to Father Pepera's bullshit.

Then she dozed off. Just as her nose slipped beneath the layer of bubble-bath foam, she woke up and almost leaped out of the tub. A little weirded out, she wondered if Earl would have popped into the bathroom to wake her up before it was too late.

Four hours later, she sailed into the autopsy room. Henry was there, and she did a little two-step by way of greeting. It was just the two of them, no body on the slab. He was staring at a digital X-ray, and he lowered it and looked at her as she beamed at him.

"I'm so glad you're back," she said. "I have this vic—"

"Lena left me a note," Henry broke in. Then, pointedly, he added, "With her letter of resignation." She blinked, but he went on. "But you were right to keep Zachary Lacey, Grace. I noticed that his left ankle was bent at an angle, so I ran an X-ray. Fracture dislocation of the talotibial joint."

She parsed. "Meaning that his ankle was broken when he fell into the river? Or that he caught it on a rock?"

"I'm leaning toward that the ankle was struck by a blunt object before he went in. And that someone wielded that blunt object."

"Ha. Gotcha," she blurted. "So someone hit him, and he fell into the drink and couldn't swim." She pondered that. "Or someone made certain he would drown before they threw him in."

"I've got quantitative tox results, too," he continued. "Lena put them in stat for you before she cleaned out her desk. Negative for antidepressants but positive for rohypnol. Roofies."

"Date-rape drug."

"Good thing Lena ran the tox screen as fast as she did." Henry set down the X-ray but he kept scrutinizing it. "That stuff breaks down fast."

She detected more than a hint of disapproval. "You liked her," she observed. "You think I had anything to do with her quitting?" She touched her chest. "Henry, I invited her to Louie's. She was going to follow me over."

He peered at her over his glasses. "You also asked her to retain custody of a body so I could check her work."

"You're senior to her," she insisted.

"And how would you feel if the tables were turned?"

"They're turned all the time," she shot back. "Between Captain Perry and IA, I get checked and double-checked." She stuffed her hands in her pockets. "And I was right to do it. She didn't catch the ankle."

"It would have been difficult, with all the bloat," he began, and then he pursed his lips. "I could have trained her."

"We're not here to train people." She was incredulous. "We're here to put away bad guys and protect innocent citizens."

He huffed, as if she'd opened a valve and his slow leak was showing. She wondered if his mood had anything to do with taking his mother to the family reunion. Probably all the relatives his age had spouses and families. They were on their second or third sets of kids from different marriages. And Henry still lived with his mother. And she had turned down all his attempts to repeat their cat-pity sex.

"I'm sorry, Henry," Grace said. "We're losing all these cases, man." She raised up on tiptoe and kissed his cheek.

He softened, mollified just a smidge, and his cheeks went pink.

"Is everybody going to Louie's tonight?"

"Absolutely," she declared. "Butch had a missing kid but we found her last night."

"Oh? That's great," he said, warming up a bit.

"Yeah." She smiled at him. "Thanks for the catch on the ankle."

"It's my job." His face softened a bit more, as if he just couldn't stay mad at her. Good to know. Plus, she really liked Henry.

She patted his arm and went to visit Rhetta. Rhetta had fibers consistent with the interior of a Chevy truck manufactured after 2000, and she was interested in the report of rohypnol. If they could match fibers and traces of roofies to a specific vehicle . . .

"Yeah, I'm loving that thought," Grace said. "Hey, we're going to Louie's tonight. Right?"

"One drink, sure," Rhetta said. "Then I have to go home and muck out stalls. All this rain is turning the whole farm into a mud pit."

Grace nodded. "I think it's God's wrath for all the sin and easy living. I think our days are numbered."

"You're always so cheerful," Rhetta drawled.

About an hour later, Grace and Ham were canvassing Flaco's haunts on foot, showing Zack's picture and offering rewards for information. It was a chilly day; the smell of coagulated oil warred with that of wet newspaper and trash pressed against the cyclone fence along the street. There were parts of OKC that were breathtaking; this was not one of them.

It appeared that Flaco had not left town. He'd been seen at the minimart; he'd been at the bus stop. But he was never where they were. The information on his driver's license was bogus, and a water bill in his name turned out to be listed for a residence he did not reside at.

The streets cleaned up as they hit a row of gay bars on West Thirty-ninth. Flaco was known to sell coke and meth to the barbacks and dancers on the circuit. But it was the same deal: He'd been around, just wasn't there today. Flaco was like the Elvis of Oklahoma City.

Grace's bad mood was getting worse. She had started out their canvass miffed because Kate had refused her request to get a warrant for the Laceys' property. A man like Ron Lacey surely owned a truck. Grace had asked Records for the file on Zack's absent mother, and had been told it would be awhile. No one wanted to help her out.

"Perry's right," Ham told her as they entered a gay bar called Pan. The black lights were on, revealing a pretty good facsimile of Elvis, naked, holding a phallic microphone. Vibey techno music thrummed low, and a couple of pretty young men in red satin basketball shorts and silver jerseys carried oval black lacquer trays above their heads, setting up for the night ahead. But it was too early for more than a table or two of patrons. Grace smelled no weed, but there were furtive scramblings throughout the place as people cleaned up for a visit from the po-lice.

"It's only hearsay that Ron Lacey beat the shit out of Zachary, and there's nothing that puts Zachary in a vehicle of his prior to the kid going into the river," Ham went on.

"Bullshit," she grumped. "Daddy practically pounded on me when I suggested his son was gay."

"But he didn't." Ham moved his shoulders. "Sure didn't seem to care much about Zack."

"Poor Zack. Mom goes missing, Dad resents him. That's how I see it, anyway." She thought of Clay, also motherless.

"Dad remarries, Zack's still in the way," Ham said.

"Hi," a waiter in pancake makeup, eyeliner, and crimson lipstick sashayed up and vogued for Ham. "Whatcha lookin' for, cowboy?"

Grace and Ham flashed their badges and introduced themselves. The waiter was even more excited to meet them, which was refreshing.

Ham showed him Zack's school picture. "You seen this guy?"

The waiter aimed a pencil flashlight at the photograph and studied it. He raised his brows and slowly nodded. "Why, yes, I believe he was in here about a week ago. I know because I had to ask him to leave." He batted his false eyelashes. "Very cute but highly underage."

"Was he with anyone?" Grace asked. She pulled out a picture of Flaco. "Like this guy?"

The waiter pressed his fingertips against his chest. "Wow, Detective, are you psychic? That's Flaco, and, yes, they were here together."

"I'm just lucky," Grace said. "Finally. So, Flaco was here with him. Did they have drinks? Do anything else? Smoke some weed in the back room?"

"Detective, shamey-shame-shame," the waiter admonished her. "Smoking marijuana is illegal."

"Yeah, okay," Grace said. "We know Flaco is a dealer."

"Well, he's been banned. For trying to bring that young man in here," the waiter said, rolling his eyes at the mere thought of such a dastardly act.

"You're sure that Flaco brought him here?" Grace repeated.

"Let me get my manager," the waiter offered. "Oh, Janet!" He bustled off.

"See, Grace?" Ham drawled. "We do it right, we get rewarded."

"Remind me to hit you at an inopportune moment."

"Harder. Harder," he mock-begged her.

But when they interviewed Janet the manager (who was a guy), they didn't get anything new—just corroboration that Flaco had tried to bring Zack Lacey in and they'd both been booted. No one had seen Antwone with them, though. Zack-plus-Flaco had been a private date.

"So much for praying away the gay," Grace said as she and Ham left. "So Flaco sells to gay bars not just because there's a steady stream of customers, but because he likes the scene himself."

"And he's a chicken hawk. Likes 'em young," Ham spun as they walked down the street. "And something goes wrong. Zack's going to tell because he's got religion now. Zack's underage, so it's statutory rape. They're doing drugs and getting it on. Flaco's on probation from the last time—"

"Let's hear it for the OKC justice system," Grace muttered.

"Flaco's been giving Zack roofies; hell, maybe Zack likes it that way so he can let Flaco do what he wants without taking any responsibility for it."

"So Zack doesn't remember any of it," Grace agreed. "Doesn't have to come clean in confession. Or whatever they call it in the non-Catholic world."

"But God tells Zack to come forward. So Zack tells Flaco he's going to tell. Bam. Dead Zack." Ham nodded.

"Sounds good," Grace said. In its way.

"Or Antwone finds out they've been together, and Antwone kills him," Ham said. "You like him for that?"

"I don't know," Grace replied. She stuffed her fingertips in the pockets of her jeans. "We need to talk to Flaco. Maybe Antwone knows where he lives. If he wants out of this he'll give Flaco up."

Ham ran his fingers through his hair, then dropped his hands to his sides. His face was sweaty, his eyelids heavy. Grace glanced over at him, wondering if he was okay. He had a lot on his mind. But she knew Ham Dewey. There was every chance that if she asked him if he was okay, he would clam up and tell her that he was. Take umbrage.

"Plus, we can go *talk* to the Laceys," she continued. "Just because we don't have a warrant doesn't mean we can't question them at their home. About various subjects including why Karen Lacey ran off. And how soon Ron and Cherie got together after Karen disappeared."

"We have to be careful," Ham reminded her. "If we see anything, we can't use it as evidence until we return with a warrant. And even though I think they both cheated on their IQ tests to hit a hundred, they might be smart enough to remove a murder weapon from the premises."

"Or their bottle of street drugs," she said.

"So we dot the *i*'s, cross the *t*'s," Ham reiterated. "We make sure we are bulletproof. Once we get the case put together, the D.A. can lose it for us."

"Yup," she agreed. "But we won't lose it for us." At his nod, she took a breath. "And I guess one of us will have to go to Zack's freaky church."

He grinned at her. "Guess so."

She licked her lips. "How badly do you want a blow job?"

CHAPTER
ELEVEN

Louie's, half an hour after the squad's quitting time. And it was raining.

Grace sat at a booth waiting for Rhetta while Ham shot pool with Butch and Bobby. Ham had actually turned down her bribe of oral pleasure and insisted that they should both go to the holy-roller church. He was drinking a longneck, but Grace had gone with a beer and a tequila shot. For starters. She needed to brace herself. As luck would have it, there was a nine o'clock healing service at the church that very night.

Antwone would get off work at the bowling alley at eleven. So much for quitting time. Not that she was complaining. There wasn't much on TV, and it was no fun to watch horror movies without Clay. She'd keep the DVD until the weekend. Clay was coming over again on Saturday night.

The jukebox was playing "It Wasn't God Who Made Honky Tonk Angels" when Rhetta walked into the bar. She was wearing jeans and that plaid blouse with the ruffles at the neck. Her hair was in a ponytail, and she had on dangly earrings and her glasses. She saw Grace and headed for her.

Grace threw back her shot of tequila so she could get another one when Rhetta ordered her white wine. Rhetta scooted into the booth with a happy groan.

"This day is over," Rhetta said.

"Hey, man," Grace said, picking her cigarette up from the metal ashtray and taking a drag. "Wait until you hear this. Zack's priest told me if it was up to him, Zack couldn't be buried in hallowed ground."

Rhetta looked startled. The waitress came over.

"Chardonnay, please," Rhetta told the woman. Grace held up her empty shot glass and the waitress nodded. "You mean because it looks like suicide?"

Grace said nothing, just took another drag on her cigarette. "You agree with him?" Grace asked her. "Suicide's the greatest sin there is if you're a Catholic. And we keep track of our sins. Big ones, little ones. Is that the one that God cannot forgive?"

Rhetta leaned toward her. Her face kind of shone. "I have faith, Grace. And I place that faith in a God who wouldn't punish a person when he is at his lowest. That priest is totally wrong. Totally."

"That's what Johnny says, too." She grinned and nodded as Rhetta's brows raised. "I haven't fully discussed it with Earl."

"That's pretty progressive for Johnny," Rhetta said.

"I'm not saying what I'm thinking about my brother," Grace informed her, blowing out smoke. Then she grinned. "It is pretty progressive of him. He told me he said Mass for a suicide victim himself."

"Wow." Rhetta was clearly startled. The waitress arrived with their drinks, and Rhetta took a moment to stare into the chardonnay. If that had been Grace's glass, the wine would be gone by now. The second tequila shot sure was.

"I'm supposed to look to my own soul." Rhetta took a sip of wine. "And my soul needs something else to talk about. I am beat." She took another sip and closed her eyes for a moment. "Dear God, thank you for wine."

"At happy-hour prices, amen," Grace added, crossing herself. "You get anything else on Zack?" Not exactly changing the subject, but it was just about the best she could do at the moment. Maybe it was no accident that her sweet puppy Gussie was an American bulldog.

"Fibers, rohypnol," Rhetta said. "River water. Pathology found diatoms."

"Diatoms are bullshit. Any semen?"

Rhetta shook her head. "He was semen-free."

"Henry didn't say anything about marijuana, either."

"No cannabis residue," Rhetta confirmed.

"That's weird. He and his boyfriend were dealers."

"Maybe after he accepted Jesus, he stopped using." Rhetta took another sip.

"I'm going to his church with Ham tonight," Grace said, smirking. "Pentecostal type of place." She lifted her fingers in the air and wiggled them. "Praise the Lord."

"And pass the ammunition," Henry said, coming up beside them. He looked very happy. Grace assumed the King of Darts had hustled an unsuspecting citizen for beer money, shameless Corona coroner guy. "*You're* going to church?"

"Gee, yeah, except I'm a little worried the holy water will boil when I walk in," Grace drawled.

"They don't have holy water," Rhetta said. Henry nodded.

"Holy shit, no holy water?" Grace said. "That's also weird."

Rhetta grimaced, mildly scandalized. Henry chuckled. Over at the pool table, Ham raised his cue over his head with a shout. His resemblance to a baboon was startling.

"Creamed 'em," Ham crowed. "Praise the Lord." He walked over to the booth and high-fived Grace.

"Are you practicing for tonight?" Grace asked him.

"I am," he confirmed. He turned to the others. "Please feel free to join us."

Grace grinned at Rhetta. "When we were in school, the nuns told us it was a sin to go inside a Protestant church. Having a friend who was a Protestant was like consorting with a known felon."

"This is true," Rhetta agreed. "Johnny threatened to tell my parents when I went to a dance at the Methodist church."

"Horrors," Grace said, widening her eyes and touching her cheeks. "He *did* tell my parents when I went to the drive-in with a hot young Lutheran. Of course, I don't think it was his religion that flipped them out."

"I'm going to go back to my place and take a shower," Ham announced.

"Cleaning up for church?" Grace asked, startled. She looked down at her light blue, long-sleeved leotard top, jeans, and muddy boots. "Is this okay to wear to a healing service?"

"It's a working-class church, right?" Rhetta asked, assessing her. "I think you look fine."

"You look great," Henry agreed jovially.

"Okay, so I'll meet you in the church parking lot at about ten to nine," Ham said. Off he went, him with his fantastic, sorry ass. Grace wondered if they could get some sexual healing in before they called it a night.

Henry was still smiling. "Henry, is something up?" Grace asked.

He smiled more broadly, all mysterious. She and Rhetta traded looks, shrugged, and looked back at him. He didn't give it up, whatever it was. Then he trotted back to his special moneylender zone in the den of iniquity.

"I should go, too," Rhetta announced, leaving more than half her glass of wine as she gathered up her purse. *More than half*. "We've got a mountain of rotting hay because of all this rain."

"That's a drag," Grace said sincerely. "Maybe Earl can

ask God to turn off the faucet. Well, I have time before I'm saved to go home and feed Gus." And to fortify herself with a little more alcohol for the coming ordeal.

"Shall we?" Rhetta asked her.

She rose and sauntered toward the exit with Rhetta.

"What is up with Henry? I haven't seen him smiling like that since . . ." Grace blinked. "Shit, Rhetta, do you think Henry's getting some?"

"Hmm." Rhetta considered. "That would be nice, wouldn't it?"

Grace chuckled. Rhetta opened the door to Louie's and they both stared at the rain. The parking lot was a minefield of puddles, even though that was a mixed metaphor at best. Rhetta would have put it better.

Their umbrellas were in the stand to the right of the door. Rhetta fished around for hers, then handed Grace's over.

"Thanks, man," Grace said, popping it open. She hopped over the transom like a skydiver leaving the plane, followed closely by Rhetta. She heard some laughter inside the bar, caught sight of Rhetta waving goodbye to her, and jogged on over to her beloved Porsche. She snapped the umbrella back into its compact size and dumped it on the floor of the passenger side. Connie awoke with a purr, and Grace zoomed home to her dog.

Earl was loitering at her breakfast bar, examining what was left of the pizza she had shared with Clay. He smiled as she tore off her sopping wet jacket and she gave him a nod.

"You're soaked through. Where's your umbrella?" he asked her.

"Left it on the porch to dry." He gazed at her with humor twinkling in his eyes. "What?" she asked.

"You're going to church."

"Undercover. For a case."

"You're going to church," he repeated.

"You said you don't care if I go to a church. I can go to a tree if it brings me closer to God." She leaned over to give Gus some love. Gus yodeled and snuffled and looked back at Earl. Earl smiled at him. As she scratched Gus between his ears, she remembered the brown, long-tongued dog that had appeared in her backyard and elsewhere upon occasion. Maybe that dog was not actually God, but Gus's last-chance dog angel. Not that Gus had ever done anything that would send him to dog hell.

"All dogs go to heaven," Earl said.

"Stop reading my mind, man," she retorted, but she felt a bit uplifted. "I'm going to put on some warm clothes."

"Get *gussied up* for church?" He chuckled.

"Oh, and you're the first person who's ever come up with that," she salvoed over her shoulder.

"I ain't a person, Grace," he called after her.

"Wanna jump in the shower with me?"

He smiled and shook his head. "How *do* you put up with her, Gus?" he asked the dog.

"Hey, I heard that," she called.

"Funny how she only hears the things she wants to," Earl said to Gus. Gus made happy panting noises; he tap-danced on the wood floor and Earl escorted him to the door. Gus looked up at him expectantly and Earl shrugged.

"Much obliged, Gus. I don't really have to eat, and I never have to take a piss," Earl informed him. "But you go right ahead. Enjoy."

Gus scooted across the threshold—as much as a big dog like that could scoot—and Earl cocked his head, listening.

Stepped outside after all, and furled his wings.

Leon was sitting in his cell, less likely to do any exercising now that he'd gotten the news: His boy would not be visiting him that week. Leon's ex, Tamara, and her fiancé were taking him to visit the fiancé's family. Taking Benjamin out of school and everything.

It was a blow, and Leon was not taking it well.

"Bitch," he muttered between his teeth. "My son is all I live for. She knows that."

"I'm sorry, Leon," Earl said, appearing in front of him. "You want to play some cards, pass the time?"

"I want to get rid of that son of a bitch." He clenched his fists. "Stole my wife."

"No, you don't," Earl said. "Leastwise, I hope you don't." Then he lifted his head. "I gotta go to France," he announced.

"I just wish I could go . . . anywhere," Leon said. He flopped down on his cot and covered his eyes with his hands. Earl knew Leon wanted to break down and cry. Earl really wished he would. It would do the bitter convict a world of good. Jesus cried so hard in the garden of Gethsemane that he wept blood. But the hard shell Leon had put around himself was one of the reasons he, Earl, had been assigned to him. Plants couldn't grow in cement. They sprouted out through the cracks. Same thing with the souls of men. And women. A broken heart was often God's best garden.

Grace spent so much time detesting Leon for murdering people that she failed to see how alike they were. She had to see that, someday.

If she wanted to see the light.

You live your entire life in a place and you assume you had seen it all. But somehow a large white temple with a sloped roof and white marble stairs leading to four big white columns had passed Grace by. She parked down the street and walked with the crowd streaming into the church, greeting each with hugs and "praise Jesus's."

It was drizzling, but she left the umbrella in the car

because it was *not* her umbrella; Rhetta must have been in on the switcheroo for the one that was now folded and dripping on the floor of Connie's passenger side. The wording on its outside surface read FOR A GOOD TIME CALL JESUS. 1-800-JCHRIST. Ha. Payback, when it came, would be sweet.

Scanning for Ham, she reached the double doors of the Ark of the Covenant Pentecostal Tabernacle. Two men in dark suits with carefully arranged white hair were handing out programs, saying, "God bless you" to each person as they took one and filed into the church. They had on blue tags with USHER written on them in white letters, followed by a white cross.

Grace had a brief, sharp moment when she remembered being dragged to church with her mother and father, and all six of her siblings. She felt herself tense up, and reminded herself that Father Patrick Satan Murphy was definitely in hell now. Or so she hoped.

"We hope you'll receive the Lord tonight," another usher said as she passed the two older guys with the programs. This one was much younger and cuter. He grasped her hand, squeezed it, and gazed into her eyes as if he wanted to propose marriage to her.

"Thanks," she said, moving on in the steady stream of people entering the church. Most of them wore shiny, expectant smiles, but a young woman to Grace's right, with auburn hair pulled back in a ponytail and wearing a navy blue peacoat, was crying. Instantly, an usher in a chambray shirt and a pair of dark brown trousers broke ranks and came over to her.

"Are you troubled, sister?" he asked the woman, taking her arm and gently pulling her out of line. "Let's pray about it together."

A lady with blue hair was riding in a wheelchair pushed by another young usher. They were chatting amiably. There were a hell of a lot of ushers.

Past the double doors, a foyer with a vaulted ceiling that belled heavenward in an inverted lily shape. An enormous crystal chandelier sparkled like a comet. Prisms danced on a large oil painting of Jesus standing on a mountain with His arms wide open—no marks of the Crucifixion in His palms. Large sprays of lilies arced out of white vases embossed with crosses.

A drum, a guitar, and voices raised in jaunty song wafted beyond a second set of doors as a woman near Grace's own age greeted her. She was wearing a red and pink floral-print blouse, a black jacket, and a matching skirt. She took one of Grace's hands in both of hers. She had an usher tag, too. Janet.

"Are you new tonight? Do you have a special need that you would like Pastor Andy to pray for?"

Yeah. I would like Zack Lacey's case to be solved. If he was murdered, I'd like the sacks of shit who killed him brought to justice.

"No, thanks," Grace replied sweetly.

"Praise Jesus," the woman said, giving Grace's hand one last squeeze before Grace walked through the next set of doors into the sanctuary.

It was massive, with stairways that led to seats way up in the nosebleed section. Dozens and dozens of rows. Hundreds of seats. Maybe a thousand. And the pews were crammed with people chatting, laughing, embracing. Ushers were directing, escorting, and handing out slips of paper and stubby pencils. People were handing them back the pieces of paper, which went into white cans labeled PRAYER REQUESTS.

The main attraction was a huge stage dominated by an enormous white cross banked with pots of lilies. On either side of the cross, a golden church candelabra gleamed with long white tapers. Stage left, on a dais sat a band of six men dressed in suits, and one woman in a ruffled white gown. She was banging a tambourine against her palm. Two of the men were playing guitars; two were singing into a mic; one was beating the tempo on a full drum kit. And the last one was playing a sax. The song was familiar, yet not. Maybe she'd heard it on the radio.

Then she raised her head to see a screen, and the words of the song appeared, line by line, as scattered members of the congregation began to sing.

Washed in the blood of the Lamb, I am.
Washed in the blood of the Lamb, I am.

It wasn't really a song; it was a chant. More of the worshipers joined in as a full choir in white robes marched from stage right, waving their arms. Applause thundered through the dome. Some congregants raised their hands, threw back their heads, and closed their eyes. They smiled. Others began murmuring to themselves. Praying.

"Jesus, we give you the praise. Oh, Lord, Jesus, come into my heart."

The choir turned and sang. An organ joined in, vibrating through Grace's feet.

Teenagers gathered in clumps on the risers, getting into it, swaying, murmuring. One kid started to cry. Another took note, and *he* started to cry. The first crier upped the ante, swaying and murmuring as tears streamed down his face. The second guy sank to his knees. Whether they realized it or not, they were egging each other on, competing over who was more filled with the Holy Spirit.

This was *so* not like Catholic Mass. It was more like a pep rally. She could sense the rising emotion, as manufactured as a designer drug, and gave her head a little shake.

The band and the organ played faster and louder, and the lights started to dim. She broke into a grin as the cross on the stage lit up. She'd figured that would happen. The praising increased in fervency, need, urgency; the drummer and the organ player found a special pulse

and tapped into it. More voices chanted the endless re-
frain. Hands raised in the air. Folks swayed, wept.

Grace whipped out her cell phone. "Hey, Ham, where
the hell are you?"

"Sister, I'm sorry, but you need to turn that off," said
the usher she'd seen pushing the wheelchair as he darted
toward her. His name tag revealed that he was Luke,
and he practically had to yell at her to be heard. "We have
some wonderful seats close to the cross. If you feel led to
answer the call tonight, you won't have far to walk."

"Yeah, sorry," she said. "Thanks, but—" Then she saw
Ham standing up to wave at her. Third row from the
stage. Good job; he was about fifteen feet away from a
mahogany podium that at that very moment was rising
out of the stage floor like a magician's trick. The congregants began to cheer. The cross on the stage blazed; she
half-expected fireworks. Or a fog machine. Or both.

"My, um, significant other's over there," Grace said,
nodding at Ham. "He saved me a seat, God bless him.
I've been saved." The usher looked both confused and
crestfallen.

"I'll take you to him," the usher said. "Is this your
first time with us tonight?"

Then a trim, middle-aged man walked out from the
wings, carrying a cordless mic. He had a muscular build
and military posture; he was wearing a dark blue suit but
it was a nice suit, adorned with a white carnation bou-
tonniere. The crowd went completely batshit at the sight
of him.

"Bless you! Bless you tonight!" he shouted. He held
up a hand and the love intensified. People were practically doing the wave. Grace looked up at the seats, stu-
pefied. Wow.

"Is that Pastor Andy?" she asked her escort.

The man beamed at her. "No, sister, that's Pastor
Jimmy, our music director."

"Washed in the blood of the Lamb, I am," Pastor Jimmy sang, and then he held the last note. The band copied him; they hung there, drawing it out. Then he signaled for a downbeat and sang:

I am God's loving Son; He is my only One.

They all started singing the new line, her usher included, as they finally reached Ham's row.

"Thanks," she said.

The usher reached into his pocket and handed her a printed form the size of a three-by-five card and a little pencil. "If you write down your name and a prayer request, I'll get extra points," he told her. He looked so excited.

"Really? Well, shoot, okay." She scribbled a few words down and handed it and the pencil back to him.

"Praise Jesus," the usher said.

"You got that right." She smiled and winked at him, then scooted into the row. Half the people she stepped over didn't seem to realize she was even there.

Then she sank down next to Ham. He was wearing court clothes—jacket, dark jeans, and his black boots. He smelled great, of soap and a hint of something spicy. She saw water droplets on the ends of his hair. He had shaved. She wanted to go home, watch TV, and jump him.

"Oh, my God, Ham," she said. "This is just . . . nuts." She gazed around. "No wonder the Catholic Church is losing people. This is way more fun."

"I used to go to revivals with my great-uncle when I was a kid," he said. "The kind in the tents."

She was impressed. "Were there snakes?"

"Naw. I always hoped."

"Well, you should have filled out a prayer request," she said. "Tonight might have been your lucky night."

"I saw you fill one out." He raised a brow. "What did you ask for?"

"I asked Pastor Andy how long he's been practicing

medicine without a license." She fluttered her lashes. "Telling kids to dump their meds."

It was obvious he wasn't sure if she was kidding. She made a show of looking around.

"Do they sell refreshments at these things?" she asked.

"Is your soul singing?" Pastor Jimmy asked the crowd.

"Amen!" the congregation shouted.

"Is your soul lifted up to the Lord?"

"Hallelujah!"

"Are you ready to stand before the Master?"

"Yes, Jesus! Hallelujah, amen, sweet Lord. I give you the praise, oh, my sweet Jesus." They were shouting loud and strong, bellowing and hollering.

"Poor Zack," Grace murmured. "He didn't stand a chance."

"Hallelujah!"

CHAPTER
TWELVE

In yellow rain boots, a raincoat, and an old cowboy hat, Rhetta slipped and slid in the mud as she trudged toward the barn. She was cold, wet, and very worried. They were already behind on payments and now the barn roof was leaking in two new places, and her daughter was coughing and talking about feeling hot. Rhetta took her temperature, slumping with relief that, so far, it was still 98.6. If she had to stay home from school tomorrow, she and Ronnie would have to flip a coin to see who stayed home from work. If the Zack Lacey case broke, there would be more evidence, and Rhetta wanted to be the one to process it. For Grace.

But now . . . warmth.

Happiness.

She stood at the entrance to the barn, loving that she owned a barn (well, along with the bank) and loving that there were animals inside it that she raised and fed and named. She put the worry away as she silently counted her blessings. Her life was filled with life. There were homeless people all over the country, all over OKC, and she and her family had one another. And their menagerie. And Grace.

She smiled faintly at the thought of Grace at a holy-roller church service and slogged through the damp to the first bucket catching the rain from the barn. It wasn't as full as she expected it to be, so there was some more good news.

Holy Cow lowed.

"How are you doing this fine evening?" Rhetta asked her as she ran a hand down Holy Cow's flank, admiring the markings that looked like Jesus. "Would you like to be milked?"

Holy Cow mooed. Rhetta smiled at her. "It's going to be okay," she said. "We just have to have faith."

And from the hayloft, Earl smiled down on Rhetta.

"Praise God! Miracles are happening here tonight," Pastor Andy shouted, king of all creation. He smiled like he was high as he gazed down on his flock. The woman beside Grace was sobbing. "Miracles everywhere. Behold the power of Jesus!"

The old lady who had been wheeled in was walking on her own steam across the stage. Four men in suits stood with white blankets in their arms. Pastor Andy high-stepped toward the woman as she shuffled toward him.

"Satan took away her power to walk, but Jesus gave it back! Hallelujah, sister!" He darted forward and tapped his fingers on the woman's forehead. "You stay out of there, devil. This sister belongs to the Lord!"

The woman stiffened. Then she began to shake all over. The band thrashed in an acceptably religious manner. The organ pumped like it was time for the kickoff. On your mark, get set . . . Boomer Sooner!

The entire auditorium was thrilled as the old lady flung her arms straight up, jerked back her head, and fell backward. Two of the men with the blankets broke her fall and laid her gently on the floor. The preacher man strutted backward as the crowd cheered. The woman kept on convulsing and thrashing.

"That's what I'm talking about!" the weeping woman beside Grace shrieked. "Oh, my dear Lord Jesus, hal-lelujah!"

"Holy sh—" Grace blurted, covering her mouth with her hand. She looked at Ham, who grinned in a superior way. *Been here, done this.*

It went on and on, as the ushers brought up their white coffee cans filled with requests and Pastor Andy went through them by the handful. Arthritis, hallelujah! Chronic fatigue syndrome, we give you the praise! No job, you're gonna get a job. Who has a job right here right now for this sinner? Will work for soul food, yessir, I hear you, brother.

After a while it got boring, because it actually got predictable—if you knew how to play against the house, and Grace did. Pastor Andy called out a malady; the ushers had the afflicted ready to hop onto the stage; Andy zinged them on the forehead, and they went into convulsions. It was quite orgiastic, and it reminded Grace of the previews for the zombie movie she had seen with Clay.

"There's not much point in sticking around," she said to Ham.

"Grace, it's just getting started," Ham told her. "We could be here hours until it's time to see Antwone."

"Hours? And you *knew* this?" she said. "Why didn't you warn me?"

"There is someone here tonight who has lost someone. That person died by his own hand," Pastor Andy announced. "He was lost, and alone, and he did not know that God had a plan for his life, a beautiful, unfolding plan."

Ham raised a brow at Grace. She raised one back. "I'll bet you there's a dozen people who fit that description," she said.

Then, Pastor Andy bounded to the edge of the stage and pointed at Grace. A spotlight fastened on her.

"Come up here, Sister Grace. We know you loved him, and we know you are grieving for him. Let God heal your heart!"

"Praise Jesus!" the congregation roared.

"Undercover," Grace gritted, as Ham slapped her on the back. "*Ham,* stop it."

"Hey, you wrote it down. And you used your real name?"

"Yeah, that was genius," she said. "I thought maybe they'd keep track of me, ask questions so I could—"

"Sister Grace!" Pastor Andy yodeled.

"How the mighty are fallen." Ham reached into his jacket pocket and pulled out his cell phone. He shot off a couple of pictures as the usher, Grace's best friend forever and ever, hallelujah, beckoned her from the end of the row to come on up. His face was shiny with perspiration and his cheeks were apple-rosy. He was on the verge of doing his own happy dance. His sinner had been picked. God was good. All the time!

"Put that camera away, Hamilton, or I swear I will never—"

"Ssh, ssh, Grace," he urged her. He started laughing. "Don't make a scene."

"You guys set this up," she hissed at him. "I don't know how you did it—"

He held up his hands, protesting his innocence, but he was laughing so hard that tears were streaming down his cheeks. She wanted to belt him one, and she would have, but the usher had maneuvered his way down the row and was eagerly grasping her hand. *Break the case, break the case,* she reminded herself as she succumbed and allowed him to parade her toward the stage. Floodlights surrounded Pastor Andy's head like a halo as he held out his arms like Jesus, urging her to come forward and testify.

Last time we testified, the guilty got probation, she thought. Her mind was racing as she clattered up the steps in her cowboy boots. Pastor Andy started doing his chicken walk toward her and she pulled back her jacket, flashing her badge. His smile didn't falter and he just kept hopping toward her.

"It's all right, sister," he said into his headset mic. "God loves everyone." He swept his arm to include the coliseum of onlookers. "Isn't that right?"

High up in the nosebleed seats, Earl waved at her. "I am going to kill you," she gritted through her teeth. Then she had the hopeful notion that all this was one big stupid dream and she was going to wake up any second.

"You lost a brother, a friend," Pastor Andy said, "through a death of his own choosing." His eyes welled. "How that must tear at you."

Only because I have to—

Without warning, a wave of grief washed through her. It wasn't sadness; it was something deeper. It descended on her like a stone, pushing her down. She was suddenly drowning in it, almost unable to catch her breath.

"Psalm 18:2," Pastor Andy intoned. "The Lord is my rock, my fortress, and my deliverer; my God is my rock, in whom I take refuge. He is my shield!"

He stomped the floor on the word "shield." The choir began to sing. *The Lord is my Shepherd, no want shall I know!* The audience joined in.

"And the horn of my salvation! He is my stronghold!" the pastor bellowed. "Hallelujah!"

Then he started toward her, his hand raised up as if he were about to smack her on the forehead. She glanced over her shoulder to see the guys with the blankets ready to catch her.

And she narrowed her eyes at Pastor Andy.

He kept coming.

"Back off," she gritted, certain he couldn't hear her; he probably couldn't see her lips, either. She hoped—*prayed*—her body language would keep him from making a scene.

"Praise Jesus," he cried.

And then, as she braced herself for a head rap, he slowly laid his hands on her shoulders, and gazed into her eyes. "It's all right," he said in a low voice. "God knows your heart. He knows what you need."

There was a hushed moment, just one heartbeat in all the nuttiness, and then he threw back his head and yodeled, "Jesus, Jesus, Jesus!" and all the other lunatics did, too.

Lights blared at her; the music was deafening as her escort led her back toward her seat. People reached out their hands to her, squeezing her fingers as she stumbled past them. They said, "Bless you, sister; praise God, sinner," patting her, touching her.

Grinning from ear to ear, Ham waited for her to plop down. Then he leaned over and whispered, "Can I have your autograph?"

She didn't answer him. She seethed privately for a few seconds, and then she turned around to look at where Earl had been sitting. The seat was empty. Figured.

"Did you write down Zack's name?" Ham asked her.

She shook her head. "Figured he wouldn't know who Zack was, either. I just asked if people who commit suicide go to hell."

"He assumed you were talking about a guy."

"A black guy. A brother," Grace drawled, but the joke didn't go anywhere.

There was a lot more swaying. The woman next to Grace started jabbering—speaking in tongues—and the man behind her took it up. The energy in the room reached a fever pitch; ushers started running up and down the aisles checking on the people who were rolling around having fits. They handed out some water bottles but let most of the holy rollers roll on.

"Come up and receive the Lord!" Pastor Andy shouted. "He is waiting to save your soul from Satan! Stand on the conviction that you are His beloved!"

Streams of people rushed to form lines. They descended the stairs, guided by the ushers, hands in the air, murmuring, swaying, yelling. Ushers stood at the head of each line and held both the hands of the convicted. They fell to their knees at the foot of the stage while the choir sang and the band played and Pastor Andy bounced forward, shouting, "You are saved, brother! You are saved, sister!"

Grace's usher looked over at her. She smiled at him and nodded, and stayed planted.

"I'm going up," Ham said breathlessly, and then he grinned at her to show her that he was kidding.

"You'd better pray that someone is going to save your ass," she shot back. "From *me*."

The parade kept marching forward. Grace started checking the exits and planning a strategy in case there was a riot. There was an incredible amount of energy, pressure, and high, high emotion. This was how people died after soccer games in England, or on Black Friday, the shopping day after Thanksgiving.

Then somehow, miraculously, it was over. The old lady who had walked across the stage was back in her wheelchair. Some people were drooped over the backs of the chairs in front of them, like pews, weeping and smiling or shaking their heads. There was a powerful eau de B.O. hanging in the air. And relief. And joy.

On the way out, Grace's usher caught up with her. Color crept up his neck and across his cheeks. He smiled at her shyly and dropped his gaze.

"I, um, hope you'll come back," he said. He smiled at her, and then at Ham. "With your husband."

"Thank you." She resisted the impulse to wink at him. *I could take you to heaven, baby.*

"Your husband?" Ham asked, jostling her arm. "Is that what you told him?"

"These guys make assumptions," she shot back.

Out into the fresh air. Ham breathed it in and pointed upward, at the ring around the moon. "It's gonna rain. Some more."

"Bobby's got mold."

"I know. He's really worried about it."

"Maybe we can have some kind of work party, help him out." Grace glanced at the church. "We should have prayed for him." She pulled out a cigarette. "Not mocking prayer, man."

"Did you feel anything when you went up there?" Ham asked her. "Some kind of spirituality? I thought your hair was going to stand on end." His mouth twitched. "And that you were going to bite him if he tried to hit you in the forehead."

"Right. Assault a beloved minister in front of six hundred witnesses." She struck a match, for which she received some glares from others in the multitudes headed for their cars. "God deliver me from this filthy habit." After she lit her cigarette, she blew out her match and carried it in her hand. "Your church isn't like that, is it?" She wiggled back and forth.

"Much more sedate," he assured her. He was waiting.

"Naw," she said. "I didn't feel anything. Not a damn thing."

CHAPTER
THIRTEEN

Ham's truck was parked closer to the church. Grace let him drive her to her car and described how to get to the taco stand. Antwone was due there in twenty minutes. Just enough time to get there and park.

As Ham followed her over, she checked her messages. Evan Johnson. Very distressed, wanting to discuss the "situation" with Juanita. A message from Juanita, ditto. And then, an older, halting voice:

"Detective Hanadarko, my name is Emily Prescott. I'm Zachary Lacey's grandmother. Father Pepera phoned me. Please, call me back. It doesn't matter what time it is." Hard, wracking sobs ended the call. Deep grief. Grace was sure Father Pepera had proved to be *such* a comfort.

She passed the taco stand, scoping it out as she left her message system. She'd call Emily Prescott later. If she was Zack's maternal grandmother, maybe she knew where Zack's mom was.

A streetlight caught the chrome on Ham's wheels as he slid in ahead of her around the corner. They both got out and walked toward the tables where she'd met Antwone the night before. They were right on time, but he wasn't there.

They waited a few minutes. Grace grabbed a taco and started crunching away like a starving woman. Ham got a soda. A man collected a to-go order and a lowrider slithered past. Not their Chevy Impala.

"Maybe he has overtime at the bowling alley," Ham said.

"Or else he chickened out and bailed," Grace countered, talking with her mouth full as she snaked out her cell phone. She called Antwone's cell. No answer. She disconnected and polished off her taco, thought about ordering another one, decided against it as she wadded up the trash and threw it out. She nodded at Ham.

"You go to the bowling alley. I'll wait here."

He nodded and jogged across the street to his truck. Grace stretched her back, then walked the perimeter, scanning for people and things that shouldn't be there— like bad guys dealing dope on the corners, bad girls waiting to be picked up by bad guys—but all was calm. No misdemeanors, no felonies.

Then she heard something farther down in the alley behind the taco shop. She froze. A scuffle; the sound of a fist hitting a body; a low moan. Silently, swiftly, she drew her weapon and darted into the shadows, pushing her spine against the wall. She peered deep in the darkness, making out nothing past the tips of her boots.

Another blow. "Faggot . . . ," a male voice said.

Shit. Antwone.

Keeping her gun out and up, she glided soundlessly into the blackness. The gray began to shift as she waited for her eyes to adjust; for the moment, she focused on listening. She needed both hands for her gun; otherwise, she would have slid her fingers into her pocket to demon-dial for backup. Draw out her pencil flashlight. Thank God her phone was on vibrate.

The alley reeked of rotten lettuce and dog shit and maybe a whiff of dope. Pieces of darkness began to thicken into shapes. Possibly two individuals bent over something on the ground. Make that some*one* on the ground. Probably Antwone. One of the guys arced back his foot and kicked. Hard. The shape on the ground grunted.

She gathered in all the details she could. The kicker was around six feet tall, two hundred pounds. It was too dark to make out the other guy. She was not seeing a gun on Kicker, but that didn't mean no guns were present. For all she knew, the guy on the ground wasn't Antwone and he was just biding his time until he could pull out his Glock and blow somebody's head off. She couldn't just sail into the situation expecting impunity because she wanted to help. On the streets, you got extra points for taking out a cop, especially if someone else was kicking your ass.

Then No Kick separated himself from Kicker. He was much smaller, definitely a kid. Damn. Grace kept her weapon aimed at Kicker.

"Someone's here," No Kick announced. He started sprinting in the opposite direction, sloshing through puddles, stumbling around a trash can. It fell with a clatter-clatter-crash.

Kicker swore under his breath and took off after him.

Grace wanted like anything to pursue. She strained like Gus when he was watching the stick fly end over end through the air. But she had a mandate to protect and serve. So she raced over to the prone figure, sweeping with her gun, then fanning with her flashlight over the muddy army jacket and Antwone's swollen, bruised face.

"Antwone, it's Detective Hanadarko," she said. "Are you armed?"

"Ow," he said, gasping. "No."

"What hurts?"

He was silent. She shook his shoulder. No response. She flipped her cell phone open with her teeth and dialed the dispatcher, identified herself, and requested an ambulance. She got confirmation that one was on the way just as Antwone tried to sit up. She dropped to one knee and helped him, slowly. He looked like he'd been in a prizefight. His lips were bleeding. One eye was swollen shut.

"Can you see me, man?" she asked him. "How many fingers—"

"Shit," he hissed. "Shit."

"Who were those guys?" she asked him. She demon-dialed number three, which was Ham. "He's here. He was jumped. Beat up. I called for a bus."

"On my way," Ham told her.

"I don't need an ambulance," Antwone said, wiping blood away from his nose.

"Maybe you do," Grace countered. "You got kicked pretty hard. Who were those guys?"

"I don't know." He wouldn't look at her.

"You definitely do. Were they guys from school?"

He hung his head. Stayed frozen that way.

"Guys beating you up because you're gay?"

He did the sullen thing like a pro.

"Antwone, don't wuss out on me now," she told him. "Guys you sold weed to?"

Nothing.

"Guys from Flaco?"

"No," he said stonily. He was mad, blaming her for getting in his face, more afraid of legal trouble than physical pain. She got that a lot. She didn't care. She just wanted him to talk to her.

"Did they go after Zack? Beat him up for being a faggot, too?" Was his death a hate crime?

He sniffled. She felt in her pockets for tissue. Found a paper napkin from Louie's with a phone number on it. Another UPS guy. Oh, well. She handed it to him while she found another one and folded it over, preparing to dab at his cuts.

"Don't touch me," he said. "I'm bleeding."

"Are you HIV positive?" she asked matter-of-factly.

"Hell, no." And then, "I don't know. I don't want to go in an ambulance. I'm okay." He stared up at her. "Please."

She held up two fingers. "How many?"

He grinned tiredly and flashed her his middle finger. She stifled a guffaw. The kid had guts. Maybe he didn't want to go to the hospital because drugs would show up. She had promised to leave him out of it as best she could.

"Walk back and forth," she said, watching him. He did so, well. No weaving or stumbling.

"Okay. Maybe you're going to live." She called back in, canceling the bus and the backup. She could feel the weight of more paperwork descending on her weary shoulders.

She walked him back to the taco stand and made him sit at the picnic table. She bought a Sprite and asked for an extra cup of ice. Dumping the ice in a wad of napkins, she pressed it against his forehead. He jerked; she grabbed his chin and made him stay still.

"Tell me their names. I need to question them," she said.

He clenched his jaw and she huffed at him. "Do you think if you don't tell on them they won't hurt you again?" Then she thought a minute. "Are they customers? Dope customers?" A bigger, brighter lightbulb went off. "Or did they front you the cash for a drug buy?"

His eyes flared. Bingadero. She made a mental note, leaning toward him. "Were you and Zack going to make the big buy together? From Flaco?" She waited. "Were you moving up the distribution chain? Were you going to buy something else? Something stronger?" *More expensive?*

"They're just asswipes," he spat. "I was going to take them out." She gave him a look. "I *was*. I was just—"

"Resting up first," she interrupted. "Give me their names and I'll stop bugging you." She moved her makeshift ice pack to another bruised spot on his face.

"Ow. Drew Covel. Brian Bradford."

"Which one was the shrimp?"

"Drew."

"Do they go to your school?" When he clamped his mouth shut, she ran her free hand through her hair and dropped it to her side. "Antwone, you already told me their names. I can find out if they go to your school. Save me the effort, okay?"

He was still silent, and she cursed the idiocy of idiots everywhere. "They didn't see me. They won't know you talked to me," she said.

"Yes, they go to my school," he ground out. "Brian's on the football team."

"Figures. Guess Brian is the quarterback."

"Yeah, but second string," Antwone said.

"There's a tiny bit of justice, there." She smirked; he smirked back. "I hated high school, man."

He balled his fists. He hated high school, too, oh, yeah. High school was such a weird disconnect—you weren't an adult yet, but you could get beat up like one.

"How did they find you tonight?" Grace asked him. "They come along, see you, pull you out of your car? Where is your car?"

"Around the corner. They must have followed me from the bowling alley. They go there a lot." He lowered his voice. "Mess with me while I'm working."

"Did they mess with Zack, too? Call him a faggot?"

He nodded.

She held up her fingers and counted off suspects. "Lots of people messed with Zack. His father. Guys at school." *How do I detest thee? Let me count the ways.*

"Yeah." Antwone's voice was mournful, angry. He jutted out his swollen lower lip and exhaled.

"Do you know where Drew and Brian live?" Had to be in the school district. "Have they helped you buy drugs before?"

He hesitated. She wanted to smack him upside the head and tell him just to tell her, goddamn it. His boyfriend was *dead*. Antwone was a juvenile; she didn't have to read him his rights because she wasn't charging him with anything. He could ask for a lawyer. He probably wouldn't. And she needed to keep him talking.

"It was going to be a bigger buy than usual," he said at last, praise God, hallelujah. "Oh, God." He twitched, beginning to panic, realizing he was unburdening himself to an actual police officer. Grace had facilitated the process many times, and she couldn't help the satisfaction that warmed her heart against the cold night. And the colder reality that this sweet, mixed-up boy was mixing it up in bad shit. He was just like Zack: He never had a chance.

"It's cool, Antwone. We're good here, you and me. Like what? Like when?"

"I don't know now. It was supposed to happen a week ago. Then Zack . . ." He took a ragged breath. "I guess they have their own customers who want their shit. Drew and Brian took their money to help me make the buy. Now no one's got shit."

"They called you a faggot."

He nodded wearily. Warily. He looked up at the moon and Grace wondered what he saw. How old and how bad did you have to be to have a last-chance angel? Was there a shortage? What happened if you needed one but they were all out of them? Did God wave his magic wand and, lo, there were more?

Birds cackled in the darkness. A lowrider spray-painted with a mural of a Hawaiian sunset drove past playing *norteño* music, maybe Los Tigres del Norte. A brown masculine face stared out from the driver's side, checking Grace out. He whistled at her. She ignored him.

Eventually, Antwone stopped bleeding.

A few minutes later, Ham showed up. Grace filled him in on Antwone's run-in with his investors, culminating in their kicking the crap out of him and calling him names. Ham pursed his lips and blew out his cheeks.

"Same thing happened to my brother," Ham told Grace and Antwone. "Guys at school used to hassle Nick. Me and my brother Rafe, we looked out for him. Bashed some heads."

"You have a gay brother?" Antwone asked.

"Are you kidding, man? The dude owns an art gallery," Grace said.

Ham nodded, and Antwone smiled a little, then winced and touched his mouth. Grace lit a cigarette, offering her pack of Morleys to Antwone, who shook his head.

She blew out smoke. "We started looking for Flaco today. Hit a string of gay bars, and it turns out he and Zack went to at least one together. What do you know about that?" She looked back at him.

Grace saw a world of hurt in Antwone's beautiful eyes. "I hate that dickhead," he said. "We should've never gotten involved with him."

Ham walked over to the taco stand, got a refill on the soda, and handed it to Antwone, who guzzled it thirstily.

"He the one who get you started in all this?" Ham asked.

Antwone nodded. "We thought we could make a bunch of money, save it up . . ."

Escape, Grace finished silently.

"We need to get you to the doctor," Grace said, grabbing his chin and scrutinizing his face. Cuts, contusions, but now that she could see him in the light, nothing permanent-looking.

"I'm not going. You can't make me go," he said, pulling back. "You're not my mother."

Yeah, what about your mother? Where is she in all of this? "Get some onion rings before they close, Ham," Grace told her partner. He nodded and walked back to the take-out window.

"There was so much shit in Zack's life," Antwone said, as if there were none in his own. "He had this laptop he carried around all the time. There were stickers of metal bands all over it, like he was trying to be cool." He shook his head. "He said he was going to bust his stepmother with what was on it. But he wouldn't tell me what it was. He said when the time came he'd share it with me."

Ooh-la-la. "What do you think he knew?" Grace asked.

Antwone reached for Grace's pack of cigarettes after all. She let him take one, handed him her lighter. The doofus thing about smoking was that it did make you look older and cooler. He looked *great*. Blame it on the media.

"I think she was cheating on his old man," Antwone opined as he blew out the smoke. "I think Zack found her e-mails to and from the other dude."

"And what, like, copied them onto his laptop?" Grace asked. "As evidence?" Antwone nodded. "Where did you last see this laptop?"

"I don't remember." Antwone fell silent. He lowered his head, and Grace raised her brows at Ham as he returned with the onion rings. Because it was obvious that Antwone sure did remember. Maybe he had it.

"Did you keep it for him?" Grace asked, as she dipped an onion ring in ketchup. "Do you have it?"

"I just *told* you—"

"You kept it for him, and those guys who beat you up took it from you," Grace spun. "You sold it so you could buy more supply from Flaco."

"No," Antwone bit off, frowning at her. "I would never do that. It was Zack's."

"Do you think his stepmother found out and took it?" *And killed him over it?*

He looked sick. Maybe the streets were a bit too . . . streety for him. Battered, minus his boyfriend . . . it had to suck to be him right now.

"I don't think she's that bad," Antwone ventured. "Mrs. Lacey. I don't know her that well, but she's always been nice to me. Her son is a total asshole."

"She's got a son?" Grace repeated. No one had mentioned anything about a son.

"Paul. He's on the baseball team at school." Antwone was getting tense again. "I steer clear."

A blunt object, Grace thought. *Like a baseball bat?* From the way Ham's brows shot up, she deduced he was thinking the same thing. *Warrant. Warrant, warrant, warrant.* But it wasn't enough to go on, and she knew it.

"Are you sure you don't want to go to the doctor?" Grace asked him. "Do you have a place to go home to?"

He got quiet. Then he nodded. Grace took note. She wondered if he, a juvenile, was living on his own. Decided for the moment not to press too hard about that. Ham was on her wavelength; she watched him watching Antwone and felt a rush of pure joy. They were good at this; they were good at this together. That was what made the sex so great.

"I gotta go," Antwone insisted.

The three rose. Ham moved to one side of Antwone and Grace shifted to the other. Antwone noticed but he kept walking. Grace offered him another cigarette, and he refused it, like a bitter, condemned man headed for the gallows.

"We went to Zack's church tonight," Grace said as he led them to a beat-up Corolla. No gangbanger's car for

Antwone, no sir. He was leading the life—minus the dealing—that Grace might have imagined for Janaya—humble but respectful. Minus the dealing. Yeah, there was that. She glanced at his license plate. Oklahoma. She'd check who the car was registered to.

Antwone looked at her expectantly. She quirked up her mouth in a lopsided grin. "That church was weird, man. Jesus, Jesus, *Jesus*." She shook all over, and he smiled sadly.

"They told him he would go to hell unless he changed. He was so scared of hell."

So, suicide not likely, unless going off his antidepressants got him all jumpy, so to speak.

"That totally sucks." Grace shook her head. "We're going to ask you for your help some more. Are you still willing to help us? After getting beat up tonight and admitting that you sell drugs?"

His eyes narrowed. "I'm more willing. If someone killed Zack . . . you know they do shit to—to *faggots*. Tie them to car bumpers, hang them."

"Drown them?" Grace asked softly.

Antwone put his hand on the door handle. His knuckles were skinned; bloody red tissue glistened on chocolate-brown in the overhead streetlight. "Did he . . . was he in pain when he died?"

"We don't know," Grace said. "Help us find out."

"Yeah," he said.

"I'm serious. I want you to help us. We'll try to keep the dealing out of it. I can't promise . . ."

Ham gave her a look. She avoided his gaze.

"I . . . whatever." Antwone's hands were shaking. With some difficulty, he unlocked his car, opened the door, and slid in. Grace let him shut the door and stood back from the curb, beside Ham. With a squeal of tires, Antwone peeled out. The air was damp and smelled of Oklahoma crude. And trash and dashed hopes.

"Maybe he's a flight risk," Ham said as they watched the night swallow up Antwone's car.

"Maybe he's not," Grace murmured.

He turned to her. "About the dealing. Grace, we know what we know."

"We didn't charge him, didn't read him his rights." At his frown, she sighed heavily. "He's got so many strikes against him, Ham. Black, poor, gay. If those guys turn out to be good suspects, we'll use it. If not, let's let him go. We've done that before."

"D.A.," Ham said.

"Shit, look at Butch's informant. Lowlife piece of crap has actually *bragged* to Butch about some of the stupid shit he's done."

Ham nodded. He stuffed his hands in his pockets. "Speaking of stupid shit, how about that holy-roller church telling Zack he's going to hell because he's gay?"

"Catholic Church says the same thing." She waggled her shoulders and smiled. "Come to heaven with me?"

"Yeah," he said, as though the sun had broken over his face. Ham happy was a beautiful sight. "Let's go."

Blastoff, baby.

CHAPTER
FOURTEEN

It was pouring buckets by the time Grace and Ham arrived at Casa Hanadarko, Grace twirling her Jesus umbrella, then tossing it onto her porch and letting Ham chase her into the house. She tripped through it, threw the side door open, and charged back out into the rain, in the privacy of her own soaked yard. Gus was on her bed; he came to see what was going on and barked with joy as Grace yanked off her boots and ripped off all her clothes in the freezing rain and twirled in a circle, laughing her head off.

"Jesus, Grace," Ham cried as he darted back inside. She taunted him, swinging her ass at him, while he stripped down. "Are you crazy? It's freezing out there."

She pushed into the house, laughing, and flung her soaking wet self into his arms. He picked her up firefighter style, and she whooped like a siren as he carried her into the bedroom. Thrilled by all the activity, Gus followed them back in and scooted under the bed.

Ham flopped Grace down onto the mattress, and she rolled back and forth to dry herself off, then over onto her stomach to grab a condom out of the nightstand. Like most men, Ham wasn't fond of rubbers; like all of Grace's men, he wore one because she wanted him to.

"Put that on your Jesus umbrella," she told him, biting her lower lip and making waggly Groucho eyes at him.

He did as he was told; then he kissed her, lacing his fingers through hers and pushing her arms over her head. He straddled her. Her skin was covered with goose bumps, and he blew on her neck as she laughed and rolled her pelvis beneath him. His fingers moved down her leg.

"Grace," he whispered. She writhed, throwing back her head in sheer abandon. Sweet release was on its way, courtesy of OCPD Major Bangs.

"Oh, God, Ham," she murmured. His fingers zoomed to the sweet spot, and she opened up to it, all of it; sex was so amazing, especially with him. Sex was the best. Ham Dewey was the best.

He was rock hard, and he wanted to move to the main event, but he pleasured her until she was soaring. Then he anchored her down to the bed with his sex, stroking, building, heating her up. They flew together.

"Oh, Grace," Ham whispered, and then a low, gut-deep moan escaped him as he climaxed. She came soon after, uninhibited, joyful, satisfied.

For a while, they lay like spent animals, while Gus remained under the bed. Grace was a puddle. Ham looked like he had died.

She decided they needed to top off the evening with some bourbon, and traipsed naked into the kitchen to grab her bottle. She spotted the flyer for Helping Hand, and her cop brain began to rev up. She gave her head a serious shake to prevent the synapses from synching. Took a quick swig of booze to confuse them even further. The cold pizza was still there; she grabbed the box and the bottle and sailed back into her bedroom. Ham was under the covers, and it looked like he might fall asleep.

So she hopped onto the bed and wafted the bourbon bottle under his nose. He chuckled.

"I'm toast," he moaned. "I can't move a muscle."

"Then I'll eat the rest of this delicious pizza myself," she announced. She took a huge mouthful. "How much of what Antwone told us is true, do you think?"

"I can't believe you got him to admit that he sells drugs," Ham said into the pillow. He rolled over onto his back. She loved his hairy chest, flat stomach, fine equipment. "Is he really that naïve?"

"He's really that grief-stricken," Grace said, holding out her pizza slice to him. "Completely off his game."

"Yeah," Ham replied quietly.

He lay back down, snuggling into her damp sheets and started looking too comfortable. Grace glanced at her radio alarm clock. It was after one. Tomorrow was a workday. There'd been a lot of tough, late nights this week. Tomorrow was Friday.

"You can take a shower if you want," Grace said. "I'm going to go check on a few things." She had a copy of the coroner's report and Rhetta's lab findings. And the pictures of what used to be Zachary Lacey. Nothing new, probably nothing that would give her anything new, but it would get her out of her bed. Hopefully, it would do the same for Ham.

She heard his sigh but didn't respond to it as she stuffed the rest of the pizza into her mouth, slid to the edge of the bed, and got up.

Grabbing her robe, she belted it around her body, using the edge to dry herself off. Gussie came, too, leaving Ham alone in her room. Point made, perhaps, that neither of the Hanadarkos were interested in the afterglow thing.

She plopped down onto the couch with the bourbon and opened the case files on her lap. It was so obvious to her that they needed a warrant, to go looking for blunt instruments and Zack's laptop. She just needed something that would get her past a judge with her golden ticket in hand.

Her eyelids fluttered. Maybe she was too tired to do this after all.

She and Earl were treading water so clear that when she looked down, she could see her toes. Both of them were fully dressed, except that she was barefoot.

"Hey, it's a wet T-shirt contest," she said to him. His light blue T-shirt was silkscreened with a couple of red Chinese characters in a rectangle.

"All you have to do is dunk your head under," he replied.

She gave him a look. "Dunk my head? . . . So I'll be baptized or something? Earl, I've already been baptized Catholic." She moved her hands. "It's a life sentence." She splashed water at him. "Or a death sentence, if you're gay. Are angels gay?"

"I have no idea," he replied.

"Do people who kill themselves go to hell?"

His features sagged. "People who kill themselves are already in hell, Grace."

The warm water cradled her. "What about this unconditional love you keep talking about? God stops loving us if we commit suicide?"

"Suicide is about annihilating the self," Earl replied. "God can't love you if there's no you to love."

"That's bullshit." She floated on her back. "It's about stopping the pain."

"Maybe direct suicide. But what about indirect suicide? Dying slowly. Smoking, drinking too much, bringing home guys you don't even know."

She bobbed on the water as wavelets massaged her backbone. "Hey. When did this become about me?"

"Having a death wish, being too fascinated with death," he continued. "Maybe being a firefighter. Or a cop."

Her mouth dropped open, and water poured into it. Sputtering, spitting it back out, she glared at him. "Hey, what the hell are you saying? That a cop . . . that Kane . . . committed suicide because he died in the line of duty? That is totally screwed."

"It's not how, it's why," he said. He looked at her. "You lied tonight. Again. Because you *did* feel something at that service."

She scowled at him. "Earl, it was a manufactured experience. Those guys are experts at crowd control. Group psychology."

"Most abuse victims numb out during sex," he said. "You let yourself enjoy it. Revel in it. But you numb out during religious experiences."

"That wasn't a religious experience. It was bullshit."

She followed his gaze. Zachary Lacey, intact, swayed beneath the water like a piece of seaweed. He was dressed in the clothes they'd found him in, undamaged. His eyes were incredibly shiny; and tears, like bubbles, swam toward the surface.

"That bullshit religious experience killed him, too," she said. "He needed someone. He trusted them. And once he let down his guard, they threw him in the deep end. That poor kid didn't know how to swim."

"Maybe they did their best," Earl said.

"Maybe the diocese knew Father Murphy was screwing all of us, and looked the other way. Maybe Evan Johnson told Juanita to send her callers to church." She stared down at Zack, watching the fish approach. Watching death claim him. "Maybe I have never had a religious experience in my entire life."

"And I'm just a brain aneurysm, waiting to pop."

"I don't know, Earl," she said. "Are you?"

Then Zack tipped back his head and stretched up his hands toward her. She couldn't tell if he could see her. A couple of deep breaths to oxygenate herself, and she dove beneath the surface. The water charged with golden light, and it was as warm as sunshine. The sensation reminded her of something, but she couldn't quite place what it was.

Down she went, deeper; beginning to feel the pressure on her lungs as she clasped Zack's wrists and swam back toward the surface. But the boy was too heavy; he was dead weight. She began to sink. She held fast, blowing out air bubbles a little at a time, emptying herself out. She knew how people drowned; they couldn't stop themselves from inhaling. It was a reflexive action and, of course, what they inhaled was water, not air. That was how Lena had known that Zack was alive when he went in.

She was going down, and the water remained golden and warm. Should be colder, should be darker. God, she wanted to take a breath. Her body was straining, her stomach contracting.

If she let go of Zack, she could go back up, get a breath. But as she released his right wrist, he slipped away, sagging downward as if pulled by gravity. Which was wrong. The dead floated.

I gotta let you go, man, Grace thought. But just as she loosened her grip on his left wrist, he began to struggle. *Damn, he's alive.*

She couldn't let go if there was a chance of saving him. Her stomach convulsed, and she bit her lips to keep herself from trying to breathe in. Her lungs screamed at her and her legs kicked. She had to let go of him.

No, goddamn it. I won't.

Then Earl appeared beside her. He took Zack's other hand, and he and Grace began to swim together. Zack was waterlogged; he weighed a ton.

When they broke the surface, Zack was not there. Grace gasped in oxygen, on the verge of throwing up or passing out. Once she stabilized herself, she looked back down through the water. The boy had vanished.

"Where is he?"

"Stone's rolled away, I reckon," Earl said. He wore a T-shirt that read LIFEGUARD. His hair was slicked back and his eyelashes were wet.

"What the hell are you talking about? What stone?"

He shrugged. "Actually, that was something I was talking about with Leon Cooley. But it could just as easily have been you. You two are alike. You just don't know it."

"Don't even start that shit."

He held up his hands.

"So where were you when Zack went in the river?" Grace demanded. "Was anyone with him?"

"God was with him," Earl replied. "The whole time. Even when the needle went in."

"What are you talking about?" Grace asked. She looked down and saw—

She *saw*—

Grace jerked awake on the sofa. Her front door had just shut and her phone was ringing. She grabbed the phone as she walked to the door and checked the peephole. Ham, leaving.

She took the call. There was weeping on the other end.

"Miss Hanadarko, I'm so sorry," the caller hiccupped. "This is Emily Prescott, Zack's grandmother. I'm sorry to call you but I can't, I just can't stand this."

"It's all right, Mrs. Prescott," Grace said. "I was going to call you first thing in the morning. I was just waiting for the sun to come up."

"Oh, please." Mrs. Prescott wept for a good, full minute. "*Please* tell me what happened to Zachary."

I wish you could tell me.

"How did he die? Did he—did . . . Father Pepera said . . ." She dissolved into more weeping. "That father of his. He scared off my daughter and then . . ." She sobbed. "I should never have left. I wanted to stay for Zack, but, oh, my God . . ."

"We're trying to determine what happened," Grace said gently. "Mrs. Prescott, can you tell me where your daughter is?"

"We lost contact. Karen told me she was leaving Ron, and I—God forgive me—I told her divorce is a sin. Marriage is one of the holy sacraments and she had married Ron Lacey. She had a child with him. She told me she hated me because I wouldn't support the divorce. She said I would rather have her be good than be happy. And—and she was right."

Sounds like God, Grace thought.

"Were there any letters between you and Karen?"

"After a while, they stopped coming. I haven't heard from her in at least eight years."

"What about Zack? Did Karen stay in touch with him?"

"No, and it tore my heart out. A child needs his mother."

"Was Ron Lacey abusive?"

"I don't know. I knew Karen was unhappy with him." She lowered her voice. "They had to get married. She was pregnant." Grace could hear the humiliation in her voice, even now. "You know, you try to raise a child to be God-fearing and . . ." She started to cry again. "Father Pepera won't say Mass for Zachary if he took his own life."

"There are other priests who will," Grace told her.

"No. Church law is clear," she said hoarsely. "He'll go to hell. Or he . . . he's in hell."

"Ma'am, with all due respect, my brother's a priest, and, and he says that the Church's position on suicide has changed."

"Zack, Zack," she moaned.

"My brother," Grace tried again, but the woman was crying too hard to listen. She made herself some coffee, listening to Mrs. Prescott until she wore herself out.

"Listen, Mrs. Prescott, I have to go now. I need to go to work. I'll do everything I can to solve this case . . . mystery." She winced. Zack was not a case. Zack was a person. Or a lost soul, according to some.

"Thank you," the old lady said, calmer now, if no less sorrowful. "Thank you with all my heart."

Grace hung up and stared at her phone. "So what do you want me to do, fabricate evidence?" she said aloud.

She squinted at the side door. No rain, and a rosy dawn. Everything smelled fresh from the rain. It was the kind of Oklahoma morning that made her grateful to be alive, and she smiled as she let the moment wash over her, wash right over her, like a baptism.

She couldn't remember what she had seen in her dream, but when she tried, darkness moved inside her, and chilled her to the bone.

She went into the bathroom. Her neighbor was up, so she let him see her boobies. They waved at each other in a neighborly way, and then she took a hot shower, sluicing away Ham's scent. As Gussie ate his breakfast, he told her a few things about life. He was so cute that Grace had to get down on the floor and wrestle with him for a few minutes.

As he slurped up water, she tossed back coffee and took some aspirin. She didn't have a headache yet, but she had a feeling it was going to be a stressful day.

A deep calm washed over Butch as Captain Perry gathered the squad in the interview room. Everyone took seats except for her. Bobby gave Butch a thumbs-up, nodding soberly as he drank his morning coffee. Off to one side, listening intently, Ham reminded Butch of a hunting dog watching a duck fall from the sky. This was the work they loved, not paperwork and desk jockeying. This was the real deal, OCPD style.

Although she wasn't late, Grace was the last to show,

looking mighty fine in a damp sand-colored top and tight flared jeans. As Captain Perry announced the mission—they were going to October's alleged drug buy accompanied by the mighty forces of Tactical—Butch watched a huge grin spread across Grace's mouth—those lips he had kissed so many times, her thumbs hanging off her pockets as she rocked back on her heels. Sassy cowgirl ready to jump on that bull and ride him well past the eight seconds you needed for a win. That woman had thighs on her.

A map of the warehouses and their alleys had been blown up and hung against the whiteboard. Blueprints of the interior of one warehouse in particular flanked the map. Tactical's names were written on the whiteboard on the perpendicular wall. Butch thought back to a time when that list included Kane, the cop who hadn't made it when they'd gone against Big Time Reynolds. Big Time, Big Money. Big sleep. Bullshit.

Butch took a moment in prayer; his shoulders began to tighten, but he did not let himself react to the memory of Grace herself taking a hit, her flak jacket bearing the lifesaving brunt; still, the round had stopped her heart. He made himself stand down. He would protect her with his life, but he sure as hell wouldn't get in the way of her doing her job.

"We're going tomorrow night," Captain Perry said, inclining her head at Butch. "Butch has someone on the inside. Not entirely reliable, but he's the best we've got."

"He might have been given disinformation," Butch warned them. "They might be testing him to see if he's loyal. In which case there might be no deal, or it's a trap. For him and for us."

"We've got people watching the warehouse," Captain Perry went on, holding up a picture taken from behind the steering wheel of a car. "About an hour ago, this black man in his midtwenties, bald, about six-two, unlocked the warehouse door and went inside. He spent forty-five minutes there, exited, and got into the same car you all were searching for last night." She smiled as the squad shifted in their chairs. "If Big Money was trying to thumb his nose at us, I'm thinking he did a pretty good job."

"Or if he's trying to bait us." Grace moved her shoulders as if she were trying to stay loose. "I mean, c'mon, the *same* car?"

"Sixty-four Impala, I'd drive it every chance I got," Butch said. A beat passed. "If I was a scumbag lowrider."

"Listen to me. I know you've been wanting this guy since way before I came on board." Perry walked over to the big whiteboard and put up the surveillance photo with a magnet. "But we got to be careful."

Nods all around from the Careful Posse.

"We let them go in. We set up a parabola microphone if we can get close enough to a window and listen in on them. We wait. For as long as it takes to get a clear signal."

"What about wiring October?" Bobby asked.

Kate turned to Butch. "Butch and I talked about a wire, but we've decided not to risk it."

"And I'm not sure I could get October out of there long enough to get it on him," Butch added.

"When's the last time you heard from him?" Grace asked. "He call you today?"

"Not since the night before last," Butch said. "But I wasn't expecting him to."

"So we're not going in with guns blazing," Captain Perry said. "We're going to take every precaution. If it looks wrong, we are backing off. I don't want any dead heroes."

Looks went around the room. Everyone wanted that son of a bitch, and they knew Butch wanted him most of all.

"When's your birthday, man?" Grace asked him. He told her. "Well, happy early birthday, Butch. I'm going to wrap this asshole up in ribbons just for you."

"What did I just say, Detective?" Captain Perry gave Grace the stink eye.

"No more dead heroes," she said. "Yes, ma'am."

They ran down the operation repeatedly. Discussed things that could go wrong—and there were a lot of them. The longer the briefing lasted, the more Butch thought about Merrie, and when he hit a full tank of uncertainty, he asked to see Captain Perry in her office.

She was sympathetic. To a point. She sat behind her desk and glanced through a dozen phone messages, took a sip from her OU cup, and sat back in her chair.

"Butch, we've been over this. She's in foster care. Her mother is in custody. The court's not going to release her to her father."

But she might have relatives. October and Janaya have families somewhere.

She grabbed her cell phone and flipped it open. "Tell you what. Leslie Jones, that family court judge? I'll run it by her. If she concurs that Merrie's safest where she is, I'll see if she can assign placement for the next twenty-four hours. We'll proceed as planned tomorrow."

He took that in.

"Then Social Services will have time to evaluate the situation. I sure as hell would not hand that child back to either of her folks." She peered up at him through her lashes. "Would you?"

"No," he allowed.

"You know that if you tell Patrick Kelly what's going on, it'll just rattle him. So let this happen, Butch. We all want Big Money. He butchered that little girl." Captain Perry's eyes flared; she reached for something on her desk and held it out to him.

He took it. It was a photograph of Priscilla Jackson in

a maroon and cream cheerleading outfit. Her dark brown hair was pulled back into a ponytail, and a sprinkling of freckles dusted her brown skin. She had heavy eyebrows and she was wearing braces. Enamel rubber-ducky earrings completed her outfit.

"Thirteen," she said. "Gang-raped. First Big Money cut off her feet. Said she would never need them to give him a hand job. I have the crime-scene photos here, too," she said, her nicely manicured nails scooping up another photo that Butch had memorized and that haunted him in his sleep. Or his nightmares.

He gave his head a quick shake.

"So, we both know where we stand," she concluded.

"Yes, ma'am." A muscle jumped in his cheek and he stood up. Slung his thumbs in his belt.

"Something else bothering you?" she queried, making a steeple of her hands.

"No. Just thinking about what kind of man could do something like that."

"A walking dead man." She gave him a hard look. "We'll get him. If not this time, then the next."

His silence was his agreement. And his vow. And his thanks.

"Okay, then," she said. "We'll meet with Tactical in an hour and break down the op." She looked down at her desk—reports, case files, more reports.

He returned to the bullpen, to discover his desk decorated with the October pages from several copies of a charity calendar for an animal shelter in Norman. Little kitties and puppies gazed up at him. Everyone knew about Merrie. There was a 4-H calendar, too, featuring pictures of kids and their livestock. The picture was for March but someone had crossed that out and written OCTOBER. One of Butch's colleagues had drawn a dialogue balloon above the head of a big-eyed calf. It read LONGHORN!

He didn't say anything, just cleaned it all up and turned the Longhorn magnet on his file cabinet right-side up. Captain Perry was right.

Maybe he could get October out of this shit with a job and some counseling. Maybe Janaya would put it back together. She was in custody, shrieking that she had been denied her rights and insisting that Merrie be brought to her at once.

Travel light, cowboy.

The squad shelved a lot of plans for the day, including a lunch trip to Home Depot for Bobby's mold problem. Grace had to back-burner her kid case, and Butch knew that hurt her heart. He decided that once this was over, he'd do some more canvassing around Bricktown and along the riverbanks to see if he could help her out. Even if it was on his own time.

They met with Tactical and went over and over their plan of attack. There were no new calls from October. If there was no new information, there was nothing to say.

Except maybe good luck. Or good-bye.

CHAPTER
FIFTEEN

After the squad's meet-up with Tactical, Grace and Ham made the time to follow up on the information from Antwone. Grace watched from the bleachers at the baseball field as Cherie Lacey's kid, Paul Finch, came up to bat.

He curled back his lip and stepped away from a bad pitch. He was a big kid, almost fat; he had thick lips and really short hair. Piggy eyes. He had on sweatpants and a sweatshirt. It was really football season, not baseball yet. But these guys were serious ballplayers, determined to rout anyone who dared to play against them. Grace understood that this was "independent P.E.," meaning that teams were allowed to hold practice and have it count toward their grade. A few heads turned her way— *cougar!*—but she didn't react and, eventually, they gave up trying to figure out who she was.

Another pitch. Too low. Grace would have let that one go, too, but Paul took a swing. He missed it, of course, and hoots and howls of protest rode the crest of his little defeat. Paul slammed the bat down on home plate in frustration. But he didn't say anything, which spoke to his self-restraint.

"Hey, Finch, don't swing at the shit ones," one of the guys in the dugout called. He was tall, skinny, red-headed.

Paul didn't respond. He set his jaw and got into position. The batter's helmet gave him a bizarrely mechanical look, like he was a cyborg. Grace wondered how he was taking his stepbrother's death. That was on her list of questions for him.

Batter up. Next pitch. Low again. Finch swung again. Moron. The dugout protested, whooping and catcalling.

"Shit!" Finch shouted, slamming his bat on home plate again. "Gimme something to hit!" His piggy eyes narrowed.

Grace watched. Something to hit. Could she see him smacking his stepbrother on the leg, breaking his ankle? She sat back, resting her elbows on the riser behind her, letting the watery sun hit her face. The bleachers were wet; she'd dried off a spot and plopped her scrawny ass down. Evan Johnson and Juanita were still on the list of things to do.

Another bad pitch. Paul started swearing like crazy, and the pitcher grew pale and held up his hands as if to placate him. Grace wanted to smoke. She wanted to smack Paul upside the head and tell him to behave like a human being. On the other hand, his anger issues might make her job easier.

Ham was off checking out Brian and Drew. Antwone's mom had called him in sick from school. Grace was going by his house in a bit.

Paul struck out but he was saved by the bell. Literally. Last period of the day, Friday. The whoops of joy and hand slapping made her grin as the players broke it up and headed for the showers.

Paul walked with a couple of guys, heads bent together as they made batting motions. Paul nodded, and one of the other players slapped him on the shoulder. So Paul Finch had friends.

Her gut told her that now was not the time to detain him for a little chat. She'd keep him fresh, and use him later.

She trotted down the bleachers and dropped onto the wet grass. With a quick call to Ham to let him know what she was doing, she hopped into Connie and drove on over to Antwone's house.

His sad, sad house. Cracked brick shack, weeds in the yard, the driveway just one pothole after another. The windows were covered over with aluminum foil. Evidently the drug trade was not the lucrative side business one might expect.

She climbed two steps made of dry rot and rang the bell. A dog started barking. That cheered her up a little. At least he had a pet—

Holy shit!

Racing from around the back of the house, a Doberman slobbered and growled at her. The dog had to be at least as big as your average mastiff—i.e., enormous. It showed her its big mean teeth, all the better to rip off her hand with, as she hissed at it to back off, shouting for Antwone to open the frickin' door.

The dog ran for her; its eyes gleamed; ropes of drool bungee-jumped out of its massive jaw. Its growl was a preparatory windup; he was going to leap at her any second. She'd be damned if she'd shoot it, but she wasn't going to stand there and get mauled. With tremendous misgivings, she unholstered her service weapon and pointed it at the animal.

"Antwone!" she bellowed. "Get the hell out here or I'm going to have to shoot your dog!"

The front door burst open and Antwone stood there, yelling, "Obama! Get your ass in here!"

Grace grinned at Obama's name; then took four giant steps backward as the dog raced on over to Antwone. Antwone dropped to his knee and Grace made a face, wondering where those ropes of drool were going to land.

Ewww.

Wiping his cheek, Antwone straightened, and guided Obama into the house by the collar. The dog whimpered and panted, but he went willingly. Antwone shut the door behind himself and stood on the rickety porch. He had a bit of five o'clock shadow. He was wearing a black T-shirt and ripped-up jeans. No shoes. It was cold today.

"Did you stay home from school because you're hurt?" she asked him, peering around him at the closed door. "Can I come in?"

"No," he said quickly. "No, you can't."

"Maybe if I looked over your stuff, things Zack gave you, it might help me understand—"

A shadow crossed his face. He was conflicted. He knew she had a point. And yet. He lowered his gaze and shook his head.

"Do you live alone, Antwone?"

"No. My mother is at work." He said it too quickly and he crossed his arms. What was in there, a goddamn meth lab? His mummified mom drinking gin?

"Right. Heard she called in for you today," she said, and turned to go.

"Hey. Wait."

She turned back around.

"Thank you," he said. He didn't smile, so she didn't, either. But she wanted to.

"You're welcome," Grace replied.

At the school, Ham caught up with Drew Covel and Brian Bradford as they walked out of the main building together; and when he identified himself, the guilt on their faces was a joy to behold. He got them to give him cell phone numbers for their parents. He called both sets and told them that an OCPD detective had witnessed Brian and Drew beating a juvenile the night before, and that they were going to be charged with battery. No mention of the drug deal for the moment. He and Grace could use it later to add some pressure if they needed it.

Drew's mother agreed to drive him down to the station. She sounded frightened, but maybe a bit relieved, too. Brian's father said they would only speak to the police if they could have a lawyer present, and Ham told him that was just fine.

Grace was busy with Antwone, so for the moment, Ham was on his own. As he prepared for his meet-and-greet with the Covels, his stomach clenched in a weird way and the beginning of a headache knocked at his temples. His thoughts flew to tomorrow's raid. He could not get sick.

Massaging his forehead, he walked into the interview room, where Bobby had already seated Drew and Mrs. Covel. Drew was hunched over in his chair, sitting on his hands. He was about five-six, maybe a hundred forty. Close-cropped hair, almost like a skinhead. He had on a dark blue hoodie and a pair of baggy jeans. He didn't particularly look like a thug. He just acted like one in alleys.

Mrs. Covel was dressed in a dark gray raincoat over a pair of dark green cords and some brown leather boots. Her red hair was pulled back into a ponytail and she had on minimal makeup. She had pierced ears but she wasn't wearing any earrings. When Ham walked in, she absently touched her hair and let out a ragged breath. Her folding chair was placed farther away from her son's than Ham would have expected, given the circumstances. And she wasn't interacting with him. In fact, she was unconsciously leaning slightly away from him, as if he frightened her.

She knows, Ham thought. *She knows her kid's a volatile asshole.*

With another tight stomach cramp, Ham set Zack's case file on the table, close to the handcuff ring so Drew would be sure to glance at it—a subtle reminder of who held the power in the room. He bobbed his head at Mrs. Covel, who nervously returned the gesture. Drew didn't look up at him.

Ham sat down and placed his fingertips along the bottom of the file. His head hurt worse. Drew's gaze ticked up at the manila folder, then back down to the square inch of table in his line of sight.

"I think you know why you're here," Ham said. He waited. He made as if to open the file, then didn't. "A witness placed you in an alley last night on South Newcastle Road. You were assaulting Antwone Abboud. Do you want to talk about that?"

"No." Still no contact. Ham could feel the anxiety pouring off the kid. He was scared shitless that Ham knew more than he was saying.

"The witness heard you calling him a faggot."

"Oh, my God, Drew," Mrs. Covel said, covering her mouth. "No."

"I watch TV," Drew informed the dull surface of the table. "You have to give me a lawyer."

"And I have to read you your rights," Ham said, "and charge you with a crime, if you want to roll that way. Let me tell you something else first. Your classmate, Zachary Lacey, was found dead a few days ago."

"I know that. Everybody knows that," Drew flung at him.

"It was discovered during the autopsy that he was beaten prior to drowning. Badly." It was admissible and legal for cops to lie to get other people to tell the truth. He waited. "And Zack was a 'faggot,' too."

Mrs. Covel jerked hard and swiveled her head at her son. Ham pitied her; her expression said, *You finally did it, you monster.* How did a mother and son get to that place?

"Badly beaten," Ham said, sliding his finger inside the

folder, as if he might flip it open at any second and show Drew the horrific pictures of a dead boy. "Just last year, a gay teenager was tied to the bumper of a truck and dragged—"

"I didn't do anything to Zack Lacey," he said.

"I talked to some of the kids at school. They said you harassed him and Antwone a lot. Cornered them in the gym, rammed their heads in the toilets and flushed. Called them names like fudgepackers—"

"Everyone did," Drew cut in, leaning forward and wrinkling his nose. He looked proud, not contrite. Ham was amazed that he was so forthcoming. At the very least, he could be expelled for this shit. "Those two fags were so obvious about it. They, like, pushed it in everyone's face."

Mrs. Covel was shriveling up. Shame, disgust, and horror waged war on her face; she bit her lower lip and her shoulders silently shook as she began to weep. Ham figured her total ignorance of the situation was part of the problem. Drew didn't have to answer to her. Maybe he figured he didn't have to answer to anybody.

"I thought your school had a no-bully policy," Ham said.

Drew snickered. "No one would have done anything to them if they'd kept it to themselves. It was so gross."

"If you want gross," Ham said, tapping the file, "I can give it to you."

"I want a lawyer," Drew said. "I'm supposed to get one, right?" He glared at his mother. "Don't just *sit* there."

Her face went dead white. Her eyes seemed to fix on a point above Drew's head—maybe back to happier times, when he was still a sunny little boy and not the monster beside her. Ham let the moment expand to fill the tension; he thought of a time when Rafe and he caught up with five guys who had been hassling Nick.

Rafe held them and Ham doled out their punishment. Luckily it was football season; the pricks told everyone they'd gotten hurt during practice.

There'd been a lot of that, watching Nicky's back. Making sure he was safe when he walked home from school, or worked the late shift at his job at Tacoville. For Nick and Zack, Ham was going to hold this dirtbag to account. So he stared at Drew, who was twisting in his chair.

"Get your phone out and call someone, for Christ's sake!" Drew yelled at his mother. She burst into tears and began to dig in a brown leather hobo bag. You wake up; get your kid off to school; work a job; go to the police station; call a lawyer.

"Hate crimes are up in Oklahoma City," Ham went on. "Juries are tired of them. They convict fast."

Weeping, Mrs. Covel pulled out her cell phone. She stared at it as if it were a grenade. As if . . . maybe . . . she should put it back in her purse.

"Jesus, Mom, get it together!" Drew shouted.

"Please," Mrs. Covel said in a rush, "I—I don't know anything about hiring a lawyer." She looked up at Ham with her big brown doe eyes, and he wished he could help her, really help her. Take her kid outside and beat the living shit out of him. Ship him off to military school.

"We can give you a phone directory," he said. "You can stay in here to make the call, if you want. I can step outside."

Ham picked up the case folder and exited the room. Left alone, maybe Mrs. Covel could get through to her son. Make him realize he was about to jump off a cliff and there was no water to break his fall. But probably not.

"Hey," Bobby said from his desk. "Brian Bradford, his

father, and Hunter Beaumont are waiting in B. Captain Perry wants to observe. I'll babysit this one for you."

Ham nodded. He was loaded for bear. If these two dirtbags hadn't directly contributed to Zack's death, then they'd made his short life miserable. Hunter Beaumont was a well-known defense attorney who cost serious bucks. And caused serious trouble for the department— one of the most recent six cases that went south had been a Hunter Beaumont special, coached testimony loaded with innuendo and false witness that got the job done.

Ham's head throbbed. He shoved open the door to Room B and slapped down the case file, letting it fall open so Mr. Bradford, Beaumont, and Brian could see the post- mortem photograph of Zachary Lacey. Beaumont nar- rowed his eyes at Ham, an acknowledgment that the gloves were off on both sides this time, not just his. Brian paled, and Mr. Bradford said, "I object to your showing my son this picture," as if they were in a courtroom TV drama.

Ham left the picture faceup on the table. "Drew Covel told us that you and a bunch of other guys used to beat up on Antwone Abboud and Zachary Lacey every chance you got. That you drove by their houses late at night and left shit on their porches. You broke their car mirrors and spray-painted their lockers. There's lots more."

Brian's eyes were huge. Ham had scored a direct hit in this game of Battleship.

"You don't have to respond," Hunter Beaumont said. "Have you read this young man his rights, Detective?"

Ham reached in his pocket to get his wallet, where he kept his Miranda card. "You have the right to remain silent."

"Drew's a lying sack of shit," Brian announced.

This was going to go well.

*　*　*

"Brian Bradford gave me over a dozen names of kids who bullied those two guys," Ham told Grace as she came in from her interview with Antwone and another fruitless search for Flaco. "And 'bullied' is a goddamn politically correct word for what they did. Beat them, stole their shit, texted them hundreds of messages every day."

"Who can afford that?" Grace wondered aloud. "Texting that much?"

"I've got lists of suspects," Ham said. "I'm thinking hate crime, Grace."

"Hate crime, whether they did it to Zack himself or drove him to it," she agreed.

"I wonder if he told Juanita or Pastor Marc about any of this."

"Well, we'll have to ask them," Grace said. "Evan Johnson asked us to come in. He's going to talk to Juanita." She blew air out of her cheeks. "I just want to go to Louie's and unwind."

"There are other ways to unwind," he said. Then he winced.

"You okay?" she asked him.

"I've got some stomach thing," he admitted. "Headache." He pressed his teeth together.

"Shit, Ham, the raid's tomorrow. You should pack it in." She knit her forehead and peered at him. "You look bad."

"Not yet," he said. "I want to bust this open."

He was the best partner in the world. That was one blessing she would count, time and again.

CHAPTER
SIXTEEN

Evan Johnson was staying late to talk to Juanita Provo, and he wanted Grace there. Despite not feeling well, Ham said he would go with her to Helping Hand, so that made it a better deal. They drove over separately. The sky was dark and the clouds were low; were Rhetta and Bobby ever going to catch a break?

Grace got there first and licked her lips invitingly as Ham got out of his truck. Without consulting each other, they both made for the deli. Some coffee and maple bars might ease the tension they were about to experience upstairs—the court-martial of Juanita Provo, Meddler Extraordinaire. But it was nearly six at night, and the donuts were long gone. Grace substituted bagels and cream cheese; she carried the white plastic sack while Ham got their coffees.

"More cream. More sugar," she ordered him as he slaved over a hot condiment table.

Then they headed over to Helping Hand, and Grace rang the bell; they got buzzed in and went up the tottery, gloomy stairs. As before, Johnson stood there in nice clothes with Ragdoll, the cat, circling his ankles.

"Detectives, hello," he said kindly, but without his previous warmth. She and Ham both said their hellos and Grace handed him the bag of bagels. "Let's go into one of the phone rooms. We'll have a little more privacy."

They followed him into a softly lit hallway covered with kid-style artwork, photographs of gatherings, and some framed thank-you letters. There was a whiteboard with names and hours. The shift lineup. Grace scanned it. No Juanita.

They went past a door on Grace's right, which was cracked open. Grace made a show of drinking her coffee but in actuality, she was listening hard.

"Annie," a male voice said, "you *do* matter. You matter to me."

Good luck, Annie, Grace thought fervently.

"Here." Johnson moved in front of Grace and opened the second door, which was on her left. A couch faced her, and Juanita sat on it with her hands around her knees. Her expression was guarded. There was a cheap seventies-style oak coffee table in front of the couch, and on it, piles of notebooks and a Yellow Pages. Also, a laptop and a phone.

And a Bible.

And a rosary.

Oh, brother, Grace thought. Clay was studying martyrs in Faith Formation; looked like Juanita was hoping for a little reprieve because she was so tortured and God-fearing.

"Hey, Juanita," Grace said.

"Why did you tell them?" Juanita snapped. It took Grace a minute to realize that Juanita was speaking to her about her inappropriate interactions with Zack. Grace figured she had confessed, but apparently someone had narced on her.

"Didn't. Not a word." There was nowhere else to sit, so she and Ham stood side by side inside the door, drinking their coffees.

Juanita looked at Ham. "Did you tell them?"

"Nope," Ham replied.

Silence fell. No one was eating any bagels. *Antwone,*

Grace thought. *Maybe he told Evan Johnson. Or maybe Pastor Marc the gay youth leader made the call.* Zack might have confided in either one of them. Maybe he coded the Helping Hand phone number for his asshole father.

Grace hadn't met Marc yet. If he'd been at the pray-o-rama last night, she hadn't seen him. She had a lot of leads. People she wanted to talk to. But first they had to catch Big Money. There was always too much to do.

And then . . . paperwork. She was going to do more illicit sexual things to Ham to make sure he did hers for her.

"So . . . we didn't tell on you," Grace said. "We didn't tell Evan here that you met privately with Zack Lacey and told him that being gay was a sin. We didn't tell him that you prayed with him to remove his homosexual orientation so he could go to heaven. Possibly to be with his mother, who has been missing for ten years. And we also didn't tell him that you encouraged Zack to go off his antidepressants." Grace mentally crossed her fingers, hoping she was right.

"*What?*" Johnson cried, staring at Juanita. "You did what?"

"I did not," she bit off. "I didn't tell him to do that." Her eyes strayed to her Bible, as if it were a teleprompter. "But I told him . . . I told him that if he had enough faith and he prayed, God could cure anything."

Including war and world hunger, Grace thought, but that was an old joke between her and God, har.

"So *Zack* screwed up," Grace said. "He didn't have enough faith. So he died."

Now Juanita looked a little less sure of herself. A little more likely to reach for her rosary, although she yanked her hand back and clenched it in her lap. She swallowed hard. "I didn't mean it to sound that way. I meant that if God hears, really hears your prayers, then He can make miracles."

Unless God's not listening.

"But Zack might have thought that you meant it was up to him, Zack, to somehow prove himself to God," Ham said. Grace was grateful he was there. This was excruciating. She wanted to punch that woman out. She'd rather be doing paperwork than this.

"I didn't mean that. I didn't want him to think that." She pressed her fingertips against her forehead. "I wanted to give him hope."

What you gave him was more pressure. Another way he wasn't measuring up. You stupid bitch.

Grace remained tight-lipped and silent.

"Do I need a lawyer?" She glanced up at Johnson. "I—I'm sorry to drag Helping Hand into . . . this." She looked at Grace and Ham. "What's going to happen to me?"

"Juanita." Johnson perched on the arm of the sofa. "Why did you do this? Why didn't you come to me, tell me what was going on? None of this was in your log."

Juanita sniffled. Grace dug in the bagel bag for a napkin. She didn't give it to Juanita.

"She didn't come to you because you would have interfered," Grace said. "And she knew best." Grace cocked her head. "How many other kids have you done this to?"

"None," she said. She kept her gaze focused on her hands, so Grace assumed she was lying. "*Ay, Dios*, Zack was special. We had a connection."

Lucky Zack.

Grace sipped her coffee. Her hand was shaking, and her stomach was tight. She was pissed off. Ham must have felt it; he glanced over at her with a neutral face, but she knew he was checking in with her.

I was special, too, she thought. *That's what Father Murphy told me.*

"*Did* you know he was taking antidepressants?" Ham asked Juanita. She shook her head.

"That he was a loose cannon?" Grace finally managed to say. "Someone you had no business getting involved with? I downloaded the Helping Hand volunteer handbook. You violated nearly every rule you agreed to follow when you signed on here."

Johnson moved off the sofa arm and stood, a protective gesture. "I know Juanita didn't mean to do any harm. If there's a lawsuit . . ." He blinked.

It was sinking in that there might be a lawsuit. And a scandal. Headlines. TV. Bad juju for Helping Hand and its leader, one Evan Johnson. Grace wondered how far he'd back up his volunteer. She ruined kids' lives in her spare time, but this was his *job*.

"We're not here to talk about a lawsuit, sir," Ham said. "We're investigating the death of Zachary Lacey. We have established the cause of death as drowning. But we don't know if he committed suicide, or if there was an accident, or foul play."

"Foul play?" Juanita said. Her eyes got huge. "Like murder? Who? . . ."

"That's why we're here," Ham continued. "We're detectives with Major Crimes."

"I didn't kill him," Juanita said quickly. She reached for Johnson's hand. "Evan, you *know* that, right?"

"Yes." Grace heard the hesitation in his voice. The poor guy didn't know anything anymore.

"We have a list of minors who harassed Zack. Beat him up, bullied him. Did he mention anything like that to you?" Ham asked.

Juanita looked at Johnson as if for permission to speak. He looked back at her encouragingly, but Grace could see the love was gone between them. Maybe Juanita could get a pet to take care of.

"He told me that some boys hassled him," she said. "Made fun of the way he walked. Things like that."

Things like that.

Ham nodded. "Did he give you any names?"

"Drew, I think. And someone named Kathy," Juanita told him.

"Any other names?" Ham asked. "We have a list but I'd rather you told me yourself." That way, the department couldn't be accused of leading her.

"Brian, I think. Paco, and someone they called the Fatman."

Ham wrote the names down. "Did the school do anything about it?"

"I—I don't know," Juanita said.

If you wanted to help him so badly, why didn't you contact the principal? Do something that would really help him, instead of telling him to pray? Grace stared at her. *Or do you believe that God helps those who help themselves?*

"Did he talk about running away? Ending it all?"

"Most kids who call us talk like that," Johnson put in.

Grace gave him a sharp look but said nothing. She was chewing the inside of her lower lip to keep herself from losing her temper. For his part, Ham was rubbing his forehead. He didn't look good.

"I'll be right back," he said, handing the list to Grace. To Johnson, "May I use your bathroom?"

Johnson pointed down the hallway. Grace faced off against Juanita and Johnson alone.

"Did Zack mention drug use to you?" she queried. "In any form? Did he tell you that he used drugs? Or sold them?"

"No," Juanita said, but her cheeks reddened and her mouth pulled tight. So she was lying, or she had guessed and never confronted Zack. If she'd pursued it, maybe she could have suggested something he could do to help himself. Do some real good.

"I am not a therapist," said Juanita, glancing over at Johnson. Grace was pretty sure it was too late to get his approval. At least, she hoped so. "I just wanted . . ." She trailed off.

Yeah, what did you want? Grace asked silently as Ham came back into the room. *Did you pray to God for it? Did you get down on your knees and make a bargain? Or did you doze off every night reading Bible verses, marking your place with a little bookmark that said God's angels are everywhere—and you were one of them? And you knew, just knew, that God would provide?*

Tell me about wanting. Tell Zack Lacey.

"I'll tell you what Juanita wants," Grace said aloud as she pulled over to the side of the road, got out, and began to walk one of the many trails along the Oklahoma River. Ham was clearly ill, so she sent him on home minus the booty call. "She wants him to've been murdered."

"Then he's a victim," Earl said, picking up a stone and skipping it over the gray churning water. It was actually the North Canadian River; the part that ran through Oklahoma City had been renamed. The sun was going down on another day.

"And God just loves victims," Grace replied. "That's why there are so many of them."

"What I mean is, if he was killed, that means he didn't take his own life. Being murdered is not a sin in any religion I know of." Earl brushed his fingertips together to clean off the grit. He could fly to Morocco in the twinkling of an eye, but he had to wipe dirt off his fingers just like a human. "It's hard to keep up with 'em all, though. The religions, I mean. You guys seem to invent a new one every week."

"We should throw the book at her." Grace lit a cigarette. "Sanctimonious Bible-thumper."

"Let's just walk a spell." Earl skipped another stone,

then put his hands in his pockets and strolled along, gazing at the water. Grace looked at his graying hair, the careworn lines in his face, and wondered why God had made him look that way. The ozone whiff of night fog lay over the busy water; the staccato tat-tat-tat of a woodpecker echoed the rapid-fire rhythm of her angry heart.

Earl kept walking, deep in thought. She wondered what he was thinking about. It drove Rhetta crazy that Grace didn't ask him very many questions. He turned his head slightly.

"Don't say anything," she warned him. She didn't want to hear any of his answers.

He pulled his hands out of his pockets in a gesture of innocence.

And the two kept walking.

Grace's little sister, Paige, was having a Bunco party, and she'd invited Grace to attend, which surprised Grace and Earl both: Paige was a middle-class PTA-book-club-French-manicure kind of girl, and Grace was a rebel slob. Nothing sounded more hideous than playing a soccer-mom dice game with a bunch of, well, soccer moms. It was the antithesis of Grace's perfect Friday night: Her original plans for the evening began with going to Louie's to get a head start on the evening, then bringing Ham home to finish the evening off with a great big bang. But Ham was MIA. She hoped whatever was wrong with him got cleared up fast. They needed him for the warehouse raid, to be staged in a little over twenty-four hours. Some weekend sex would be nice, too.

Then she'd realized that because of the raid, she was going to have to cancel out on her Saturday night movie sleepover with Clay. She'd found out that Doug had dropped Clay at Paige's because he had a date, so she'd called over there to see if Clay could spend the night tonight instead. And that was when Paige realized that Grace had the evening free, and insisted she come to her party. It amazed Grace that she, Superdetective Hanadarko, had been so clueless.

Grace would rather vomit, seriously, but Clay was over there, and, strangely, she actually wanted to see Paige, if not her Bunco posse. Wanted to be near her. There was no way to explain that aberration, but Grace went with it. She even put on a dress that Paige might approve of, and wrapped her hair into a chignon.

Paige had a nice middle-class house in a great school district. She also had a husband who was cheating on her, and Paige knew it. Such a good Catholic woman, keeping up her end of the deal.

It wasn't until Grace had parked and rung the door-bell that she noticed her mother's car parked on the street. She groaned inwardly. Paige plus Mom was a bit too much family, thank you very much.

Her retreat back to Connie was cut short as Paige yanked open the door. She was wearing an ice-blue cash-mere sweater and a pair of black knit pants. She had a cocktail glass in her hand.

"Grace, come in," she said warmly. "We're having mojitos."

Oh, God, just shoot me, Grace thought. But what she said was, "Cool," and walked on in. She thought she felt the warm fuzziness of Earl's approval brushing against a shoulder. But when she looked for him, she was alone.

"Butch, how could you do this to me?" Janaya demanded, as he visited her in the county jail on Shartel. They were sitting in a grimy, sad little room at a table. Gray metal table, gray cinder block walls. The matron was standing by the frosted-glass door.

Janaya was dressed in an orange jumpsuit. She was

coming down off her addictions, and her jailers weren't giving her anything to help her along. Her hair was wet and she was sweaty and, Lord, if Butch ever thought about doing drugs, all he would have to do is remember how bad Janaya smelled tonight.

And see the vomit splashed on her cheek.

"Everything was going well for you, girl," he said to her. "What happened?"

The whites of her eyes were yellow. "There was this guy," she began, licking her lips over and over.

Wasn't there always, in these kinds of scenarios?

"Does Patrick know about this guy?"

She shook her head. "I ain't talked to him for months."

"I have a hundred bucks for you from him," Butch said, throwing in a few because, after all, Janaya was Merrie's mom. "Once you get out of here, I—"

"God*damn,* I feel like shit." She ran a trembling hand across her forehead. "I feel . . . oh." She doubled over, her head curling toward her chest, her shoulders rising up. The matron went on alert as Janaya groaned and fell forward, her head about to hit the table until Butch raced around and grabbed her.

The matron hit a button and ran over to them. Together they held her, or tried to; Janaya writhed and convulsed, falling off the chair onto the gray linoleum; and she began to foam at the mouth. The stench of urine hit the air.

The door buzzed open and two prison guards blasted in. Things began to happen fast: Medical was called, rushing in as Butch relinquished his hold on Janaya and became a passive onlooker. The team hustled her onto a gurney, and he followed as far as he could, but his part was over. Janaya'd been doing so well, just a week ago—relatively speaking, for a woman who'd started turning tricks when she was fourteen and knew deep in her soul that when things started to get better they'd wind up much worse than they were before. Self-fulfilling prophecy, or the law of the street?

Flat and sad, he checked in with Captain Perry and told her what had happened. God knew what Janaya's street drugs had been cut with; it could've been anything from Ajax cleanser to flour. One step forward, sixteen back. In many depressing ways, Janaya and October were well suited.

Butch thought about calling Bobby and offering to help with his mold project. But it was the night before the raid, and Bobby might want some time with Marissa and their kids.

So he drove on down to Louie's to have a beer and listen to the jukebox. He was seated at the bar when a tousle-headed cowboy sat down next to him and ordered a longneck. He seemed vaguely familiar, but Butch couldn't place him.

"Evenin'," the man said. Butch returned the greeting with an incline of his head. "So, looks like the Bowl Championship Series is going to put the Sooners and the Gators up for the big one."

"You're crazy," Butch shot back. "Better check the scoreboard. The Longhorns will be there."

"I don't rightly understand the BCS system," the man said. "I heard there's a computer program you can buy to decipher it. Used to be football was easier to figure out than women."

"All you need to know is that Texas is going to take the whole thing."

Butch sipped his beer and smiled faintly as he thought of Grace. He figured she was off screwing Ham; he wondered if Ham had ever made breakfast for her, like he had: Texas omelet, homemade waffles. Grace told Butch she wasn't a breakfast person. Her code for "Back Off."

He'd learned the vocabulary during the short stay of his boots under her bed.

Butch thought of Janaya, who had been climbing out of the pit; some dickhead had grabbed her hand and pulled her back down. If anybody had ever made her breakfast, it was probably by tossing her a breakfast burrito into a bag after she paid for it at the drive-through.

"You look troubled, if you don't mind my saying," his bar buddy went on. "It's Friday night, time off the clock. Life is good."

Butch shrugged and made rings on the bar with his beer glass. He stared into the foam and pushed the beer away.

"Someone I had hope for . . . well, it's not working out so good for her," he said.

"I had me one of those," the man said. "But I think she's turning around." He tapped the bar with a finger. "Least, I *hope* so." He grinned at his little joke. "It can get overwhelming, pulling for somebody when their heels are dug in deep."

"Yeah."

"Feels like it might be easier not to care at all. Just saddle up and mosey on."

"Don't think I can do that," Butch said.

"Then there's hope for *you*," the man replied. He held out his hand. "My name is Earl."

"Yeah." Butch smiled. "I think we met before." They shook hands.

"Think so. Well, it's been a pleasure."

The man gestured for his check. "Be seeing you around," he said to Butch. Then he left.

After a few minutes, Butch paid and headed for the door just as Henry walked in. There was a woman with Henry—Lena Garvin, the short-hire who'd quit. Butch hadn't really met her; mostly he'd listened to Grace complain about her incompetence and kept her on his radar, hoping she wouldn't catch any of the bodies in any of his own cases. Henry was beaming at her, and she was laughing. Then Henry saw Butch and he grinned like a cat-eatin' canary.

"Henry. Ms. Garvin." Butch tipped his cowboy hat. "We haven't met but I saw you around at the station."

"I saw you, too." She smiled neutrally, probably wondering what he'd heard about her.

"Hi, Butch. Where is everybody?" Henry looked around the bar. Probably he wanted to introduce Lena, show her off.

"We got business tomorrow night," Butch said. "Everyone's resting up." *You might want to plan for some overtime.*

"Excuse me," Lena said. "I need to use the ladies'. It was nice to meet you." She gave Henry's arm a squeeze, a pleasant smile at Butch, and left the two men.

"Nice, Henry," Butch said sincerely.

"Yeah." Henry was beaming. "Grace insulting her . . . it was the best thing in the world for me. Lena wouldn't date anyone from work—"

"And now she doesn't work there," Butch finished.

Henry grinned. "Right." He looked toward the bathrooms. "She just broke up with some guy. . . ."

Oh, no, rebound, Butch thought, his happiness for Henry deflating a bit. This date came equipped with all sorts of baggage.

Henry must have caught his expression. He pushed up his glasses and his cheeks went a little pink. "Butch, I go home to my mother and a twenty-one-year-old *cat.*"

"Got it." Butch said. He was going home to . . . what? Maybe he'd do that canvassing for Grace tonight. "Good luck."

"Thanks," Henry replied.

Butch left the bar, called in and checked on Janaya,

and drove on over to Bricktown. Heard the wind crying across the little canals and the refurbished buildings, warrens of stylish bars and restaurants filled with good food and Blood Alcohol Content readings above 6 percent, the magic number for criminal penalties in the great state of Oklahoma. Kiddieland for big people.

Janaya was in bad shape. The doc Butch talked to on the phone said that her drugs had been very dirty and a war was on inside her body. Butch called Merrie's foster care but his call went straight to voice mail.

You are not a social worker, he reminded himself.

The fudge store was still open, and a middle-aged couple was peering into one of the cases. The clerk with the Victoria Beckham hair was waiting on them, and Butch thought about getting something for his sister Nell and his mother. But who was he kidding? He was really thinking of getting something for himself. And he was here to help out on the case.

His boots rang on the pavement as he crossed the tidy street and studied the green metal bridge attached to the Miller Jackson Company Building, his gaze traveling a line from the bridge to the canal. Even though this was the off season for the canal boats, someone would have seen something. Maybe the body didn't start out here, as they had assumed. Maybe it had started on the other side of the lock from higher up on the Oklahoma River.

He got back in his car and went farther upriver, by Regatta Park. The sky was black, the moon ringed with prisms. More rain was on the way. The drug raid would likely take place in the rain; one more variable to contend with.

He pulled over to a more secluded spot of the river, moving past the berms of rocks to the dark waters. Looked up, down, thinking, assessing. Walking farther back up onto the grass, he pulled a flashlight and studied the sloshy mud. Not even Rhetta would be able to ferret out clues from these washed-out banks. Plus, there were seven miles of river to examine. It wasn't even a needle in a haystack; it was the memory of a needle in a haystack that had long since scattered.

He continued on, weaving his flashlight in arcs. The moonlight kissed the brim of his Stetson. There, a shape.

Beside a large cardboard box, a man was bundled up inside a sleeping bag, reading by flashlight. As Butch approached with the light full on the reader, the man looked up warily from his book and squinted at him. A skel—short for skeleton, a homeless man so thin and wiry it was amazing he was still alive.

The man put up his hand to block out the light, and Butch lowered it to the man's other hand. Empty. Then Butch flashed his badge.

"I'm a police officer. Please get out of the sleeping bag, sir," he said.

"I will, I am," the man said in a tremulous voice, setting down his book. "I don't have a gun. Please don't shoot me."

"I won't," Butch assured him as the man snaked out. He got onto his knees and crawled toward his hands, flat on the gritty earth, pushing himself to a standing position like someone doing yoga. He was wearing a filthy, shredded OU baseball cap, a flak jacket, a pair of mud-caked sweatpants, and tattered running shoes.

Butch ran his flashlight over the sleeping bag. The title of the book the man had been reading was stamped on the cover in plain white letters: *Being and Nothingness* by Jean-Paul Sartre. Heavy reading for somebody in a place like this.

"I'd like to ask you a few questions," Butch said.

The man looked up at Butch. Rheumy eyes, gray dying skin. "Hell is other people," he said in a nasal New Jersey accent. He raised both his brows as if he'd just delivered the code word, and Butch had to respond appropriately before he would reply. Butch had been down this road a hundred times, maybe a thousand: The other guy wanted you to play by his rules. Butch was okay with that.

"That's from *No Exit*," Butch said. "Also by Jean-Paul Sartre."

The man blinked. "A cop with a soul."

"So I hope," Butch replied.

"What do you want?" the man asked.

"We're looking for information. A teenage boy might have jumped in the river, or been pushed in. We don't know."

"A kid," the skel echoed.

"Have you seen anyone go into the river?" Butch asked. "About a week or so ago? It was raining very hard."

The man licked his lips. He looked very tired. "I have seen way, way too much. That's how I wound up here."

"But did you see someone go into the river? I might have something for you if you did."

The man drew himself up, looking insulted. "I don't need money. I live off the grid."

An owl hooted. Butch thought about those two jerkwater kids Ham had interviewed today, loaded with entitlement and cruelty. He looked at this filthy man, and sighed.

Don't even try, Butch warned himself, but he was fresh from his philosophical chat with the cowboy in the bar. *To protect and serve.*

"There's a shelter near here," Butch said. "It's run by a church. You might have to listen to a sermon." *And try to avoid our drug raid.*

"I'm very comfortable here," the man informed him succinctly. "And I have a lot of reading to do."

"They have showers and two hot meals a day," Butch added. The man stared at him as if Butch were speaking Swahili.

Damn it. Come back on into the world. Start over, he willed.

"It's going to rain some more," Butch said, his last gambit.

The man shrugged.

Defeated, Butch turned to go. His boots crunched. Thunder rumbled.

"I might have seen *something*," the man declared.

CHAPTER
SEVENTEEN

I gotta stop chugalugging these wimp-assed drinks, Grace thought as she topped off her mojito glass from the pitcher in the kitchen and opened Paige's fridge. She was starving. Every single one of Paige's girlfriends was on a diet, and Paige had refrained from serving much in the way of snacks so as to "empower" them.

"Grace, what are you doing?" her mother said sotto voce as she came into the kitchen with an empty salsa dish.

"Paige said it was fine if I raided the fridge," Grace lied. She emerged with a package of sharp cheddar cheese and carried it to a cutting board. She grabbed a knife and whacked off a hunk. "Want some?"

Her mom looked over her shoulder in the direction of the festivities and gave a barely perceptible nod. Smug, Grace carved two healthy slabs from the rectangle and handed one to her mother. Her mother blanched at this breach of protocol. No plate, no doily, just cheese. Then she made a guilty little "oh-what-the-heck" face and toasted her wild child with it.

Together they gobbled them down.

"Paige is so happy you're here," her mom said, wiping at the corners of Grace's mouth with a manicured fingernail. She was all rosy and joyful. Maybe it was part hooch, but mostly it was her delight that her daughters were both accounted for, and under the same roof. With smooth jazz playing, even, like a movie. She picked up a cocktail napkin decorated with shoes and handbags that said GIRLS NIGHT IN! "You should spend more time with her."

"I have a very demanding job," Grace reminded her mother. "Stakeouts, double homicides . . ."

"Johnny told me about that suicide." Her mother cut herself another piece of cheese. Aha, a fellow starver. "The parish priest doesn't want to say Mass for the boy."

"He's *refusing*," Grace corrected her. "Says that kid is already in hell." She looked over at her mother, leaning against Paige's immaculate counter and draining her most recent drink. "What do you think?"

"I think . . ." Her mother took a deep breath. "The Church has so much more to contend with these days. When I was your age, we didn't have many other influences. Everyone I knew was a Catholic. We all understood what that meant. We had the same values." She smoothed errant strands of Grace's hair away from her face. "It's a lot more complicated, now that we . . . mix."

"Why?" Grace asked, cutting off more cheese for herself. Between them, they'd wolfed down almost half. "Why should it be more complicated?"

"It just is," her mother said.

"It just is," Johnny said, his voice tinny on Grace's cell as she curled up in her pajamas on her couch. After the ordeal by Bunco finally ended, she'd hung out with Clay for a few. But he had his cousins and the Wii, and although he loved her dearly, she knew she should make a clean getaway. Accordingly, she'd gotten out of Paige's house as fast as she possibly could. She'd won the Bunco game, and was now the proud owner not of a pot of money, but a trio of scented candles and matching hand lotion. The Bunco money would be donated to Catholic Charities, and who knew *that* when she was playing like a gunslinger at high noon? For the love of Christ.

"The Church is eternal," Johnny continued. "From one age to the next, we have abided by the commandments set down by the Savior. There are rules that govern the behavior of Catholics that are consistent no matter where he or she lives."

Grace nodded. She was smoking. Gus was sniffing at the little gift bag brimming with her scented candles and hand lotion. She picked the bag up off the floor in case he decided to pee on it.

"Right. No birth control even if you live with your sixteen kids in a Brazilian slum. No women priests even though you don't have a priest in your parish because there aren't enough to go around. Oh, and no screwing kids."

"Grace . . ."

"And suicide is a sin. Only maybe if you're, like, possessed by mental illness, you might get a Mass out of it."

There was a silence. She smiled sourly, glad she was pissing him off. Call her petty. Call her bitter. Call her someone who wished she'd never even heard of the Catholic Church.

Then he surprised her, Johnny did, as happened on occasion.

"That's actually fairly accurate," he said. "And Grace? Zachary Lacey being gay? God loves the sinner, hates the sin. If Zachary didn't indulge in homosexual acts, then he didn't sin."

"Well, thank God you cleared that up," she said wryly. "Tell that to his grandmother. She's losing her mind."

She heard a beep. "I got another call. I really do, Johnny. Thanks for the catechism lesson." She switched over.

"Guess what I have in my hand." It was Ham.

She slid down on the couch a little, grinning to herself. "You must be feeling better."

"Yeah. Maybe it was a bad bagel. But I'm okay now." A beat. "Want some company?"

She calculated. If he came over now, he might try to spend the night. That was starting to occur too often, that pushing toward an actual relationship. Men could be so needy. Ham tried to stay over; Butch had made her breakfast when she was injured on the job. She took another draw of her cigarette and watched the smoke rise toward the ceiling. Her house was a one-seater.

"I'm going to bed," she told him. "But we could have phone sex. Guess what I have in *my* hand."

His laugh was amused, lusty.

Hang 'em high, sheriff.

Then she got another beep. She checked the number and groaned. She had completely forgotten to call Mrs. Prescott. She told Ham who it was, and he sighed long and hard. *Long* and *hard.*

"Night," she said regretfully. And then, "Hello, Mrs. Prescott. I'm so sorry I didn't get back to you today."

"Miss Hanadarko," she said. Her voice was slurring, like maybe she'd had a bit too much to drink. "I spoke to Father Pepera this evening, and he said that Ron hasn't requested a Mass. Is Zack . . . has Zack been . . ." She sniffled.

Jesus. Mrs. Prescott didn't know if Zack had been buried. For her part, Grace wasn't sure if Henry had released the body or not. They were kinda done with it. Henry had taken more X-rays but all he had found was the one broken ankle.

"Ron hasn't returned my calls," she said. "And I—I want to know . . ."

"Would you be coming into town for the service?" Grace asked.

"I'm disabled, Miss Hanadarko. I have severe fibromyalgia and I live with an aide. My husband died last year."

"I'm so sorry," Grace said sincerely. She made a fist and lightly pounded her forehead, her mea culpa that she hadn't phoned earlier. Gus snuffled at her feet; he loved her no matter what, especially if he could have hand lotion for dessert. "I'll find out what's going on for you."

"Oh, would you, please?" Her voice cracked. "God bless you, child."

They disconnected and Grace put out her cigarette. She shooed Gus away from the gift bag, dug inside for one of the candles, and plopped the bag on the breakfast counter. Then she blew french-fry bits off the nearest plate, placed the candle on it, and carried it into her bedroom.

Grabbing a book of matches from Louie's, she lit the wick and put the plate on her nightstand. Brushed her teeth, and lay down on her crimson sheets. Her twinkle lights glittered like stars.

She watched the flame. A kid who thought it was his fault, whatever it was. All over Oklahoma City, children were trying to atone for things they'd never done . . . and never would.

Dying because of the lies their parents told them. And the biggest liar? God the Father.

This little light of mine . . .

She was going to let it burn all night, in memory of Zachary Lacey. Keep vigil for justice. Make the wrong go away. Her lids flickered; she forced them open and shifted in the bed to keep herself awake. Weariness sank her more deeply into the mattress, as if she herself were being lowered into the earth.

After a time, her eyelids closed; and she was unaware of Earl standing at the foot of her bed, watching her in the candlelight, moved by the kind thing she had done by keeping the boy alive in her heart.

"Yes, God bless you, child," he told her.

As she slept.

They walked through the Garden of Allah, Leon Cooley and his son, Benjamin. Nightingales sang in pomegranate trees on the banks of a gently flowing river of honey, which was festooned with rushes and overhung with date palms. The sky glowed.

"You didn't die, did you?" Leon asked Benjie, gazing at his boy's dark skin, his big brown eyes, his nappy head. His kid through and through. A little bit of Tamara in him, too, but Benjie looked like his father. "You're not here because—"

Benjamin smiled at him. "I'm always with you, Dad. I'm part of you." Then his expression changed and he pointed to the river. "You have to save her."

Leon looked. Grace Hanadarko lay facedown in the honey-water as it burbled past them. She was wearing jeans and her sheepherder jacket. Her hair floated around her head like yellow seaweed.

Leon took a step toward her, then looked back at Benjamin—or where Benjie had stood. His son had vanished. The pomegranate trees swayed; incense and orange blossoms permeated the air. He was alone on the riverbank.

"Benjie, where are you?" he yelled. He whirled in a circle. "Son!"

The waters pushed Hanadarko past him. If he ran he could catch up with her.

"Benjie!" he screamed.

Then he heard Benjie shout from the river. "Dad, help me, save me!" And it wasn't Hanadarko in the water. It was his boy.

Leon Cooley stood rooted to the spot. He clenched his jaw and balled his fists. And before he knew it—before he realized what he was doing—he was jumping into the water to keep that bitch from going under.

"Stop messing with me, Earl," he said when he woke up. He stared up into the blinding golden light filling his cell, forcing his eyes to stay open as he searched the brilliance for his last-chance angel. "That dream was bull-shit."

"I didn't give you a dream last night," Earl said as the light died down. "Whatever you dreamed, it came from somewhere else."

In the morning, Grace rolled out of bed, drank a lot of water and coffee, and took Gus for a run. Then she called the Laceys and got Ron, asked if she might come out to their place to take a look around. She had the perfect excuse—Mrs. Prescott's desire to know about the arrangements—even though she didn't need one. And even though it was a bullshit excuse. Cops didn't go around doing crap like this. At least she didn't. Very often.

"We're still investigating his case," she reminded Daddy Lacey.

Lacey agreed, even though it didn't sound like he wanted to. People who resented cops could be defiant one minute and acquiescent the next. You never knew which way the wind would blow, but the weather was on her side that morning.

Grace called Ham and asked him if he would come with her. She repeated their mantra. "We won't do anything stupid. We don't have a warrant. But if we get permission . . ."

"Amen. Hallelujah," Ham said.

He drove over to her place, looking like a night alone had done him some good. Jeans, blue shirt, jacket. He smelled great. It was clear he wanted to take some personal time in the sack before they went to the Laceys'. Maybe he was feeling sentimental because, with a raid tonight and all, one of them might get killed in the line of duty. But Grace was ready to roll in a totally different direction.

They took Ham's truck. On the way over, Butch called and said he had a possible witness. A homeless guy had seen a kid standing at the river's edge, staring down into the water. Three nights in a row. They were working on a description but so far his witness was erratic.

"So maybe it was Paul, planning to throw Zack in," Grace said to Ham as they zoomed along the Forty. "Or Zack, planning to jump in."

"Or another kid altogether," Ham suggested.

They got to the Laceys', not half as bad a bastion of right-wing paranoia as Grace had anticipated. Beneath the gigantic American flag on a flagpole, a cyclone fence separated the Lacey property from all comers. NO TRESPASSING PRIVATE PROPERTY THIS MEANS *YOU* hung in several places on the chain link. Also I HUNT AND I VOTE. There was razor wire along the top.

On the private property sat a light blue ranch house with a composition shingle roof, maybe three bedrooms and two baths. Wild grass and verbena grew in profusion. Across a blacktop roundabout was a detached garage with a closed door painted buff brown. Grace crossed her fingers that there was a truck in there.

Ham pulled off the road and parked next to the fence gate. Grace hopped out, missing a muddy berm, and discovered that the padlock was hanging open, possibly in anticipation of their visit. She pushed on the gate and Ham drove in.

Lacey himself opened the front door. Grace scrutinized him. Flannel shirt, work boots, canvas pants. Coffee cup in hand. He hadn't shaved. He looked beyond irritated.

"Good morning," Grace said. "Thanks for having us over."

Lacey scowled at them both and gestured for them to come in. Grace and Ham scanned the entryway as they kicked the mud off their boots. There was a free-standing oak hat rack loaded with baseball caps and surrounded by muddy shoes. The floor was hardwood, and while it had seen better days, it wasn't in bad shape.

In the living room, there was too much furniture—a sofa and a settee both, two overstuffed chairs, a coffee table and three side tables, all of it on the appalling side, wooden curlicues and Granny Smith–green velvet; God, where did you even *buy* shit like that? Thomas Kinkade knockoffs lined the walls—lighthouses glowing in the fog, English cottages. Lots of pink, red, and purple silk flowers in cut crystal vases with doilies underneath them. There was an oversized shopping bag from Crossroads Mall on top of an oak sideboard, but Grace couldn't exactly paw through it without asking. Still, she sidled over and tried to peer in. Looked like black jeans.

Lacey sat down in one of the Granny Smith–green chairs. He didn't invite them to do the same, but Grace took a spot on the sofa and Ham sat in the other chair. This was not a guy to tower over. He would be especially infuriated that a woman was the instrument of his intimidation.

"I called Cherie," Lacey said. "She's shopping for clothes. She don't wear much black." He looked at them as if they would catch his drift.

"For the service," Grace supplied. His silence was her answer. "So you've made plans."

"We haven't made shit," he countered, settling back into his chair with his coffee cup. "So what did you find out? Did he do it or not?"

Grace realized that he thought that was why they were there: to deliver the verdict. "We're still trying to find that out, sir. We thought if maybe we could talk to you, and your other son, Paul—"

"My stepson." A tiny flash of pleasure washed over his face. Hmm, liked the stepson better than the dead son. Heartless bastard. "He's in his room." Then he bellowed, "Paul! Get your butt out here."

After about a minute, Paul Finch emerged from a hallway to the left. He was wearing gray sweatpants and a white T-shirt. White socks. He looked muzzy, as if he had just awakened. He stopped short when he saw Grace.

"Hey. You were at school yesterday," he said.

Lacey raised his eyebrows at Grace.

"Yes." She stood and showed him her badge. Ham did the same. "We're investigating the death of your stepbrother."

"I thought he killed himself," Paul said blandly. He was definitely not broken up over the idea.

"We don't know." Grace turned back to Lacey. "Mrs. Prescott called. Father Pepera contacted her."

Lacey's face soured. "It was her fault Karen left me. And she babied Zack something fierce. She probably turned him gay."

Ham stayed cool. Grace struggled to do the same. These were data points coming out of the mouths of parties they were interested in, nothing more.

"When was the last time she saw Zack?" Grace asked as she sat back down.

"Couple of years. She lives in Kansas. He'd stay over there for a couple of weeks."

"Was that before she became disabled?" Grace asked.

Lacey guffawed. "That old witch is not disabled. She just wants to get a free ride. Me, I'm a workingman. Paying for her lazy ass." He looked at Paul. "Isn't that right? I work hard to put food on this table."

Paul said nothing, and looked over at Grace and Ham. "Why were you watching me at school?"

"Procedure," Grace said. "We have to interview the victim's relatives. But I didn't want to disturb you in front of your friends. School was out for the day. I didn't want to hold you up."

Some of the wariness left his face. She decided to press her advantage.

"That pitcher, man." She shook her head. "I hope he's not the best you've got."

Paul laughed. "He sucks."

"He sure does. I'll bet it's hard to win games with a loser like him on the team."

"We do okay. At least, we did last year."

"League champions," Lacey said. "Kid's got trophies, ribbons. MVP . . ."

"Oh, could I see that?" Grace asked.

Paul looked at his stepfather. Lacey shrugged. Grace would take that as consent if it came to trial. Lacey was a lot less hostile on his I-HUNT-I-HAVE-A-GUN-I-VOTE-I-DON'T-PAY-STORAGE-FEES-FOR-THE-CORONER'S-FREEZER home turf. And he wasn't acting like a murderer who was afraid of getting caught.

"Okay." Paul headed back down the hall. Ham and Grace followed him.

His was a typical messy boy's room, with pennants and baseball posters on the walls; computer game CDs piled around an unmade oak twin bed with scratched bedposts and a half-eaten banana on a napkin; and dirty clothes scattered like autumn leaves all around. Grace noted a black baseball-equipment bag and wandered over to it.

"What kind of bat do you use?" she asked him.

"I had a brand-new Plasma Gold, but someone stole it," he said. "I'm just using my old shit Easton until I get some bucks scraped together."

Blunt instrument. Grace forced herself not to look at Ham. She could feel that he'd made the connection, though, via their partner ESP. "How long ago did it get stolen?"

"A couple of weeks. My mom was so pissed."

"We had words over that," Lacey said from the door-way.

"Where was it stolen?" Grace continued. She knew Ham would stay silent and let her run the questioning. If they both chimed in, it would rattle their subject. Paul would know it was a big deal to them.

"I don't know. Just, one day, it was gone." He opened the bag and pulled out his glove. "This is a Nokona. Walnut leather."

"Cool," Grace said admiringly as she slipped it on. It dwarfed her hand. She took off the glove and handed it back to Paul, aware that Ham had been surreptitiously snooping around as only the best could snoop.

"Would you mind if we looked in Zack's room?" Grace said to Lacey. "We might learn something useful."

Lacey hesitated. Grace took note. Then he said, "I talked to Father Pepera today. He said Zack never came to him about any gay stuff. Zack told that shrink those tranquilizers were making it hard for him to sleep. I think I'm going to sue that Jew doctor."

Antidepressants, not tranquilizers, she wanted to say, but that wasn't the point, was it? *And* of course Zack never talked to Father Pepera. The good father was an asshole.

"I knew he was gay," Paul said. "It was so obvious."

Grace swung her head around to look at him. "Did that bother you?"

Paul glanced at his stepfather, then back to her. "Hell, yeah. How would *you* like to have a faggot stepbrother?"

"Who is dead," Grace reminded him.

He didn't say anything. Wow, cold.

"Did you talk to your priest about having a funeral Mass, Mr. Lacey?" Ham asked.

Lacey looked down and away. "Yeah, well, we're having a disagreement about that at the moment."

"Mr. Lacey," Grace said, "my brother is a priest. He told me that the Church does not refuse Mass to people who commit suicide. Especially minors. And we're still investigating what happened to him. For all we know, it could have been a tragic accident."

Lacey's lips parted and he started to say something, then turned and led the way farther down the hall. Paul came, too. The door was shut, and Grace mentally crossed her fingers.

Laptop, she thought. *And he lets me take it.*

In they went, into the catacomb. While Paul's room was All-American Boy, Zack's was a dark, stinky altar of death-metal love: outsized posters for Megadeth and Carcass covered the otherwise plain white walls. His sheets were nondescript white and his blanket was dark brown; on the floor, a jumble of black T-shirts and jeans. There was an old PlayStation, but it was covered with dust. It was almost as if he had never actually lived in his room, only unpacked a duffel bag in preparation for a short visit.

His closet door was open. *Laptop, please.* Grace said to Lacey, "May I?"

"It smells in here," Lacey announced, as if he had just noticed it. "He used to eat in here. Didn't eat with the rest of the family."

"He was so frickin' weird," Paul muttered.

Grace waited. Lacey ignored her and looked at Ham, as if he was the go-to detective on the case. The *man.* Grace let it roll off her; if she ever let sexism bother her, she was in the wrong line of work. The only thing she did with it was try to figure out how to use it to make progress in their investigations. So she let herself go innocuous and invisible while Ham nodded and walked in front of her, placing a hand on the sliding door of the closet.

"This okay?" Ham asked him.

"I guess," Lacey grumped.

Ham pushed it back and bent down, examining a pair of Doc Martens and a more prosaic pair of muddy black Converse slip-ons. An Army jacket and a heavy black winter coat. A white dress shirt that seemed remarkably out of place.

Grace moved to a battered oak dresser covered with band stickers and opened the drawers. On top of some rather gray tighty whities was an amber plastic prescription bottle for Prozac. Grace rolled it with the edge of a pair of white underwear so she wouldn't get prints on it: ZACHARY RONALD LACEY. His prescription, definitely. Filled in September, two months ago, and it was close to full.

Suicide remained the front-runner theory.

Ham moved from the closet to peer under Zack's oak bed. Grace heard Lacey huff but he did not withdraw permission, so she kept combing through the chest of drawers. School track shorts. A receipt for one admission at the group rate to Frontier City, dated twelve days ago. A Sunday. The psychological profile they had put together of Zack didn't include Oklahoma City's premier amusement park. She tried to form a mental image of him screaming his head off on a roller coaster. Nope.

She left it there and turned as Ham searched a free-hanging shelf beneath an Iron Maiden poster. There was a jumble of old paperback books, many of them fantasy novels, which puzzled her; and then Ham lifted *The Lord of the Rings* and retrieved a pamphlet that said *GAY? NO WAY! SAVED BY JESUS!* It was identical to one of the ones the boys had hung like a mobile from the ceiling above Grace's desk.

Ham showed the pamphlet to Lacey. Purple rushed up his neck. He balled his fists and sucked in air. If looks could kill: BLAM-BLAM-BLAM-BLAM-BLAM.

"What's that shit doing in my house?" Lacey said. "Gimme that."

Paul snickered.

"It might prove useful," Ham began, but as there was no warrant, they had to do as he asked.

Lacey ripped it into tiny pieces and Grace had to swallow down her whimper. Ham looked from the shelf to Grace and back again, signaling that there were more pamphlets, and she kept her face neutral as she went back to her chest of drawers.

"I think you both better leave," Lacey announced. He looked as if he was about to stroke out. Paul stood beside him, gaze wandering back to the bookshelf. He headed for it; maybe he realized Zack was not coming back for any of his stuff and he could help himself to whatever he wanted.

Grace was disappointed but not very surprised. She wanted like anything to ask Lacey if he owned a truck, but she kept her mouth shut, aware that he was hovering behind her and that he wanted them off his property because they knew the horrible secret of Dysfunction Drive.

"Thanks for having us out," Ham said, as if it had been Lacey's decision.

"This is bullshit," Lacey shot back. "This whole thing." And Grace could see that Ron Lacey was waking up to the fact that the bullshit he was referring to was his life: He marries a woman who disappears; he fathers a homosexual who commits suicide. No wonder he preferred bat-swinger Paul and Paul's hot if somewhat dim and trashy mom to Ron Lacey the Prequel.

"We're trying hard to figure this out," Grace said, like the rodeo clown deflecting the bull after the rider falls off. "We're real sorry to bother you."

He glared at her as if he wasn't sure if she was being sincere or sarcastic. Paul was watching his stepfather as if he was trying to figure out how to act—what the family stance on all this was—and said, "He was real weird. None of my friends liked him."

Oh?

"I can see why," Grace said, shaking her head. "I've

got a nephew into goth stuff. He's in the vice principal's office every other week."

Ham didn't react to her blatant lie. He never did. He lied, too, if he thought it would help their work. How come if he was an adulterous liar *he* didn't have a last-chance angel?

"That's the kind you have to look out for," Lacey opined. Then he fell silent again.

They walked back down the hall. A bathroom door hung open, and Grace took a lightning-fast inventory: a pile of flat packing boxes and a couple rolls of packing tape. For Zack's belongings? That would not be good.

"Thanks again for your time," Ham said as the front door closed in their faces. Don't ask, don't tell, don't bother us again.

"Shit, Ham," Grace said as they walked back to Ham's truck. "Did you see all the packing boxes in the bathroom? What if he throws out all the good stuff?"

"Paul's missing a bat," Ham said, and she grinned.

"Yeah. Maybe we should have asked outright about the laptop." She shook her head. "Then the evil stepmom would know we were onto her. That we know Zack was collecting shit about her."

"She might not be evil at all," Ham said. "She might just be horny, picking up guys when Ron goes on the road." He smiled faintly. "I mean, would you want to sleep with Ron Lacey?"

"I would rather die of horniness." She smiled. "Paul's missing a bat. We have found missing murder weapons all over this great city in the past, Ham. In Lake Hefner, even."

"Zack gets hobbled and can't swim. Drowns."

"Murder in the first degree," Grace concurred. "And we will find that bat."

"Let's go to your place and celebrate."

Even if they fell asleep, they had to get up to go on the raid. Plus it was daylight. So technically, it would not qualify as staying over.

"Gotta take our victories where we find 'em," she said.

CHAPTER
EIGHTEEN

Butch worked out and showered. It was six p.m. They were due to rendezvous a few blocks from the warehouse at eight. October had told him the buy was set for eleven.

Two phone messages came in while he was cooking mushrooms in butter and fajita seasoning for the steak he was broiling. The first was from Captain Perry. The other was from October, on Butch's fake-pizzeria cell number.

As long as Butch had known Captain Perry, she hadn't pulled any punches, and she didn't do so now. Straight and direct, and he was grateful to her for it.

"Janaya Causwell didn't make it," she told him. "She had a heart attack about two hours ago."

Damn, girl. He spared a moment of silence for the tragic, wayward woman. Another for her daughter.

"I have a call from October," he reported. "I haven't checked it yet."

"If he doesn't know about Janaya, you shouldn't tell him."

"Yeah," he said, stirring the mushrooms.

"Butch, we have a chance to get Big Money tonight. If your informant freaks out, he could blow this entire operation sky-high. Get someone killed. Maybe one of our own."

"I know," he said. "I'll see what he wants."

"Let me know. Call me back," she ordered him.

Butch checked the message.

"Hey, Butch, it's all set. But after this, I want out," October said. "Janaya's friend LaKeisha got a message through to me that Janaya wants to talk to me. We're going to make it work. You can help with that, right? Help us?"

Butch's heart pounded. What the hell was this? Was LaKeisha setting October up?

He called Captain Perry and repeated the message. She grunted, sighed.

"How did he sound?" she asked.

"Happy." It was the happiest Butch had ever heard him, in fact. "Eager to get out."

Captain Perry swore. "This is a surprise, and surprises are not good."

He agreed. His mind raced. The scent of steak and baked potato filled the room, but he was losing his appetite.

Surprises were not good.

"Let me think this over," she said. "I'll call you back."

She hung up and he called Grace. Since she was a woman, she might have a take on this.

Her voice was muffled, as if she had been asleep. He imagined her in bed, then turned that channel off and took a sip of water.

"Shit, that's weird. But it sounds like high school," Grace suggested when he told her what LaKeisha had done. "Girls did shit like that, pretending to help a guy get back together with his girlfriend when the one pretending was really after the guy. And all these people are definitely stuck in high-school land."

"Janaya died a couple of hours ago," he told her.

"Shit." Grace was quiet for a moment. He heard the strike of a match.

"Maybe LaKeisha's in with Big Money and it's a trap," Butch said.

"Trap for October," Grace said. "Not us." She exhaled. "He knows he's one step away from a fatality, being in a gang."

Not really. October tuned out the parts of reality that he didn't like. Always had.

"Yeah," Butch said. Butch knew the score; he wasn't some rookie cop working his first informant. And if this went south for October, he wouldn't be the first one Butch had lost, either. He thought of Merrie Kelly.

"Butch, you okay, man?"

"Yeah." And he was. He put his heart elsewhere and kept his cop blood beating. "Captain said she was going to think it through and get back to us."

"She'd better go for it," Grace said. "I'm ready to rock and roll." She giggled a little, and her voice moved away from the phone. He heard a smack. If Ham wasn't with her, someone else was. Not his business.

"Me too," he said.

"See you at eight."

"This is a no-knock warrant," said Marston, tonight's Tac lead. "We will move into place at one and two." He flashed a laser light on the plans of the warehouse and adjoining alleys, showing a large one at the front door of the warehouse, a two at the rear. "Red goes in first. Blue activates once there is activity in the rear."

Yeah, baby, activity in the rear, Grace thought, sharing a smirk with Ham.

Marston nodded at Grace when he concluded. "Detective Hanadarko?" he said.

"Everyone standing here knows what kind of scumbag Big Money is," Grace began, addressing Major Crimes and Tac both. "He cut a thirteen-year-old girl named Priscilla Jackson into pieces and fed them to his dog. He's recruited kids as young as eight to courier weapons and drugs to his gang and serve as lookouts." She passed out copies of Big Money's surveillance photo. Tac examined it more closely than her team, since he was not as well known to them.

They put on their amulets and good-luck charms. Bobby kissed a picture of his wife and kids. Butch slithered into his Longhorn shirt. Ham fastened his St. Christopher medal to his chest with black duct tape. Grace placed a wrapped paper tube of white sage in her boot.

"Sound check," she announced. She and Ham jumped up and down for Bobby and Butch. No jingling. All was silent.

"Sound check," Butch said next, as he and Bobby did the same. Ham and Grace gave the all-clear.

Grace glanced at Ham as she adjusted her type-three body armor. He was looking at her with a dangerously soft expression. She tipped her head back and he gazed down on her. "Are you feeling okay, Ham?"

"Butch is worried about his informant," he said. "And I'm fine."

"I know, man. It is what it is." Then, chuckling, she added, "Whatever the hell it is." A beat. "Show me an informant who's not a squirrel, and I'll show you a dead informant."

"Yeah," he said. His smile widened. "Baseball bat."

"Laptop." She shimmied.

"Pastor Marc."

Grace's smile fell. "Yeah, about that. The youth group meets at nine a.m., and I was thinking, you know, that you're more of a morning person than I am." She waggled her brows hopefully.

He laughed. "You're so full of shit. C'mon, Gay Youth Pastor is our main attraction."

"Speak for yourself. I'm liking Dad. *Storage fees,* can you believe it? And he goes ballistic when all we find is one pamphlet. God, I hope he leaves the other ones alone. Maybe Rhetta can get prints. Clues. Leads."

"We push the right domino, everything collapses," he agreed.

Butch and Bobby approached. Ham and Grace nodded at them. Bobby was quiet, focused. Butch looked loose, but Ham could tell he was on his guard. It was Butch's guy who'd brought them here tonight. And nobody on the squad wanted Big Money worse than Butch.

"It's gonna happen, man," Grace said, patting Butch's forearm. He nodded.

"Captain Perry said if we get done in time, she'll buy us a round at Louie's." He grinned. "I told her to ask Louie to stay open late. Just in case."

"I went to Paige's last night and drank mojitos," Grace informed them all. Ham and the others cracked up. "I played Bunco and I *won*. Candles. And hand lotion." She held out her hands. "Gardenia."

"Mmmhmm," Butch said appreciatively.

Ham figured Grace was not going to mention that they'd used up half the bottle during sex. Grace's sheets were a mess. But his ass smelled like a flower garden.

"Okay, let's roll," said Marston.

Tac drove them over to the warehouse district in their van, and everyone silently climbed down, MP5's in hand. Ham let go of everything in his life but the op. Grace was his partner. Butch and Bobby were on his squad. Tac had the parabola mic and the battering ram.

He, Grace, Butch, and Bobby were part of the Red Team. Red was going to sneak down the alley and assemble around the back door. Their deficit was the fact that the alley was narrow and crowded with Dumpsters and garbage. The warehouses were covered with aluminum siding, which could cause ricochets, but everyone was packing heavy shit, so that wasn't too likely. Rounds would just tear through. They'd made as sure as they could that no one else was inside those warehouses.

The Blue Team would take the front of the warehouse. Their deficit was that they were vulnerable to attack from late arrivals and/or reinforcements. Although Tactical had already swept the area for bad guys hiding in adjacent warehouses or staked out on the roofs, they might have missed someone.

"Make sure your clips are loaded," Marston said by way of parting.

Grace's team moved silently into position and waited for the signal from Blue. Blue would be the first to act; they would hoist up the parabola mic and confirm that the players were in place, and that something actionable had occurred—i.e., the buy. Or a murder. Whatever.

Grace and the boys crouched into position, helmets on, guns up, waiting. Grace listened to her heart, sure and steady, a little trippy from adrenaline. She was as focused as an eagle. No one spoke. No one moved. A bomb could have gone off but if it wasn't their bomb, no one on the Red Team would so much as blink.

There was a white towel on the Dumpster. Butch shifted his gaze to it, staring at it as if it were a snake about to strike. October's signal. Trouble. Danger. For Butch's team? Or for October?

Shit, he thought. He nudged Ham, who looked questioningly at him. Butch looked at the white towel. Ham got it—Butch had told him about it—and he pursed his lips. There was nothing to be done now. You planned and strategized and practiced, and you had procedures you were not to violate, and then there was a white towel. And you didn't know what the hell to do. Being a police officer was not like being an accountant. It was mostly about winging it. Shooting from the hip.

And not dying if you could help it.

So what did the white towel mean?

*   *   *

There were sounds inside the warehouse, muffled and echoing. Grace kept track of them in case they got louder near their door. She didn't look at anyone; she stared at the door. She was as motionless as a statue; her mind was clear of chatter; and rarely had she felt so alive. This wasn't just what she was born to do; it was what she was. The tornado and the calm eye; the whirlwind and the silent aftermath of the blast. No one else existed because everyone on Red Team was one being: Justice. If Big Money died tonight, it was Justice. If any of those scumbag assholes went with him, Justice.

And then:

"GO! GO! GO!" roared inside her helmet speaker.

Grace aimed her MP5 as the door burst open. Blurs of dark skin, brown skin, sallow skin; do-rags and guns. Bullets blazing past her helmet; she was rolling to one side without conscious awareness of doing so. Propping herself up on her elbows. Scooting back and racing around a trash can.

Rounds from a submachine gun threw up mud, splattering her face. Bullets tore into the siding above her head. Buffeted by the wall of sound, her ears filled with cotton and her headset crackled in her helmet: *eleven guys count them officer down armed dangerous they are exiting toward Red go go go . . .*

She was coated with mud; it began to rain and a big mofo wove in the doorway, then barreled back into the warehouse, squirting blood. She got up on one knee and stood her ground. Blue would chase them through; she was supposed to stay in the alley, and mow the bad guys down when they tried to escape, rats from the *Titanic*. She waited, her finger on the trigger; and she aimed her gun right into the chest of some scrawny guy who was crying—

—*October*, she thought—

and she hesitated.

And Scrawny Gun shot right at her.

BLAM-BLAM-BLAM-BLAM-BLAM! replied her team-mates.

Something stung very, very badly, and everything went away.

White light, white light, white light.

Got you, now, Earl thought as he extended his hand in the white tunnel. *Girl, I got you—*

Grace woke up in the hospital, surrounded by loved ones: Rhetta, Butch, Bobby, Johnny, Ham. And Paige. She groaned. Not because Paige was there. Well, okay, *maybe* not.

"Not again," she muttered.

"A bullet grazed your left thigh. You weren't hurt badly," Rhetta said. "But you got knocked out. So you're under observation for a concussion."

"Shit," Grace said. "I love those jeans."

"I'll patch them for you," Rhetta promised.

Standing apart from the others, hovering on the threshold of her room, Earl smiled the sweetest smile at her, so not like any other smile of his she'd ever seen, and walked—or vanished—into the hall. Her last-chance angel had come for her again, as he had before.

Maybe God just doesn't want me to die, she thought.

Then she looked up at Ham, who waved a catheter back and forth like a hypnotist with a pocket watch. She grimaced at him, then smiled gently at Butch.

"Hi, Scarecrow," she said. "Where's Toto?"

"October's gut-shot," Butch said, coming to the bed and taking her right hand in his. "They're not sure he's going to make it."

"That's a bitch, man," she said sincerely, even though she was fairly certain it was October who had shot her.

She gave Butch's hand a squeeze. "Johnny, maybe you should go see him," Grace said to her brother. She let go of Butch's warm big hand and tested her forehead. Her fingertips came away clean, meaning that Johnny hadn't performed Last Rites on her. Johnny didn't say anything. Maybe October wasn't a Catholic—i.e., one of the lucky ones.

"Who else?" she asked. "Did we get Big Money?"

Butch looked grim. He shook his head. "Big Money didn't show. We got everybody else, though. Two fatalities for them, but we caught them in the middle of the buy, so they've all been put away wet. Couple of injuries on our side, but you're the worst."

"That's something, Butch," Grace said. She was so sorry. And so pissed. "We got some poison off the streets."

His jaw was clenched. Now Big Money would be more cautious than ever, sinking into the sludge like a sewer gator. They might never see him again in their lifetime . . . or in their city. If he'd just leave . . . he'd still carve little girls up in someone else's town.

When Henry's cat died, I slept with him, she thought. *Hell, I'd sleep with Butch just because, but I would also do it to ease his pain.* She looked over at Ham. *Well, that sure would complicate things, wouldn't it?*

"Hey, guess what," Ham said. "Joey Amador was in the warehouse. We shot him. He had a gun in his hand when he went down."

"Are you shitting me?" Grace cried.

"Shit, no," Ham replied.

"No shit." Grace chuckled. Paige rolled her eyes at the language, and Grace filed that away under "Ten Ways I Can Prove My Sister Is a Superficial Tightass." "Did we shoot him dead?"

"No," Ham said. "My aim was off."

"Hey, I shot him," Bobby said.

"No way. It was me," Butch insisted.

"Well, it probably wasn't me, because I've got good aim," Grace said. "And you know he'll just get probation again, because of all the police brutality." Grace made her hand into a gun and fired it at Ham. He fired back.

"It's really not funny to talk about killing someone," Paige announced, distressed.

"We're just taking the edge off," Grace told her. She had explained police humor to Paige before. "We don't really mean it." *Except for all the time.*

"Well, I hope you don't talk like that around the kids." Paige gave Johnny a look, as if the moral authority of the Hanadarko clan should use this as a teaching moment.

"I almost died again," Grace told Rhetta, who was blowing her nose.

Rhetta shook her head. "No, this time they said you were going to be fine. We all knew it. It was just a graze. And a concussion."

Grace paused. Rhetta stopped honking, and Grace locked gazes with her very best wonderful friend in all the world. She looked at her hard and nodded: *I am telling you that I saw the white light again. And Earl.* Grace had described her first near-death experience during the squad's failed assault on Big Time Reynolds's crack house.

Rhetta's eyes widened, and she covered her mouth with both her hands and slowly sat down in a brown plastic chair. Message received.

"Well, God does work in mysterious ways," Grace said to Ham, as he came up beside the bed. "Looks like you get to interview Pastor Marc alone tomorrow."

"I'll get them to discharge you," he promised, picking up a bedpan and making as if to place it on her head like a hat. They grinned at each other.

Paige cleared her throat, clearly ill at ease with their juvenile antics. "I can stop by your house and feed your dog."

The thought of her fussy sister seeing her dirty dishes and possibly her sheets and floor slathered with prized Bunco gardenia hand lotion made Grace wince. Paige was already gathering her purse and Grace half-heartedly raised her head off her pillow in protest.

Ham stepped up and said, "I have to go by Grace's for the case file," which was a damn lie, but Grace nodded vigorously.

"It's on the counter. You know," she said, yawning. "He has to go anyway, Paige." She yawned again.

"Okay." Paige modeled her signature expression of mild frustration, one that had taken Grace years to understand: She was being spared the hassle of doing the errand, and yet her will had been thwarted.

"On the counter," Grace repeated to Ham.

Everyone took that as their cue to leave. Rhetta, Butch, Bobby, and Ham kissed her good-bye. Her own two siblings did not. Hanadarko family weirdness. Grace, however, was an equal-opportunity smiler as the gang filed out. She was about to turn out her light when Doug and Clay walked in. Clay's face was dead white, and his eyes were swollen.

"Hi, Aunt Grace." He looked up at his father, who put a hand on his shoulder.

"Hey, Clay," she said, reaching out her hand. "It's so nice of you . . ."

A big tear rolled down Clay's cheek.

"Clay, I'm all right," she said. "I'm fine. It was just a scratch."

He lowered his eyes and nodded. "I know."

Doug sighed, and Grace saw the resemblance to Clay around his eyes. Clay's grandpa and mom, both gone. His aunt . . . make that *favorite* aunt, damn it, back in the hospital with another bullet wound. So *was* being a cop a form of indirect suicide?

"This is getting kind of old," Doug said. "Do you always have to be such a hotshot?"

I hesitated, she thought. *I wasn't a hotshot at all.*

She said, "Hey, I'm getting out of the hospital tomorrow. Can Clay come over and spend the night? You could give him Monday off. Call the nuns and say he's sick." *Lying to nuns. A hellfire offense for sure.*

"Oh, *wow,*" Clay breathed. "Dad, please?"

"Not on your life," Doug said, shaking his head at both of them. "But he can come over next weekend."

"Damn, I'm spending a fortune in video-rental fees," she muttered as she smiled at Clay. "Cool, man." She lowered her voice. "We'll eat so much crap we'll puke."

"Yeah." He grinned at her, shiny eyes and white teeth. "Chomp!"

You had to take life's pleasures where you found 'em.

CHAPTER
NINETEEN

It was almost nine when Butch stopped by October's hospital room. There was a guard outside who let him in, and a young nurse inside who informed him visiting hours were over . . . until she saw his badge and gave him an excited little smile. She was a short little blonde, very cute. Her name was Terri.

October looked terrible. He looked like Butch's homeless Sartre-reading philosopher, only dead. There was a cannula in his nose and grizzled beard on his sunken cheeks. As Butch turned to go, October's eyes drifted open.

"You got me out," he whispered.

Butch swallowed back whatever he might have said, and nodded. "Where was Big Money?"

October coughed lightly. His breathing was shallow. "He had a fight with his girlfriend." He took another short breath. "She's a bitch."

Damn. If only Big Money had traveled light, too . . .

"Sorry," October said.

"I saw your towel on the Dumpster. Your signal. I wasn't sure what it meant. If you were warning us to abort." *Caused a bit of confusion, and Grace got shot.*

October shook his head. "Wasn't mine."

Butch took that in. Had someone else known about October's signal? Was it some kind of coincidence?

"LaKeisha said Janaya wants to make up," October said.

Cold certainty washed over Butch. He couldn't lie to this guy anymore.

"October . . . Patrick," he began.

But October's eyes rolled shut, and his mouth dropped open. Butch looked at Nurse Terri, who checked the readouts on October's heart-rate monitor.

"He's just very tired," she said. "We're giving him morphine for the pain."

"He probably loves that," Butch said as he turned to go.

She was studying him. When he caught her eye, she dimpled slightly. "So, you're a cop."

"Yeah."

"He's your prisoner? From a shoot-out?"

He nodded. *At the Not-Okay Corral. Grace got shot.*

Her eyes got a little wide. "Wow."

All that, and I cook, too, he thought. But that was the little head talking.

"I have a break," she said, smiling. "They'll watch Mr. Kelly from the nurse's station. Want to go to the cafeteria for a cup of really bad coffee?"

"Sure," he replied, and told himself that was the little head, too. But maybe . . . it was a little cold and a little dark back at his place, right about now.

Ham was sitting in Pastor Marc's office at twelve thirty on Sunday afternoon while Pastor Marc himself buzzed around like a meth addict. The walls had posters of Christian rock groups and one of those Not of This World logos against a sunset. There was a stained-glass rectangle hanging in the window, which depicted a cross against a rainbow. Rainbows could be symbols of diversity and/or gay pride. Ham could hope.

Morning services were over, and the youth group was

meeting back at the church in an hour. They were going to the rez to build a house. Ham had called Bobby, asked him if he might also wander over once they hit Native-American property. Butch was over at Bobby's, helping him with his mold.

Pastor Marc had some nachos with ground beef and a soda on his table. He offered some to Ham, but Ham passed. Now the detective sat in a wooden chair backed with a few inches of blue fabric, observing the whirlwind, all the time looking for clues regarding Marc's sexual orientation. Weak chin, check.

His gay brother, Nick, would kill Ham if he knew he was thinking like that. But hell, sometimes you *could* tell.

"So to answer your question, yes, we *are* an inclusive church." Pastor Marc's last name was Grayhill. He had chubby cheeks, a low forehead, and a sort of mullet haircut Ham could not believe. He wished Grace was there to see it. She had gotten discharged, wasn't even limping, but she'd made him go by himself. Payback would be sweet.

He smiled at Ham with capped teeth. "Jesus really does love everybody."

"So . . . does the church allow commitment ceremonies?" Ham asked.

Pastor Marc didn't miss a beat. "By 'inclusive,' I mean that we accept all who have sinned against the will of God. That includes you, and that includes me. No one is worthy of the glory of the Lord. But He gives it to us if we are truly repentant and live clean, just lives."

"And Zachary Lacey went to Frontier City with the youth group," Ham said. "Two weeks ago."

Something washed over Pastor Marc's face. His jaw tightened; the blood rose in his cheeks. Ham remained neutral, letting the clues come to him.

Old joke: So there were these two bucks in the forest, an old one and a young one. They were standing on the crest of a hill, looking down into a meadow filled with does. And the young buck says to the old one, "Let's run down there and screw one of those does!" And the old buck says, "Let's *walk* down and screw *all* of 'em."

Ba-da-dum. A younger Ham would have started asking questions right then, to see what was ailing the good minister. But the older Ham remained patient. Partnering with Grace had taught him the wisdom of patience. A little.

"Yes, Zack went with the group." He was speaking carefully, his back turned to Ham as he rooted through a red metal toolbox identical to the one Ham's mom owned. Virginia Dewey had walked Ham through his first oil change when he was still in elementary school.

"How'd he seem?" Ham asked. "At Frontier City?"

"Where's that hammer?" Pastor Marc muttered.

Blunt instrument.

"He seemed . . . detached." Pastor Marc turned around and huffed with his hands on his hips. *Gay.* "He said things weren't going well at home."

"We have a witness who told us he had an altercation with his father shortly before he died. Did he talk about that? Did you notice any injuries?"

"He was a private person." Pastor Marc wasn't looking at him. Ham could just feel the anxiety rolling off him and remained calm, steady as she goes, but the sounding notes of the "William Tell Overture" were on him like a fever. "I respected that. I hoped that, in time, he would feel free to open up to me. He had only been coming to the youth group for a couple of months."

"Did he bring anyone to Frontier City? Hang out with a particular group of kids?"

"He came by himself, and the group hung out together," Pastor Marc reported. He was getting superbusy with his search for the hammer. "If he was troubled, he didn't share that with us."

Us.

Pastor Marc looked up at Ham. He picked up a nacho, scooping up a dollop from the sour cream on the side of the cardboard plate. "I'm sorry, Detective, but I need to get ready."

Dismissed. "Sure, of course. Thanks for your time," Ham said, getting up as Pastor Marc grunted and held up a ball-peen hammer. Thing like that would have shattered an ankle. Henry hadn't said anything about shattering. "I'll walk myself out."

Pastor Marc nodded, clearly done. Ham went out the side door into a busy courtyard decorated with a white statue of Jesus in the middle of a rock fountain. Mexican paver tiles were inscribed with the names of donors and in memory of various people. He surveyed the names as he walked: PATHI, ATKINSON, BRAUN. People in their Sunday best chatted in groups. A few smiled his way. A friendly bunch on a Sunday morning. He used to go to a church in Chandler. He hadn't picked a new one yet, but this one was not it.

He walked out of the courtyard to the back parking lot just as three guys piled out of a truck. One of them looked familiar. He was wearing a football jersey and as he ran around to the truck bed, Ham read off his last name on the shirt, above the number 22: COVEL. He wasn't Drew Covel, the jerk kid Ham had interviewed. Had to be a brother or a cousin.

Covel scrambled into the truck bed and grabbed up a medium-sized Styrofoam cooler. Then he scrabbled back down and trotted toward the courtyard.

"Hey," Ham said, closing the space between them. The other two guys had climbed into the bed, gathering up more supplies for the trip, Ham supposed, to the reservation. Neither saw Ham approaching their friend.

Ham's badge must have caught the light; Covel glanced down at it first, then up to Ham's face. He blanched and looked back over his shoulder. His two friends were busy.

"Is your brother Drew Covel?" Ham asked.

"I wasn't there," the boy said quickly. "I had nothing to do with it."

"Well, I'll be damned," Grace said as she carried some extra-superlacy bras toward a dressing room. She was at the Crossroads Mall, in the Victoria's Secret store.

And so was Cherie Lacey, just coming out of a dressing room. Cherie was dressed in a pair of tight jeans with rhinestone swirls down the sides, a pink belt studded with gold roses, and a dark pink sort of a peasant blouse. Her nails matched her blouse. She had been trying on black bras to go with her grieving-stepmom black dress. Or else she did a little pole dancing in her spare time.

It took Cherie a minute to figure out who Grace was.

"Oh, hi. Detective . . ." Cherie was at a loss.

"Hanadarko." Grace pulled a sympathetic smile. "How you doing, Ms. Lacey?"

Cherie shrugged, hefting another big Crossroads Mall shopping bag over her shoulder. It had the black dress in it. To match the dark circles under her eyes.

"I guess I'm okay, considering what's going on. Ron said you came out to the house yesterday. Did you find what you were looking for?"

Laptop. "We weren't looking for anything specific," Grace replied. "Just anything that could help us figure out what happened." A beat, and then, "Zack's grandmother is all torn up. She's afraid Father Pepera won't say Mass for Zack."

Cherie fingered the black bra on the top of her little pile. The cups were see-through. So maybe she was cheating. Or maybe she just liked to keep the home fires burning.

"I'm not a very good Catholic," Cherie confessed. "I don't really get all that stuff."

"My brother will say Mass for him," Grace said. "He's a Jesuit. Priest. They're more liberal." She nearly choked on her words. "Hey," she said brightly, "you want to go get a cup of coffee or something in the food court? I really shouldn't be spending any money on stuff like this." She wrinkled her nose. "Mortgage payments."

"I hear you. Ronnie would kill me if he saw the bills for this stuff." She paled. "I mean, he wouldn't *really* kill me."

"I know what you mean," Grace assured her. "I don't have a man, so no one's looking over my shoulder except the bank and my credit-card company." She set down her bras on the nearest table as Cherie headed for the nearest cash register. Grace started to follow her empty-handed; then on second thought, she grabbed the black thong from her selections and followed her on over. What the hell.

Cherie paid in cash, then Grace handed over her plastic; they headed to the food court. Cherie grabbed a diet soda, and Grace ordered onion rings; they sat down at a table for two. Cherie had a sizable number of purchases inside the catch-all big bag, given that she had only one special occasion on her calendar. At least that Grace knew of. Grace had only just located her when she was buying the dress, and followed her on over to Vicky's.

They settled in, almost like girlfriends; Cherie with her pink nails and makeup—her lips were lined in a dark pink, then filled in with a lighter one—and Grace, still kind of slaggy from being in the hospital. Her thigh hurt but she wasn't even limping. Paul was the one who had answered the Lacey phone and told her his mom was shopping. Grace had remembered the Crossroads shopping bag at their house, and hit it lucky.

Lucky being a relative term. She wasn't sure what was worse, interviewing Pastor Marc or going to a mall.

Dipping an onion ring in ketchup, she gestured with

her head for Cherie to help herself. Cherie waved her hands no-no-no.

"Have to watch my figure," she said with a little wink. "It's harder to take it off the older you get. And I'm getting up there."

"Get out." Grace guffawed. "You can't be older than . . ."

"I'm nearly thirty-five," Cherie confided.

"Wow, I guess you'd have to be," Grace said. "But still." So she'd had Paul around the age of eighteen. She wondered where Dad was.

"Ya gotta stay out of the sun," Cherie told her. "And moisturize." She made a little face. "And you shouldn't smoke."

"Keeps the weight off," Grace countered. "Ron told us that Zack ate in his room a lot. Didn't eat with the rest of the family."

Cherie tapped the end of her straw with each of the fingernails of her left hand. "I never felt like I knew him very well," she said. "I married Ron when Zack was fourteen. Just a couple of years ago. I think he had these dreams that his mom would come back." She sighed and slid her hand down the side of her cup.

"Does Ron know what happened to Karen, just doesn't want Zack to know?" Grace asked.

"She really did just disappear," Cherie said. "Which makes me think . . ." She hesitated, then shrugged and took an onion ring. "I think she did herself in, too. I think it runs in that family. Ron gets these dark moods." She shivered.

"They say that mental illness has a genetic component," Grace agreed. "Do you worry about Ron out on the road, by himself?"

"No, it's almost . . ." She looked pensive.

". . . a relief?" Grace filled in.

"Oh, no, I wouldn't go that far," Cherie said, nibbling

on the very edge of the onion ring. "We're newlyweds, after all."

"You came from Texas," Grace said. She grinned. "Or at least, you sound like it."

"El Paso," she said. "Such an armpit."

"Won't argue with you there." Grace felt her cell phone vibrate. "Excuse me." She checked it. It was Ham.

MEET UR HOUSE 1 HR?

She texted back a yes and put the cell phone bag in her pocket. Cherie had taken the opportunity to glance at her cell phone, too. She jerked her head up when she realized Grace was looking at her.

"I should go," Cherie said. "Ron's got a short run tomorrow, and we need to decide what to do about the funeral." She pressed a paper napkin against her lips. "Is there any chance you will be able to declare or say or whatever it is, about if Zack's death was an accident or if he—he killed himself?"

Grace pursed her lips and shook her head. "Can't say yet. And it could have been a murder." She picked up another onion ring and bit down hard.

Cherie looked a little sick. A lot of people did when they heard the word *murder*.

"Oh, God," she murmured, sliding back her chair. "Well . . ."

Something told Grace to go for it. There and then. "Have you seen Zack's laptop? Kid at school said he always had it with him. It had these stickers on it, death-metal bands . . ."

"Laptop," she said slowly, as if she had never heard the word before. "I didn't notice. . . ." Her hands trembled as she picked up her shopping bag.

"And Paul's missing a baseball bat," Grace added.

Cherie brightened. "*That* I knew about." As if she were actually pleased he'd lost a two-hundred-dollar piece of sports equipment.

"Is it possible one of the guys on his team took it by accident?"

"The bat, you mean? I don't see how, with his initials and all," Cherie replied. "And those are nice boys."

"Except for ganging up on Zack, of course," Grace said. "That part . . . not so nice."

She looked confused again. "Ganging up? . . ."

"Calling him a faggot, that kind of nice stuff." Grace cocked her head as if to say, *Well?*

"Oh, no, you must be mistaken. Those are good boys," Cherie insisted. "Back in Texas . . ." She stopped herself. "They're very nice," she concluded. "Oh, my God, if they hassled him . . ." Her eyes welled.

She started to cry in earnest. She was good at it. In fact, Grace couldn't even tell if she meant it or not. She grabbed more napkins and dabbed at her eyes, blotting eyeliner and mascara. Again, as the layers came off, she looked older than thirty-five.

"Did he open up to you? Tell you anything about what was going on with him? When was the last time you were together?"

"I took him to the grocery-store pharmacy to get his prescription renewed. About three weeks ago."

But he had stopped taking his meds, and there was nearly a full bottle in his underwear drawer. The date was September, nearly two months ago. Maybe Zack had faked her out, told her he needed more.

"What did you two talk about?" Grace prompted.

"He wanted to know what I wanted for my birthday." She wept harder. "He said he wanted to get me something nice because he had saved up a bunch of money."

From dealing drugs?

"People think just because he was my stepson, I'm not all that upset. But I *am*."

"I can see that," Grace said.

"I want to know what happened to him." She blew her

nose. "I cared for that boy. Losing his momma and all . . ." She took a deep breath. "Ron's so angry, but that's his way. He gets angry when he cares. I've been trying to hold it in because, well, I wasn't really family. But this is all the family I've got."

He gets angry when he cares.

"Cherie, we were told that Ron and Zack had a bad argument shortly before Zack's disappearance. That blows were exchanged."

Cherie sucked in her breath and stared at Grace with real fear in her eyes. Grace felt that frisson of electricity that told her she'd hit the right nerve, square on. She waited.

"Oh, God, please don't think that way about Ron," she begged. "I was so afraid it would get out . . . because then y'all would be thinking the way you are thinking."

"You don't know what I'm thinking," Grace said.

"I do. I knew as soon as you started talking to us in that room that if you found out about that fight . . ." She covered her mouth to keep the nightmare from pouring out. "Ron wouldn't do that. I know that man."

"Did they fight over him being gay?" Grace asked.

She shook her head. "We didn't know. It was over me. Zack didn't like me. Ron didn't tell me what Zack said about me. But . . . he did hit Zack."

"A lot."

"A lot," she said brokenly. "And I haven't done anything wrong. I swear it to you."

"If I found that laptop, what would I find on it?" Grace asked her.

"I don't know," she said, "but I wish you would find it. Then that would clear Ron, and maybe I could find out what Zack had against me."

"Ron hasn't been charged with anything," Grace reminded her.

"Okay," Cherie said, bobbing her head as the tears

came. "Right, I know that but I'm so scared. . . ." She bit her lower lip. "We honestly didn't know that Zack was worried about being a homosexual. No one ever told us that."

"Dr. Metzner didn't catch it?" Grace asked.

Cherie shook her head. "Maybe he wasn't supposed to tell us. We're plain people, Ronnie and me. I don't even know any gay people."

"Except Zack," Grace said.

"Oh, my God, why did this happen to us?" Cherie whispered.

She sank back down in her chair, rested her head in her hands, and sobbed.

CHAPTER
TWENTY

"Gay-orcism?" Grace echoed, as Ham paced in her living room. She had just returned from her talk at the mall with Cherie, to find him pacing, livid, in her driveway. They walked inside, and he slammed her door so hard the windows shook. One look at him and Gus had retreated to her bedroom.

"Yeah. After Frontier City the youth group goes back to the church, and Pastor Marc leads them all in prayer and he leaves to get pizzas. Alone."

"Leaving them alone, bad boy," Grace said, grabbing two beers out of the fridge. Ham needed to cool off.

"So while he's gone, these guys get this great idea to have an exorcism for Zack to stop him from being gay." Ham ran his hands through his hair. "They put him in a chair and tie his hands behind his back and start screaming Bible verses at him."

"Are you shitting me, man?" Grace waited for the punch line. Because Ham wouldn't be this angry about a few Bible verses. She didn't get that riled up about Bible verses, and she was the one with the religious issues.

"And Pastor Marc's not coming back from his pizza errand. So they get really into it. Someone saw this James Bond movie so they get *another* chair, only they yank the seat out of it, and they take off his jeans and his underwear and they sit him down in the chair. And they start asking him if he's gay, and when he doesn't confess, someone hits his balls from underneath the chair—"

"*What?*" Grace nearly dropped the longnecks.

"With a pool cue. They've got a pool table in their rec room, and they're smacking his balls with it and shouting at him. And Pastor Bullshit is not there. And he *should* be. He was gone for over an hour."

Grace's mouth dropped open. "He's giving them time to do it?"

"And Zack is not saying a word, not a frickin' word, and his head falls forward, so they get spooked and let him go." Ham made fists and punched the air. "And after he's gone, Pastor Marc comes back with their pizzas."

"Jesus." Grace gaped at him.

"Marc knew. He did. He acted guilty when I was in his office today."

"Another adult dangles him over the pit. God*damn* it," Grace said. She slammed down the beers. She was pissed. Really pissed.

It's a fierce white-hot mighty love.

This was such pure and utter bullshit. Unbelievable. It was so incredibly stupid that she couldn't even believe it.

"I want," Grace said, "I want to bring that asshole down to the morgue and let him see Zack Lacey now. We're all supposed to rise from the dead in our mortal bodies, Ham, so *pure. . . .*" She clenched her teeth so hard she could almost hear them crack.

"Grace, Grace," Ham whispered, taking her gun out of the holster, then her badge, laying them on the counter. Ham walked to the side door and opened it, taking Grace with him.

The world smelled like ozone, and oil refineries, and cow manure. It smelled like incense.

I hate men of God. I hate how they screw with kids and ruin their lives. If we have souls, they just tear them out.

Through the side door, the rain poured down in buckets, by the river-load. Grace stared at it, understanding the impulse to drown the whole screwed-up mess. God saying, *To hell with this.*

Ham shut the door in some parallel universe where life was normal, and carried her down the hall into her bedroom. She curled up in his arms and wished they could skip some steps and be joined now, right now; she let him roll her onto the bed and undress her. Zippers, buttons, bra hooks. He tore it off and then shot out of his own clothes like a comet. He was ready and he parted her legs and she arched her back with her teeth showing.

Gimme, she thought, as her most basic, demanding self. Nothing let her forget better than Ham inside her. She snapped into the moment, fully awake, aware, and alive; other men could do this but no man could do it like Ham. He thrust and she bucked, and there were no priests and ministers and no bullies, nothing but the amazing delight of sex with the man who played her like a screaming guitar. Liquid heat and fierce, white-hot mighty pleasure. She clung and she moved and he did the things he knew she loved. And that was the only love involved; love of the flesh, and of being alive.

"Oh, Grace, oh," Ham moaned.

And it quieted her body, if not her mind. One out of two wasn't bad. Three, if you counted her soul. Her stormy soul, bothered and incessant.

But her body, for the moment, rested. In peace. Ham lay still and quiet beside her like a dead man. Someday, one of them would die first. Maybe they wouldn't even know each other anymore, when that happened. She took comfort in the idea of not knowing when Ham died.

The rain came down in torrents. She listened to it for a while. Then Ham shifted his weight with a slow, long sigh.

"Cherie didn't seem to know about a laptop." Grace told him. "Said Paul's initials were on his bat. She confirmed that Ron beat Zack for talking trash about her."

"These are good things to know," Ham mumbled. His breathing changed, and she knew he was drifting off to sleep. Lucky bastard.

She thought about reminding him that there were no sleepovers. But it was only four in the afternoon. He'd wake up long before bedtime.

"Oh, hello again," said the coy cocktail waiter in Pan, the bar with the black-velvet Elvis singing into a penis. "How is the crime business, Detectives?"

"Can't complain," Grace said as she and Ham scanned the perimeter. Empty booths, a few scattered patrons at the tables. The jukebox was on low, more background noise than music. Sunday night in a gay bar was about as dead as Sunday night in a straight bar. "Got a question."

"Fire away." The waiter posed. *Hit me with your best shot.*

"When you saw Flaco in here with our underage guy, did our guy have a laptop with him? That he maybe left?"

The waiter shrugged. "I don't know anything about laptops. Lap dances, yes." He smiled at Ham. "I would even give *you* a discount."

Ham wondered if Nicky ever did this kind of shit. Then he said, "This laptop was covered with stickers from heavy-metal bands."

"Death metal," Grace elaborated. "Megadeth."

"Ick." The waiter splayed his long, buffed fingernails over his chest. "But let me ask Janet to check Lost and Found." He darted away.

A few minutes later, Janet came back with him. Dressed in a woman's black business suit, a black silk tank top, and big-ass stilettos, Janet was probably presurgery, but his voice was high for a man's. Grace figured he was taking estrogen. He seemed perfectly at ease with having two detectives in his place.

"Yeah, I remember that laptop," Janet said. "Flaco was carrying it and the kid kept trying to hold it. Flaco was giving him shit."

Grace wanted to kiss him, but thought better of it. So she simply nodded like Detective Sergeant Friday on *Dragnet* and tried to get more details. There weren't any. Flaco and Zack came in with a laptop, Flaco was hogging it, the end.

"You've been a big help, Janet," Grace said.

"My man is a cop," Janet replied frankly.

After Grace and Ham left, they had a great time going into hysterics and trying to decide who Janet's man was. They invented an elaborate story that starred Bobby because that was the most ludicrous choice they could come up with, except for Grace.

They canvassed the Lost-and-Found boxes of the other five bars they had visited on Thirty-ninth before. There were no laptops in any of them. There were sunglasses, cell phones, handcuffs, whips, vinyl underwear, and very expensive condoms in individual boxes—unused, thank God.

Ham got a call requesting he go back to the station to talk to Pastor Marc's attorney about the torture-ring bust. Shortly after he took off for that fun task, Antwone called. He wanted them to come over. Grace was alone, but that worked for Antwone, too.

She took Connie to his dump of a house, and who should open the door but Antwone himself. With a new black eye and a fresh cut on his lip.

"Who did this to you, man?" she asked, and this time he let her in. His dog must have been in the backyard. The living room was shabby but tidy. An old orange sofa, a leather recliner. Athletic shoes on the floor. A TV and a DVD player. A plastic tablecloth with bumblebees printed on it covered a dining-room table. Car keys, a soda, a few bills, some schoolbooks. A minor could not give his consent to search; she didn't have a warrant. She reminded herself of these facts.

"Some guys in Zack's church group," he said. "They said I told what happened. I didn't even know what they were talking about."

"They messed with him big-time," Grace said. "He didn't mention the gay-orcism?"

"The *what*?" He stared at her.

"I'll tell you later. I swear," she said. "Why'd you call me?"

"Flaco texted. He wants to set up the buy."

Oh, God. Grace's eyes widened. *Here we go.*

"On my BlackBerry," he added, pulling it from his pocket.

"Can I take this from you?" she asked, making sure he was relinquishing possession. She took it and opened up the messages.

FLACO: U READY?

"What did you tell him?"

"Nothing," Antwone said. "As soon as it came in, I called you. What is a gay-orcism?"

"It's bullshit. The church kids tried to de-gayify Zack. I'll tell you later, man."

"No. Now," Antwone said.

Grace sighed, frustrated. His dump, his rules. She sat him down and tried to go easy, but he was crazed by the end of it. Maybe even ready to kill someone.

"Antwone, I'm sorry. I really am," she said. "But you gotta stay focused with me. The last person who was seen with Zack's laptop was Flaco. If he has it, and we can get it . . ." She let the last sentence trail off to its obvious conclusion. But he was still back with the revelation that good Christian Jesus-fearin' folk had tortured the boy he loved.

"Why didn't he tell me?" Antwone moaned, doubling up his fists. He looked left, right, as if for someone to hit, something to destroy.

"To protect you," she said. "Because he cared about you."

He broke down sobbing, his abject, animal cries coming from the hole in his life. Grace sat quietly, a witness, and anger boiled up inside her. The whole situation was so wrong. So . . . unjust.

"Zack," he mourned, "oh, Zack."

She felt his BlackBerry vibrate in her hand. Looked down and saw that it was Flaco again. Shit.

"Antwone, listen, it's Flaco. I'm going to tell him you'll make the buy," she said. Antwone kept crying. She wasn't sure he heard her, but she texted Flaco back anyway.

OK.

That was all she said; then Flaco responded CALL and the phone rang. Grace looked from Antwone to the faceplate—CALLER ID BLOCKED and texted Flaco again.

POS—shorthand for "Parents Over Shoulder," which was a catchall for not being able to answer a call, among other things.

Flaco texted OK. CALL L8R.

OK, Grace texted back. GTG. Got to go.

She hung up. Antwone was going down the lonesome meltdown road; she tried to wait him out, took a seat and bore witness. She had never seen anyone cry so hard in her entire life, and she had seen a lot of tears.

The phone rang. CALLER ID BLOCKED.

POS, she texted.

No reply.

Antwone kept crying. Grace was getting so antsy she thought she might break out in hives. She checked the time on his cell phone and told herself she would wait fifteen more minutes before she tried to get him to stop.

Or twenty.

The phone rang. CALLER ID BLOCKED. She took a deep breath and said, "Antwone, if you want justice for Zack, we need to move on this. You need to answer the phone."

He just looked at her, so ragged and spent and miserable that she felt her cop self shut down. She detached and went on automatic. Her walls went up, the shell around her heart hardening, so she could do her job.

She held the phone out to him. For a second, she thought he was going to throw up.

"Yeah," he said, connecting. "Yeah, Flaco."

Grace closed her eyes and heaved a sigh. Nodded. She pulled out her notebook and wrote, "Get specific address."

"Yeah, okay, where?" he asked, then gestured for Grace's notebook. She handed him her pen. He wrote down an address on Reno.

Then he hung up. He took a deep, ragged breath. "He says this is his house. He wants me there at ten."

"Good, Antwone. I'm going with you. You go in and make the buy and I'll come in after you."

He frowned at her. "That's entrapment, man."

Grace shook her head, even though it was. "It's not. It's not at all. We think he has Zack's laptop. And we need it. We need to see what's on it."

When he didn't say anything, she folded her hands and rested her elbows on her knees. "Antwone, Flaco is an asshole. At the very least, you can help me get him off the streets. That's one less—"

He whipped his head up. "There's too many assholes. Every time I see you, you tell me about someone else who hurt Zack. And *I* get hurt. And it will never, ever stop." Tears rolled down his cheeks. "I only wanted to love him, you know? And now he's dead."

"I know," Grace said, "and you have cause, Antwone. You have cause. But you've been dealing drugs. *You're* one of the assholes. It's the truth. And you know it."

He wrapped his hands around his head. "We just wanted to make enough money so we could get away—"

"It doesn't matter why," she said, scooting her chair closer to his. "It matters that you did it." She wrapped her hand around his forearm; he tried to jerk away but she wouldn't let him. "Flaco might have murdered Zack. You need to stay with me, and help me find out what happened."

Grace left a couple of messages for Ham and followed Antwone's old Corolla. Grace realized they were back in the same part of town where they'd searched for the '64 lowrider Impala. She had a moment's pause where she tried to put Flaco together with Big Money—they both had drugs in common—and she called Antwone on his cell phone. Suddenly she felt very wrong about what they were doing. She should have called her captain, tried to get a warrant.

"When we get there, drive past," she said. "I'll call you."

They glided over wet streets, past blasted-out tenements and then one or two gentrified streets. He made a right and she stayed close behind. They were on North Twenty-third; there was a little frontage road; and they passed the street number. It was a small brick house surrounded by what appeared to be azalea bushes. The porch light was out.

She called Antwone. "Pull over now," she said.

He complied, and she felt a tightness in her chest. He was a kid. She was considering putting him in harm's way. So she could figure out why another kid was dead.

This is wrong.

She sat behind the wheel and clenched her teeth. Then she got out of Connie and walked over to the Corolla. She rapped on the driver's-side window and he rolled it down.

"Go home," she said. "Go now."

He frowned. "Hey, what?"

"I'm going by myself," she said. "You can't go in there. It's too dangerous."

"But you said," he began, and when she didn't change her expression, he shook his head. "I have to go in. He's not expecting you."

"Go home," she said again. Then she turned away and walked toward the little house. Drew her weapon. She shouldn't go in alone. She knew it. She was doing it anyway.

Antwone pulled away from the curb. Good.

Her cell phone rang. It was Ham.

"I'm going in," she said.

"Grace, no. We need a warrant," he said. "If you get the laptop without a warrant, we can't use it."

"We don't have enough for a warrant," she said. "We have no proof that the laptop has got anything we need or that it's inside Flaco's house."

"If Antwone goes in to make the buy, you can go in," he said. "It's a raid. You can do a search."

"No. I sent him home," she said.

"Grace, Flaco's a dealer. He knows Antwone."

"Zack knew him, too."

"At least wait for me," he said. "Please. Tell Antwone to call him and say he's running late."

"That's bullshit, Ham," she replied.

Her phone vibrated. It was Antwone. "Hold on," she said to Ham, switching over to Antwone's call.

"I'm at his back door," he whispered. "I'm there now."

She gripped the phone. "Shit. No. Get the hell out of there."

"Hey, man," a voice said. "I told you to use the front door."

"I'm sorry, Flaco," Antwone replied. He disconnected his cell phone.

Shit, shit, shit. She switched over to Ham. "Antwone's inside. I'm going in."

"On my way. I'll bring backup."

"No lights, no sirens." She disconnected and ran like the devil, straight up to the windy, wet bushes to find a five-foot-tall chain-link gate behind them. Praying that Flaco had no confederates posted, she climbed it—no razor wire, thank God—and landed as softly as she could in slippery mud, to one side of a cement walk. She crawled on her hands and knees past the front of the house; then rose and hunched over, wiping her hands on her jeans, drawing her weapon again, and moving, swift and deadly.

She went past a dark window and then a brick chimney; then she saw the two of them framed in a window with diamond-shaped panes, recognizing Flaco from his mug shots. He was true to his nickname—*flaco* meant "skinny" in Spanish—addict-thin, bald, with a hooked nose, and a long bandito-style mustache. He was wearing a black sweatshirt and jeans, and there was a Glock in his hand. He was patting Antwone down. The two looked to be alone.

And the back door was still open. It was a wooden door with a square of glass bounded by white wrought-iron grates.

Sucking in her breath, Grace tiptoed on the balls of her boots around the south corner and plastered herself against the side of the house directly beside the door. Her heart was pounding, and she held her breath so she could at least hear what they were saying. And then she realized she could see Flaco reflected in the glass in the door. He had the gun, had it, still had it; they were moving to a glass-and-wrought-iron kitchen table.

"Did you bring the money?" Flaco asked.

"Yeah, man," Antwone said.

Grace had no idea if that was true. All this time, she

had never asked Antwone if he could actually make the buy.

Gun up and cocked, she watched Flaco's reflection. His smile showed gaps where teeth were missing. He was not a very attractive man.

But she could have kissed him when he put down his gun to examine an envelope that Antwone had apparently handed him—an envelope she had not seen on him when they'd left his place.

Wait for it, she told herself; since Antwone was going through with the buy, she might as well make as good use of it as she could. Slowly she let out her breath and stared as Flaco held out what looked to be a brick of marijuana wrapped in plastic wrap. He pulled the film off and showed it to Antwone with the air of a waiter allowing a guest to inspect a bottle of wine before he decanted it.

"Want to try it out?" Flaco asked, breaking off a corner and handing it to Antwone.

"Stop! Police!" Grace shouted, bursting through the door. She headed straight for Flaco's gun and grabbed it before he had a chance to. Aimed her weapon at his head, placing herself between him and Antwone.

"On the floor, get on the floor *now*," she ordered him, advancing on him but staying far enough out of range that he couldn't touch her if he decided to launch himself at her.

But he knew the drill; he went down to his knees and then lay facedown, spread-eagling himself as Grace stood over him, her gun aimed at his head.

"You bastard," Flaco said to Antwone. "You are *dead.*"

Grace patted him down. Finding no more weapons—*moron*—she cuffed him.

She looked at Antwone. "You okay?"

He nodded, but he didn't look very steady. She lowered her voice. "Take a look around."

For the laptop, she meant, and he understood. He walked past the kitchen table farther into the kitchen itself, and started opening drawers and cabinets.

"Hey, what the hell?" Flaco said. "I got rights, man."

"That's right," Grace said. She reached into her pocket and pulled out her copy of the Miranda. She began to read it. "I am Detective Hanadarko, OCPD. You have the right to remain silent—"

"Screw you," he said.

"Anything you say can and will be used against you—"

"Screw you!"

"—in a court of law."

Antwone shook his head. Grace said, "Have you ever used a gun?"

He shook his head again. She gestured him over. "See how I'm holding it? Hold it like that. Flaco, on your rights? Hold that thought."

She handed the gun to Antwone. Crossing her fingers that there would be no incidents, she moved from the kitchen into a dining room packed with boxes of what appeared to be small appliances—toasters, waffle irons, juicers. Add up enough petty theft, you might reach larceny territory, but it would be a stretch.

She passed that room up. "You okay, Antwone?" she called.

"Yes," he called back.

She opened a door and found herself in a darkened room. She felt for a wall switch and found it. Turned on the light. Flaco slept on a mattress on the floor, which didn't surprise her in the least. His pillowcase was smudged and dingy. There was a crack works and a bag of marshmallows beside the mattress. Dirty clothes, muddy boots; a little TV and a DVD player. He'd been watching either porn or *Die Hard*. Had to love that irony.

There was a desk pushed against a wall heaped with clothes and an empty hamster cage. A shotgun. Loaded.

A dresser. Filled with ammo and whack magazines . . . and a laptop. With stickers. Zack's laptop.

"Oh, my God," she blurted, because most of the time, it wasn't that easy. "Earl?" she called, glancing around.

She grabbed it up and slid it beneath her jacket. Came back out to Antwone and smiled at him.

"Where've you been? What did you do?" Flaco bellowed, still facedown on the floor.

"Used your bathroom," she said. She took the gun from Antwone. "Thanks, man," she said. Then she mouthed, *Go home now.*

He shook his head, and she narrowed her eyes at him. She pulled up a chair and sat down, keeping the gun aimed at Flaco. She let Antwone see the laptop. His face broke into a smile and he swallowed hard.

Then he left.

CHAPTER
TWENTY-ONE

"You two played this one awfully damn close to entrapment," Captain Perry said as she, Ham, and Grace sat with the guy from Tech who was opening up the many locked files on Zack's computer. "You've made a mountain of paperwork for yourselves, too."

"Not me," Grace said. "Ham's doing mine." She smiled at him. Captain Kate grunted.

"I don't want to know how you struck that bargain."

"Arm wrestling," Grace told her.

What they found on Zack's laptop was mostly video games, MP3 files, and tons of e-mails between Zack and Antwone. *We'll get some money and we'll get out of here. We'll go to California. I have a cousin in Fresno.*

"*Fresno.* Have you ever been to Fresno? Oh, dear God, they might as well have stayed in Oklahoma City," Captain Perry murmured.

"This is bullshit," Grace announced. "What on earth was so great that—"

"Look," the tech guy said.

A short movie began to run: Darkness, and then a light going on. Grace recognized the bathroom where the packing boxes had been stashed, seen from the counter pointing toward the toilet. Cherie stepped into view. She was wearing a floral nightgown, and she turned and shut the door; from the forced perspective, her arm looked enormous.

Then she walked toward the toilet.

"Okay, this is getting weird," Ham said.

She lifted the lid off the tank and laid it on the counter. Reached inside and pulled out a fifth of what appeared to be gin. She uncapped it and put it straight to her lips.

The four watched in silence as she sat on the toilet seat and kept drinking. Then the movie ended.

"That's it?" Grace asked. "That's what he had on her?" She looked at Ham. "Do you think Cherie would kill Zack because he knew she was boozing in secret?"

Ham made a face and shrugged.

"Can we have a warrant?" Grace asked the captain. "There were roofies in Zack's tox results. Rhetta found fibers consistent with a truck. If the Laceys have a truck—"

She sighed. "If you can manage to talk a judge out of one, you can use it."

"Hot damn." Grace grinned.

"Ron's on a short run today," Grace said as she and Ham pulled up to the gate in front of the Lacey compound. It was midmorning, and they'd taken Connie. The American flag was not flying. Ron was probably the one who raised her every morning. "Paul's probably at school. So maybe Cherie's home alone. Maybe she's passed out cold in the bathroom."

Naturally they hadn't called ahead: *Hello, can we come over and serve you with a warrant? We're looking for anything you don't want us to see.* It didn't matter if anyone was home. They didn't need consent to search. The warrant was their ticket in.

Ham got out and pushed on the gate. Open, as before. Ham walked it wide so Connie could drive on through. Then together he and Grace went to the front door.

Grace had just rung the doorbell when the garage door opened and a big, shiny black four-by-four not unlike Ham's roared out of the garage and screamed down the driveway. Cherie was behind the wheel, and Paul Finch sat beside her, staring out of the window straight at Grace. The tires squealed as it took the corner from the driveway to the road too hard, but Cherie righted it and floored it with the finesse of a NASCAR driver.

"Shit!" Grace yelled as she and Ham slammed back into her Porsche and took off after her. Ham put her light on the roof and called Dispatch. He read the Laceys' license-plate number off the warrant and advised that they were in pursuit, and their subjects might be armed.

"Ham, she killed him," Grace said.

"Or Paul or Ron did."

"I say it's her. Blow job."

"You're on."

She burned rubber.

"You made it through Visiting Day," Earl said to Leon.

Leon grunted. "Man, I don't have that many more visiting days. Tamara knows that."

"Kinda hard for them to have a life and spend every Sunday down here, I reckon." Earl pulled a harmonica from his jeans pocket and handed it to Leon. "You can play the blues, if you want."

"Don't make fun of me," Leon snapped at him. "Or—"

"Or what? You ever wrestled with an angel, Leon?"

Leon's shoulders slumped. He dropped the harmonica on the floor; the clatter echoed as if he'd thrown it down a well.

"He's all I got to live for," Leon said.

"That's not true," Earl said. "You've got God to live for."

"So is God punishing me? Keeping my son away from

me so I'll pray better? Exercise?" He said the last word like it was the dirtiest word he'd ever spoken.

Earl looked aggrieved. "How many times do I have to tell you? God don't work that way."

"What if I don't believe you?" Leon flung at him, stomping to the opposite side of the cell.

"Well, who else are you going to believe?" Earl asked him, making a show of looking around the cell for a third party. "I mean, I think I'm it."

"It's not fair. She took him from me and it's— Not. Fair."

"Life's not fair," Earl agreed. "But life is good. Even your life. That's what God wants you to believe. If you could find just a smidge of joy—"

"Are you crazy? I'm sitting on death row."

"But you ain't dead yet," Earl said. He looked hard at Leon. "That's the gift. You have to accept that gift before you make any more progress. Or else . . . we're at a roadblock."

"Oh, my God, Henry," Rhetta said as they ate lunch together. She was having leftover tuna casserole. Henry had a ham sandwich. Grace's squad were all in the field. "A gay-orcism, can you believe it?"

Henry sighed. "It's going to be all over the news."

"That's a huge church," Rhetta said. "Grace told me they have over a thousand members."

"It fills a need." Henry drank his diet soda.

"Past tense, I'm thinking. Unless Pastor Andy can distance himself far enough from Pastor Marc. Do you think Pastor Andy knew?"

"I don't know," Henry said. "It sounds like the Spanish Inquisition."

"Part of my church's not-so-illustrious past." She took a bit of tuna casserole, sighed, and set down her fork.

"And your church survived it." Henry picked up his ham sandwich.

"Yeah, but we're not a cult of personality. Our teachings are what unite us." She thought a moment and fingered the gold cross around her neck. "I guess that's not true."

Henry smiled kindly at her.

She blew air out of her cheeks. "That poor baby, cold and alone in your cooler. I hope they find out what happened to him. My God, I would go crazy. You'd have to just lock me up forever."

"I need to make room in there. I'll have to release him to a funeral home this week," Henry said.

"Yeah." She adjusted her glasses. "How's it going with Lena?"

He sighed, too. "She's moving to Albuquerque. They had an opening there. And . . . it turns out that the guy who broke up with her . . . is going to Albuquerque, too."

"Oh, Henry, I'm so sorry." She laid her hand over his.

"I still have my cat." He gave her a weak smile, and took another bite of his sandwich.

Now they were reaching the Forty, and the bridge that crossed the North Canadian River. Ham requested a 10-52—roadblock—and any minute, Grace expected to hear the whum-whum-whum of a department chopper. Then suddenly, Cherie yanked off the main drag and raced over a frontage road that swooped down toward the riverbank.

Grace ticked her gaze from the back of the truck to the river water and *knew* the way she knew sometimes that this is where Zachary Lacey had come to die.

"This is where she did it, Ham. She dumped him here. The current carried him down into the lock, toward the canal."

It began to rain. Grace flipped on the wipers without

missing a beat. The black truck remained in her sights. She braced herself for shots, for a standoff, a confrontation. They were going to run out of road sooner or later. Ham had his service weapon out. She kept her boot against the floor, and Connie loved her for it.

"Maybe Ron gave her some kind of ultimatum," Ham said. "If she didn't stop drinking, he'd leave her. And she told him she did stop. But Zack caught her so she had to get rid of him."

"He tried to tell his father but he wouldn't believe him. So he caught her on camera," Grace continued. "It's nuts." But they'd seen people get murdered over parking spaces.

The frontage road emptied into a turnaround, with some posted signs about fishing licenses and noodling— catching catfish bare-handed. The truck screeched and slid to the left. The passenger door flew open and Paul Finch jumped out.

Then Cherie flew from the driver's side, wearing a pair of jeans and a Windbreaker. The rain was pouring down on her, and she covered her head as she staggered off the blacktop into the tall grass leading to the river. There was a small wooden pier jutting out over the river with a couple more signs and a trash can.

Grace kept driving until she almost touched the truck's back bumper. Ham opened the door and crouched behind it with his gun drawn. Grace whipped out her weapon and did the same, praying that Cherie was not armed.

"Stop," Grace called.

Ham and Grace both broke into a run. Ham was closer to Paul Finch; he got him down on the ground while Grace kept after Cherie. Cherie leaped onto the landing, and Grace swore under her breath. If that bitch jumped in the water—

"Shit!" Grace yelled as Cherie went in.

Grace lowered her gun and placed it on the pier, tore off her jacket, and jumped in after Cherie. The river was high because of all the rain; in the summer, sometimes it was too shallow for boating. And it was damn cold. She hoped backup came with blankets and hot chocolate. She broke the surface and saw Cherie's head about fifty feet away. She was going down.

Grace got to her and wrapped her arm under Cherie's armpits lifeguard style. She started swimming against the current while Cherie struggled.

"If you don't stop it, I'll knock you out," Grace promised her.

"Just let me drown, let me drown." Cherie sputtered and choked.

"Wish I could," Grace gasped. She saw Ham at the very edge of the pier. "No!" she shouted at him. "We're on our way in."

She heard the blades of a chopper above them. The shriek of sirens.

"Praise the Lord," she said.

Ham sloshed along the bank and helped her pull Cherie out. The woman was sobbing. Paul Finch, in handcuffs, looked down from the pier, and his eyes were bulging from their sockets.

"Mom!" he shouted. "Don't say anything!"

"I didn't mean to do it," Cherie said to Grace. "I just wanted him to loosen up and tell me how much he knew."

The roofies, Grace filled in. "Knew about . . . what you'd done," Grace filled in.

"She didn't do anything!" Paul said.

"It's okay, honey," Cherie told him. Then she began to cry.

"Back in Texas . . . ," Cherie Lacey whispered in the interview room at the station. She was dried off and cuffed to the ring in the table. She had waived her right to an attorney. D.A. would probably have a shit fit. "He hit me. Raped me."

"Your first husband," Grace said. "Back when your name was Charlaine McAllister. You were married to Tom McAllister. You killed him when Paul was six. Drugged him, cuffed him, and set the bed on fire. Allegedly."

She hung her head. "It was self-defense. Paul knew it. He protected me. Never said a word to anyone for eleven years."

"You ran. Committed several counts of identity theft. Then you met Ron. Wanted a shot at a normal life. But you had this weird stepson, Zack."

"And Zack . . . he told me he was onto me. And I . . . I panicked." She started to cry. "I gave him a roofie to make him talk. It wasn't working. I thought. So I gave him another. And it was too much."

"He was overdosing. You forced him into the truck." Rhetta was collecting fibers from that very truck even as they spoke.

"You can't know what Texas was like. The things Tom did . . . it was a nightmare . . . hell . . ." Tears streamed down her face. "He abused Paul. He threatened to kill me so many times."

"Cry me a river," Grace said. "Zack didn't know shit about Texas. He wanted Ron to know you were hiding bottles in the toilet."

Cherie stared at her for a full ten seconds. Her face drained of all color. "Oh, my God." She threw back her head and screamed.

"She thought Zack was dead," Grace told Gus, as she came home from the world's longest day on the job. She was chilled straight down to the bone. "That she'd made him OD on the roofies. So she decided to dump him in the river. But he woke up and tried to get away. Tried to save his own life."

"Brf," Gus said, sitting down so she could properly scratch him behind the ears. But she felt so tired and drained she could hardly lift her hand.

"Paul's baseball bag was in the cab and she went after him. And you know what she told me? 'He didn't struggle for very long.' As if that was a good thing."

She took off her gun and her badge. Stumbled into her bedroom and took off her boots. Lay down fully clothed. Gus hopped up next to her and put his head on her feet.

"Oh, Jesus, Gus," she whispered.

The rain came down and she floated in exhaustion and sorrow, her bed her ark, Gus and the ghost of Zack Lacey her two-by-two companions.

Cry, Earl urged her as she stared into the darkness. *Cry me a river, Grace.*

Two days later. The rain poured down on the cluster at the grave site, umbrellas open, faces sad and lost or maybe a little bored. The casket was shiny dark wood. Grace had sent a funeral spray of roses. Zack's dad was there, looking shell-shocked. Grace wanted to hate him for all the misery he'd put his boy through. He'd beaten Zack and rejected him. Then he'd married a pitiless lowlife murderess who killed his only child.

You had him, she thought. *You had him, and you practically forced him into that river yourself with all your bullying and your stupidity.*

But here he was, in the rain, wearing an ill-fitting, cheap navy blue suit. The pants pooled over the tops of his scuffed black work boots, and the jacket hung on his wide shoulders. His suit was too large for a large man like him, and that struck her as kind of . . . sad. He'd made the attempt, still couldn't pull it off.

He held a dirty khaki ball cap between his hands. His head was lowered, and he was staring at the casket. He was stone-faced, and Grace couldn't read his expression.

She felt dull and heavy and weighed down, as if every muscle in her body had atrophied.

O, God, by whose mercy the souls of the faithful find rest, mercifully forgive the sins of your servants and handmaids, who here and everywhere repose in Christ, that, released from every bond, they may rejoice with you forevermore. We ask this through Christ our Lord.

In his black clerical suit and white collar, Father Pepera was putting his final seal of approval on Zack's funeral. As the group began singing "Salve Regina," Grace shifted her attention to him. It must be driving him crazy, knowing he was burying a gay kid who had neither confessed nor repented, at least as far as he knew.

Ham, Butch, and Bobby stood silently, hats off and heads bowed beneath umbrellas in the heavy rain. Rhetta couldn't come; her daughter was sick. Grace had called Zack's grandmother and given her the fantastic news that her grandson had been murdered. She was grateful.

Antwone stood with a woman who was an older, shorter version of him, without an umbrella; he looked small and alone, beat up and scared. Flaco was in custody, but there were always the assholes at school and the customers Antwone would be unable to satisfy. Grace thought that he and his mother should move to Fresno, or at least get the hell out of Oklahoma.

Janaya Causwell was already in the ground. Patrick Kelly was going to recover, and Butch had agreed to sponsor him in a rehabilitation program. The goal was a job, structure, and possibly, someday, full custody of his daughter.

Big Money had disappeared. For the moment.

At the end of the hymn, the mourners began to depart. Bobby, Ham, and Butch shook hands with Ron Lacey, then hugged Grace. Ham lingered.

"Yeah," she said to his unspoken question. "Come over in about an hour." She needed some alone time first.

"I'm sorry for your loss," she said to Ron Lacey. He looked at her as if he had no idea who she was. Then he nodded. Wife in jail, kid dead. What the hell was he supposed to do with Paul Finch?

She turned to go, and saw, through the rain, the forlorn figure of Juanita Provo, standing with Joe Varisse. Maybe that was why Varisse had acted strangely during their interview; he had a thing with Juanita. As Grace walked toward them, he squeezed Juanita's hand, then hung back as she approached Grace alone.

"I'm so sorry," Juanita said.

Grace looked at her.

"Sorry I couldn't do more for him. That terrible church . . . if he'd come to *my* church . . ."

Grace's lips parted. Juanita still didn't get it. She walked past her, and Juanita started crying.

"Detective," she called, running up to her. "I wanted to help him. You know I wanted that."

Grace stopped, but didn't turn around. "You didn't," Grace said coldly.

She headed for Connie without looking back . . . until the last second, when she began to climb into the driver's seat. At the head of the casket, she saw Earl, wings unfurled, his head dipped low. She couldn't see his face, but was certain, somehow, that he was crying.

When she got home, Earl was there, too. He was wearing a T-shirt that said "Masada," with a silkscreen of a cliff. He glanced down.

"Masada's a holy place in Israel," he told her. "In 37 BC, a bunch of Jewish rebels and their families took their own lives, rather than be taken captive by the Romans."

She blinked at him. "They committed suicide?"

He nodded.

"And that's holy."

"You were pretty rough on Juanita Provo," he said. "She wanted you to forgive her. Absolve her."

"That's your boss's job, not mine."

She heard Ham's truck in the driveway. "All this worrying about forgiveness. Zack never needed forgiveness. He needed justice. And I got him that," she said. "That's what I risk my life for, every goddamn day. And if your boss thinks that's a suicide mission, He can stay on His side of heaven."

She went to let Ham in.

The rain poured down into the river, where Butch's homeless skel had seen someone else stand at the water's edge for three days, and then leave. That one didn't go in. That one chose a different way.

The rain poured down on Grace's house, where she lay in a sleeping tangle with Ham, another candle burning for Zack Lacey. She was dreaming of Leon Cooley. He was walking on the water, like Jesus. And she was sitting in a little boat, bailing like crazy.

"Come on in. The water's fine," Leon said.

Grace jerked awake. She raised her head, listening to the hard patter of the rain. She grabbed her cell phone, and walked into the hall. Dialed a number.

"Hello," said a sad, tired voice.

"Juanita," she began, "it's Grace Hanadarko."

In the living room, Earl was having a chat with Gus. "Squirrels can be fast," he explained. "You gotta ambush 'em. See, when you bark, you warn 'em. You need to be sneaky."

Like you, Grace thought, as she finished her call and walked into the living room. Gus's tongue was hanging out as he listened intently to Earl. Grace smiled faintly, wondering if Earl and Gus really did communicate in some special dog-angel language. God might have appeared on her porch a few times, posing as a reddish brown dog with an enormous tongue, matching a tattoo on Earl's back. Or if it wasn't God, Earl might have a future in law enforcement, if he could stage such elaborate practical jokes.

Earl turned to her. "That was a nice thing you did, calling Juanita."

She shrugged. "Talk's cheap." She walked to the door and watched the falling rain. "He'll never see another rainstorm," she murmured.

"Oh, I think you're wrong about that," Earl said, coming up beside her. "Zack's got a lot to look forward to. And so do you, Grace. God's got big plans for you."

She pursed her lips. Then warmth bloomed behind her, and the rain stopped. It was three a.m., but golden light poured down from the sky and made the rectangle of her door glow. Made her hands glow. She turned to Earl, and he was washed in a blaze of glory so bright she couldn't see his face.

"Why do you have to fight so hard?" he asked.

"Because that's me," she replied. "That's who I am, Earl. A fighter."

The brilliance faded, and Earl smiled at her. "You got me there."

"Sorry to disappoint you." Although in all honesty, she wasn't sorry. She really didn't give a damn what he thought. God could take her or leave her.

"I'm not disappointed," Earl replied. He chuckled. "And neither is anyone else." He cocked his head. "It's going to be okay, Grace."

"It's okay now." She shrugged. "I'm going back to bed."

"Sweet dreams."

She pointed at him. "*No* dreams. I just want to sleep." She moved past him, waving at him. "Good night, Earl."

"Night, Grace."

Gus's toenails clattered as he followed her down the hall. Ham murmured in his sleep as Gus hopped onto the bed and snuggled up to Grace's feet. She looked at the candle, and felt the beginning of a tear welling in her eye. She swallowed it away and stared, long and hard. Silent.

In some religions, what she was doing was praying. And, Earl noted with true angelic joy, she was good at it.

Earl thought of a quote by Antoine de Saint-Exupéry, one of his favorite writers: *If you want to build a ship, don't herd people together to collect wood and don't assign them tasks and work, but rather teach them to long for the endless immensity of the sea.*

Longing was praying, Grace style. Longing for life, and justice, and the whirlwind. Longing as Earl had rarely seen, in his long and endless life.

And so . . . there was hope for Grace, God's beloved lost and ever-so-wild child.

And that was enough.

For now.

ACKNOWLEDGMENTS

My deep and humble thanks to Nancy Miller, Holly Hunter, Everlast, and the cast and crew of *Saving Grace*. I am in awe. Thanks also to my fantastic agent and dear friend, Howard Morhaim, and his assistant, Katie Menick. To my editorial squad: Keith Clayton, Liz Scheier, and Kelli Fillingim, my deepest gratitude. My appreciation as well to Debbie Olshan. Thanks to Katharine Ramsland, Lee Lofland, Jonathan Hayes, Phyllis Middleton, and Wally Lind of crimescenewriters. And thanks to Dave Lindo of OKC Kayak.

Thank you, my Grace-daughter, Belle. You are a cowgirl, baby. Shake it up.

Read on for an excerpt from Nancy Holder's

SAVING **GRACE**
TOUGH LOVE

Published by Ballantine Books

"Fight," Grace told the dying boy.

Definite drive-by. Probable DOA—dead on arrival. Sixteen, maybe, and his life was nearly over.

Not yet, though. He had backup: Grace Hanadarko and Ham Dewey, OCPD Major Crimes. They were busting their humps to keep him alive. While Grace tried to stanch the flow of blood from the grievous, life-sucking wound, her partner talked to 911. Ham spoke calmly but loudly into the phone, running down the pertinent information: location, location, location; victim's condition. By Ham's questions and answers, Grace knew a squad car was en route for backup—lights and sirens—and an ambulance was practically there. But help wasn't there yet, and it might not come soon enough.

The pitch-black alley stank of rotten food and dog shit; it was a terrible place to die. Wind pitched grit, gravel, and fetid newspapers against Grace's face. The knees of her jeans were soaking up blood and rock chips as her bare hands slipped in and out of the hole in the kid's chest. The hole. The big, gaping, fatal hole that was expelling blood like an Oklahoma gusher.

He can make it, she told herself.

The hole that was too big—

He will make it. He will.

She had violated procedure by not taking the time to snap on a pair of latex gloves before she went to work. Maybe someone else would lose focus and fret about that, spin a mental mini-drama about getting a positive result on the subsequent HIV test they would take. But she wasn't someone else, and right now she had this kid's whole world in her hands.

Despite the buffeting wind, Ham held the long black flashlight steady while he stayed on the line with dispatch. Grace's world was reduced to a circular yellow glow, a spotlight. The boy's complexion was very black, almost purple-black; she couldn't tell if he had gone cyanotic, which would not be a good sign. But if this murder came to trial she was saying that there had been enough light for the shooter to see this short, scrawny boy, this unarmed teenager who was gurgling and dying. Plenty of illumination for the bastard to hit what exactly what he'd been aiming for: a one-way ticket to hell.

"Live," Grace ordered him. Then something happened to his eyes: they fluttered open, and she felt a thrill down her back as they focused on her. "Come on. You can do it. You can—"

His eyes widened. She saw him seeing her. He was aware, and with her. Ham's flashlight shone like a halo.

"Yeah," she said. "Good. Stay with me."

Then they went dull and glassy, and she knew he wasn't seeing anything. Her hands slid in the wound, and she set her jaw. If they got him to a

hospital, got a transfusion going, got a team working on him—

"Grace," Ham said softly. "Grace. He's gone."

She was silent a moment, aware that she was panting and that icy sweat was sliding down her face.
Her back muscles were spasming. Her knees felt like
ground glass was embedded in them.

Pain. Hurt. World of hurt. The boy, gone . . .

Then she said, "To hell with that," and pressed her
hands over the boy's wound again.

And she didn't let go until the ambulance came.

Around eleven that night, Grace blew into her
house along with the fierce, near gale-force winds,
her long, curled blond hair brushing the shoulders
of her black suit jacket as she shut the front door
and leaned against it, her head back, her dressy
boot heels flush. Overcome with exhaustion, she
wiped her eyes. She was wearing the change of
clothes she kept in her locker at the office: black
trousers, white shirt, matching jacket—like the
damn FBI.

A few drinks at Louie's had done nothing to dull
the knife of the condolence call she had made to the
overcome, overwhelmed, meth-addicted mom of the
victim. He had a name now—Haleem Clark—and
from the looks of it, he had bled out in that alley
after being shot while making a drug buy for his
mother. Some kids get sent to the store for a loaf of
bread. Haleem died fetching a chunk of crystal for
Mommy Dearest.

This was how Grace and Ham figured it went
down: The dealer met Haleem and they began to

conduct their business. Then Mr. Dealer saw something he didn't like, and took off down the alley. They guessed that would have been the vehicle carrying the shooter. Maybe it was someone he owed money to. Or sold bad drugs to. Or maybe he just saw the glint of a weapon.

Whatever the case, he was smart to run because someone in the vehicle shot at him. At least once. Rhetta Rodriguez, head of the crime lab and Grace's best friend since kindergarten, had extracted a bullet from the exploded remains of a pile of dog shit, and it sure looked like it had come from a Sig P220 to the two of them. Grace and Rhetta were both assuming Haleem's gut shot came from the same weapon. Rhetta would get back to Grace after ballistics made their report.

Despite the Sig's reputation as an accurate weapon, the shooter still missed the dealer. So Mr. Killer made another pass in his vehicle, leaving nice deep tire tracks in the mud that Rhetta's lab was already working on. Also, by tracing Haleem's shoe prints through the mud and garbage, Grace surmised that Haleem had run toward the vehicle, maybe assuming the occupants would recognize him, or else spare an innocent bystander.

Maybe the shooter didn't like Haleem. Maybe he didn't like black kids buying drugs. Whatever the motive, he—or she—took out Haleem on a second attempt, the vehicle hanging a U and driving by him again. They couldn't quite figure out why he hadn't been shot in the back—why he hadn't dashed headlong back into the alley to get out of the line of fire. It was almost as if he had stood waiting to take a bullet while the vehicle took the time to drive past him one more time.

That second pass was Grace's judicial ace in the hole. Coming back around implied intent and pre-meditation. That invited stiffer penalties, including the needle. If praying for an execution would get it done, then Grace was all for praying.

Okay, then, maybe just crossing her fingers.

Someone called in the shooting (though of course no witnesses came forward during the subsequent canvass), and dispatch sent Grace and Ham over, as they were already in the vicinity, working on a liquor store burglary. As first on the scene, they rendered assistance. The victim strangled on his own blood anyway.

At sixteen.

Grace went to the mom's while Ham attacked their shitpiles of paperwork; afterward, they went for drinks at Louie's. With their first toast—two longnecks chased with tequila shots—Grace swore she would find the shooter, find him and strap him to the same gurney in the same death chamber where Leon Cooley had died, unless someone else got him first.

As for Haleem's mom, she'd wailed like a banshee when family services came for her three other kids, screaming that she'd just lost one baby, and how could they do this to her? High as a kite, and there was no food in the house, and the littlest one was wearing nothing but a filthy diaper and some flea bites.

"She might as well have pulled the trigger herself," Grace muttered. She felt a million years old.

Then toenails clattered, and Bighead Gusman, her

white bulldog, greeted her with his nose against her kneecap and a low, happy moan. Without lifting her head or opening her eyes, she gave him a good scratch and a pat. Some of the storm clouds dissipated as he chuffed in response and led her toward the kitchen, where he knew that his five-star dinner sat waiting for him in a family-size can. Grace remembered only then that she had a fresh rawhide bone shaped like a barbell out in the car. With a couple of snorts, Gus assured her that he was happy to see her even if she never brought him home another chew toy in his life. He was always happy to see her. She smiled very faintly.

Okay, so maybe there was life after death, and dogs were in charge of it.

"Evenin', Grace," Earl said, as she grabbed a beer out of the fridge. One minute she and Gus were alone; the next, her last-chance angel was standing beside her in the kitchen. Earl did that, just showed up; it used to be the sight of him was enough to set her teeth on edge. Now, as with her Gussie, she was glad Earl was there.

By all appearances, Earl was a fifty-something workin' man with straggly teeth and tousled brown and gray hair. He was wearing a gray jacket with a couple of militaristic-looking badges over a plaid shirt, which was itself over one of his signature T-shirts—a photograph of a tornado and the words OKLAHOMA'S FIFTH SEASON. Ha, got that right. Jeans and black athletic shoes completed his ensemble. But he also had a pair of golden, feathery wings that he kept tucked away, unless he had to fly off to France or Milwaukee, or hold a dying child in his arms.

When even one feather brushed Grace, it made her feel stoned and orgasmic. Blissful. She needed some bliss, just about now. Haleem Sampson Clark had not died in a state of bliss.

"Hey, Earl." The fridge door hung open; she raised her brows and paused, in case he wanted one, too. Earl nodded. She grabbed three beers and checked the level on the tequila bottle that was sitting next to an opened box of pancake mix. The bottle was nice and full. Grace was counting her blessings.

Earl took one of the longnecks and held it up, toasting. "To Haleem."

They clinked, threw back. One of the things Grace loved about beer was that the seventh one tasted as fantastic as the first one. Every time.

"Where is he now?" she asked him, pushing coils of hair away from her eyes. "There a ghetto in heaven, too? Angels fly by now and then, and wave, then go hang out in the nicer neighborhoods?"

Earl smiled at her sadly with world-weary eyes. "You know heaven don't work that way, Grace."

"I don't know shit," she retorted, as she crossed to the side door and forced it open against the stabbing wind. She made kissy noises at Gus. "Go wee-wee, Gusman."

As her housemate trotted happily past her, she said, "I take that back. I do know shit. I know that kid is dead."

"Dead in this world," Earl concurred. "But in the next, he's only dead to pain and sorrow."

"Like I said." A frustrated sigh escaped her. She didn't think every single word coming out of Earl's mouth was bullshit anymore, but she also wasn't quite sure how much was lifted from the in-house marketing memos God circulated every morning, versus how much was stuff Earl made up on the spot. Or maybe some of it might actually be true.

"And Haleem knows his mama loves him, in her way," he added.

"Yeah, loved him to death." Grace grabbed the tequila bottle. "Just like God and Jesus, huh? God loved His only begotten Son so much He let Him hang there, suffering . . . " She trailed off, as tired of her own cynicism as she was sure Earl was.

"You should close that pancake mix," Earl said. "It's going to spoil."

"Clay's coming over tomorrow night. We'll finish it off." Still, she set down the tequila bottle and crimped the edges of the plastic bag together. Then she opened up Gus's can of wet food and thwunked the massive, chunky cylinder into his bowl. Broke it up nice with a spoon and then set it on the floor as she opened up the side door again. The wind slammed it wider; she jumped; Earl did not. Equally unruffled, Gus sashayed in, harrumphed his thanks, and dug in.

"Good thing he ain't a Chihuahua," Earl drawled, and Grace grunted.

"Yeah, he'd be long gone by now." She smiled affectionately at her puppy guy. "Gone with the wind."

She leaned against the breakfast bar, awash in weariness. The last of her street-induced adrenaline had long ago burned off, leaving her to crash, hard. Crashing was difficult to take, so cops pulled brutal practical jokes and swore and drank too much and had libidos to match the need to stay alert so they could stay alive. Ham got that—the prime directive to mix it up—or rather, he used to, until he started feeling sentimental about her instead of simply lustful. Now he was muddying the waters of their firecracker partnership with buzzkill feelings.

Did Earl understand that she had to drum it up to keep it up? She had a demanding profession; she had to stoke her fires to keep burning bright. Tonight he just smiled his pleasant, accepting smile and drank with her in silence. Her mind went over and over what she had done, and what she had failed to do. If they'd gotten there sooner, if she'd tried harder to stanch the wound. It was such a bitch when her best still wasn't good enough.

She should have saved that kid.